MEN OF STEAM

A Yorkshire Novel

RAYMOND FLINT
(Hull 1994)
'SANTONA PUBLICATIONS'

Cover design
Original Watercolour

'CASTLEBROUGH FLYER'

by
Adrian P Thompson
Water Colour Artist (Hull)

First Published   1994
Reprinted   1996

British Library Cataloguing-in-publication data.

A catalogue record for this book is available from the British Library.

Copyright ©1994 by Raymond Flint.

First published in 1994 by Santona Publications, Hull HU6 7UW

Typeset and designed by Jenko Graphics Limited, Hull.

Printed and bound by Fisk Printers, Hull.

ISNB 0 9507960 1 8

Also by the same author
'The People's Scenario' 1982
'The March of the History Animal' 1985.

'The Spirit of Santona'

Onward to the horizon.

'SANTONA PUBLICATIONS'
(HULL)

DEDICATED
to
JOAN

my wife of forty-four years
without whom this
book would have never been written
and
whose response when I was diagnosed

PARKINSONS DISEASE
was
"We'll have to think of it as just another adventure."

ACKNOWLEDGEMENTS

Few books can be the sole work of one person and this book is no exception. Without the encouragement of my family and friends and without the presence and help of the 'Parkinsons Disease Society' I'm sure I would have not found the spirit to start writing again.

The family and many friends helped by their common faith that there was room in the field of literature for someone to achieve the original task of bringing our steam railway heritage into the field of novel writing. They also believed I could do it. "Don't just write about steam locomotives, write about them and the people that made up the railway experience. Bring them together and bring them alive." I hope I've achieved those general objectives.

Without my son Stephen's love of railways, steam, and model making I would have never learnt of the 'magic of steam and rail' that enthuses so many people who have never experienced the dirt and toil and independence of a locomotive footplate. Also to my two daughters Julie and Carol whose interest in my accounts of the past encouraged me in my perseverance.

There are many who read the script and offered positive suggestions and expressed an enthusiasm which maintained my faith in the end result. Ken Hoole, railway historian and author, sadly now deceased but immortalised in Darlington Railway Museum's Ken Hoole Visitors Centre; my lifelong friend Don Lamplugh, sadly now deceased, whose struggle against severe paraplegia over fifty years and whose humour and love of life helped to shape mine, cannot go unmentioned for their reading of this script and for their advice. Railway authors John Farringdon of Aberdeen University, and Robin Lidster of Scarborough are likewise on the list of persons to whom thanks are directed. John Farrington's book 'Life on the lines' and his comments were an inspiration. Others to whom I am indebted are Frank Burton of Dewsbury, Jim Turner of Walkington, Roger Bateman of Thorngumbald, Mike Pearson of Hull, Doctor Paul Sutton of Hull University and his wife Lorraine Sutton, and Tim Gosden, Chaplain of Hull University, and many others.

I hope this work gives pleasure to readers and becomes a suitable testimonial to all to whom I am indebted.

Ray Flint 1994

PREFACE.

Yorkshire was the largest county in Great Britain during the Nineteen-forties; it had vast industries, agriculture, ports, coal mines, an extensive railway network and a vigorous working people. Many thousands of these people were the employees of 'The London and North Eastern Railways'; a railway system that straddled much of Britain from London to the north of Scotland.

Joe Wade, the central character in 'Men of Steam' is one of those employees. He is youthful and ambitious, reliable but in need of close guidance; he is conscious of political, social and trade union questions, he is alert to the great upheaval of the 'Second World War' that is transforming the world; but he is first and foremost a poorly educated young railwayman who has seen the war devour his chances of a full adolescence in peace time. Instead the war brought to him a man's job on the footplates of steam locomotives that worked the lines of Yorkshire. His experiences were those of countless men and boys; they were the experiences of working people whose mode of work had been decided by Victorian engineers and perpetuated well into the Twentieth Century.

Steam railways are now a thing of the past, but the not very distant past; they are within the living memories of many of us. Indeed many of the men and women and adolescents who are the inspiration of this story are alive and vigorous today; they lived and worked just as do the fictitious characters in 'Men of Steam'. Their lives, their humour, their greed, their generosity, ambitions and hopes are the raw material of the story which springs from them and the steam locomotives which formed such an important part of their lives.

This volume and any that may follow in the same theme is a tribute to that numerous body of enginemen, railwaymen and women of the steam age who operated all steam railways.

'Men of Steam' relates specifically to the north east of England; to the moors, the vales and the wolds of Yorkshire. Much of what appears in this volume as sidings, stations, signal cabins, locomotives, sheds and goods yards has now ceased to exist in our reality. Maybe that is as good a reason as any to preserve in our literature those situations and places which existed in our past.

The novel that follows is both serious and comic; it intends to amuse and entertain. It is a record of a reality that existed and indeed is very close to the lives of the people who worked on or were associated with the railways of Yorkshire.

The situations in it could have happened, sometimes did happen. Although all the situations and characters are fictitious they are most certainly part of that life that was experienced by men, women and boys who were employed on the London North Eastern Railways. The novel aims to amuse and inform but also hopefully preserve that part of our heritage and experience which was found amongst the men and women of the steam locomotive era.

★   ★   ★   ★

MEN OF STEAM

CONTENTS

Dedication		5
Acknowledgements:		6
Preface:		7

PART ONE: THE CAMEL'S HUMP.

1	A Change for the Better.	11
2	Humiliation.	16
3	The Maze and the Blackout.	25
4	The Lost Shovel.	40

PART TWO: A WHISTLE TOO MANY.

1	De-railed at the Starting Post.	57
2	Stop the Express!	62
3	The Race to the Bookmakers.	74
4	To the Finishing Post.	83

PART THREE: THE SKY PILOT.

1	A Pig's Been Killed.	92
2	The Trouble with Sleepers.	96
3	Whose books are these?	105
4	A Lesson from the Sky Pilot.	108

PART FOUR: THE GIRL.

1	The Undertaker's Visit.	114
2	The Girl in the Cab.	121
3	The Directors' Train.	130
4	The Struggle in the Tunnel.	136
5	Congratulations Driver.	154
6	A Watch to Time Trains.	164

★   ★   ★   ★

1
A CHANGE FOR THE BETTER?

The nine o' clock news had just closed as old Dick Peace rose slowly from his chair to tune to another radio station. Turning the black knob on the wireless set he searched for Tommy Handley and the 'It's That Man Again'. He was delaying his departure to bed because he was hoping soon to see his sixteen year old grandson Joe Wade arrive home from work.

"Where's Joseph, Emily? Shouldn't he be home by now?" The seventy year old retired coal miner addressed his question to his daughter Emily.

"Yes Dad." She answered loudly from within the scullery where she was preparing a meal. "Said he'd be home at eight when his shift finished but look at the time, nine-fifteen."

Joe Wade - 'War Acting Lad Parcels Porter' - at Castlebrough Railway Station had been expected home much earlier than nine-fifteen. His lateness meant that Emily his mother was having to reheat his plated meal on a pan of hot water which simmered on the ancient gas cooker.

"Do you want some supper Dad, while you listen to Itma?" asked Emily Wade as she approached him in the back living room of their council house home in Castlebrough.

"Slice o' bread and jam an' a cuppa tea. Tah."

Emily turned back towards the scullery. All of her waking hours were spent catering for the needs of her three sons, her husband, father, Billy the tom cat and the half dozen hens in the back garden. It was her first nature to serve the needs of others instantly. So when Grandfather Peace asked for bread and jam she turned away from the knitting which she had been about to pick up and attended to the fresh task.

"Joseph's not been late from work once this week." Emily said. "Don't know why he's late tonight?" She spoke from within the scullery and spoke loudly enough for her father to hear her above the music and laughter of the comedy radio programme. She was very thin and small; her black hair pinned in a bun at the back of her head, her full length pinafore tied closely around her waist. As she stooped over her scullery table slicing the homemade loaf of bread, a knock on the back door called her attention. The door knob turned as someone tried to enter. She heard a faint voice on the other side of the door in the darkness of the night.

"It's only me Emily." The voice belonged to Mrs Jean Walton her nearest neighbour.

Emily Wade reached to turn off the electric light before going to open the back door. She was always very careful about lights and about abiding rigidly to the black-out regulations. She unlocked the door and admitted Jean Walton into the darkened scullery.

"Just dropped in for a chat before bed. Now Jack's in the army I get lonely at this time. Like to see someone for a talk." The big figure of Mrs Walton whispered her message to Emily in the darkened room as though she wished to avoid waking someone. "Also, I've brought you a fish-head for the cat."

Emily closed and locked the back door and then groped her way through the darkness towards the door of the living-room. "Dad's in there listening to Tommy Handley's Itma. Come on." Her fingers found the light switch and electric light flooded the darkened scullery. She took the proferred fish-head from Jean and opened the door into the living room and stood aside for her to pass.

The Wade's living-room in their nineteen-twenties built council house was almost one quarter occupied by a large steel Morrison table air raid shelter which also served as the family dining table. It was so large that it had to stand well into one corner and beneath the blacked out window. The most accessible corner of the table shelter was covered with a cloth and set with a knife and fork ready for the laying out of Joe's cooked supper. An eye level cast iron mantelpiece carried a wooden clock and two brass candlesticks. Two top upholstered polished oak buffet box stools and a joining fender fronted the fireplace and its low burning coal fire.

Jean Walton settled herself on one of the buffet stools and clasped her hands across her knees. Facing her in a semi-slumbering position in a wooden reclining easy chair was the white short-haired Grandad Peace. She was about to speak out but noticed Emily's finger placed on her pursed lips while her other hand stabbed silently in the direction of the radio and the Grandfather's listening figure. Jean bided her time and bent her ear in the direction of the jokes and laughter being emitted by the radio.

"Here Dad." Emily disturbed the plump, semi-slumbering figure. with an offered plate of bread and jam and a cup of sweetened tea. As she did she heard a knocking on the back door so she pressed the plate and cup into his hands and hastened away. Minutes later the living-room door opened to admit Joe, or Joseph as he was more formally known to members of his family.

"I'll put your supper out Joseph, it's been waiting since eight," said his mother with a note of irritability in her voice.

Joe removed his London and North Eastern Railway porter's cap with a blackened hand and then slipped out of his black serge railway jacket. He said nothing. His eyes fell on the red-haired full figure of Jean Walton. As always when seated her ample shapely legs and knees were prominently displayed. On this occasion she unwittingly exposed her lille stocking top and a glimpse of white thigh. They quickly caught Joe's embarrassed eye and awoke his sexual feelings.

She always stirred some emotion and passion in his breast. He was old enough for his mind to be often concerned with sexual matters and she at thirty-five had a full mature figure which often aroused, in him, erotic thoughts. He moved his gaze conciously. He did not want to be caught looking at her displayed legs. It would not do for anyone, especially her, to realise that he felt attracted to a woman twice his age.

"Your hands are as black as coal Joseph. What have you been doing?" Mother's voice agitated at him.

"Been on an engine, Mam. A steam engine."

"Is that why you're late? she questioned.

"Yes, I stopped off at the loco' shed and went on some engines" Joe answered.

"Fancy making me keep your supper warm. All week you've been home at eight. Don't you think about me?"

"Leave him alone Emily. Don't go on so. Leave lad be." Grandad Peace intervened on Joe's behalf.

"I'll get mi dinner quick Mam an' go out wi'out changing."

"Without changing! Are'nt you going to wash?"

"No I'm only going to West's to see Dan."

"You're always at West's."

"Well Danny's his pal Emily." Grandad intervened again and seemed to have lost interest in the itma programme. "What were you doing on the engines Joseph?"

"When I was leaving work Tom West's engine stood in platform one. He told me to put mi bike on the tender and have a ride with them to the shed," Joe answered.

"Would'nt that have got you home quicker?" said Jean joining in the conversation for the first time.

Joe's eyes switched in the direction of the red haired Jean. Her blue flowered dress cloaked her breasts and clasped her knees enticingly. Joe felt warmed by her interest in his doings. "Yes," he replied, "but I stayed at the shed and helped Tom West do some work on his engine."

"You should have come home for your supper," mother chimed in with another show of indignation and irritability.

"I had to go to the shed Mam to get to know what to do on Monday."

"What's Monday got to do with it?"

"I start there on Monday," replied Joe.

"Start work," interjected Grandad.

"Yes."

"Mother was exasperated."You're going to start work at the engine sheds on Monday. Why when you've got a job as a porter?"

"I want to be a fireman." Joe paused ever so slightly. "One day I want to be an engine driver like Dan's dad."

"Have you changed your job just like that? Did'nt you have to apply?" Grandad raised his five-feet three figure and move to place his empty cup and plate on the air-raid shelter top close by Joe's supper setting.

"Oh yes Grandad. I applied two weeks ago an' sat an exam' in the shedmaster's office."

"And you've just told me now." Mother's frail figure trembled with irritation as she placed Joe's supper of sausage, potatoes and sprouts on the shelter top. "You know I wanted you to have a clean job as a porter. I got that job for you through Mr Bowman to get you away from Packard's Iron Foundry and muck and grease." She emphasised her last words almost to a shout. She continued angrily, "You know that Doctor Harker said that you needed a clean job to get rid of your acne. Now you tell me that you've gone and got another mucky job on steam engines."

"Emily, Emily, lad's got to think of his career an' not just his spots." Grandad stooped over his chair as he prepared to seat himself slowly, as his weakened legs dictated. "Bein' an engine driver's a good job lad."

"But I've got all of his mucky clothes to wash, an' pack up his food for all different shifts. You know what it's like for Mrs West." Mother was still harassed and irritated by Joe's news that he was to start work as a railway engine cleaner on the coming Monday morning. With a flourish of her hand she said,"Get your supper."

"I'll wash my hands first" replied Joe, inwardly glad that he had broken his news to his mother about his change of occupation on the railways. He had always had a lingering passion to work on the mighty steam locomotives which poured out black smoke and let off steam in the loco' shed yard down Sander's Road. He had lived close enough to the shed to see steam engines on very many days of his life. He had fresh memories of a childish drawing which he had made showing how steam came from a boiler to blow a fan around and drive a wheel. His father who had worked on steam locomotives in the mining industry for a short period of his life took great pains to show the young Joe how steam locomotives really worked. He had planted a seed in Joe's young mind that was to grow into an ambition to become a locomotive fireman and driver. On Monday next Joe was to start on that ambition.

While Joe ate his supper and tolerated more complaints about his now irrevocable intention to become a locomotiveman Grandad Peace moved off to bed. Conversation of no interest to Joe developed between Jean and Emily. Soon Joe was able almost without notice to slip out of the house and make his way through the blacked out night to the West household. He intended to spend two hours before bedtime with his friend Dan West who had been paralysed from his chest after falling from a tree two years ago.

Over the next few weeks Joe's mother became resigned to the filth he brought home on grease caked boots and overalls but it did not stop her complaining regularly to him. "How do you think I get these shirts clean when soap's rationed" or "I'm fed up with your mucky overalls and boots. Keep them in the coal-house and not in the kitchen" she would regularly repeat. Joe however was more interested in his job with the loco's and in Jean Walton's warm attention to his company than with his Mother's concerns.

The loco' job had its rewarding moments for Joe. Within his first three weeks he had been in fireboxes and helped Jack Mild rebuild fallen brick arches; he had helped clean engine fires, he had even driven a little six wheeled tank engine down number one shed road without permission.

More boringly he had spent many hours cleaning grease off engine works with paraffin soaked cloths, or shovelled coal and ashes into and out of wagons. He was known as 'War Acting Engine Cleaner Joe Wade.' He worked early shift or late shift as required and always went home dirty; but he went home in the belief that one day he would be asked to be fireman to one of the shed's thirty engine drivers and maybe, just maybe, fire an express to York.

* * * * * *

2
HUMILIATION.

"Can I speak to Mr Franker?" Bob Laker's grumpy tones shot into the shedmaster's office almost as soon as he had jerked open the heavy wooden door. His question was addressed to Douglas Firth, the tall wiry, grey-haired shedmaster's clerk who sat on a tall stool at a dickensian type desk.

"Yes he's in there. 'Spect he'll see you if I can't help" the clerk replied.

"I'm in here. Come in." Jack Franker's voice carried out from the office beyond.

"Come on." Bob Laker jerked on Joe's arm and pulled him in the direction of Jack Franker's office. He drew his cloth cap firmly forward on his head as a gesture of determination. His small round figure moved angrily though the doorway of Franker's inner office. His jacket swung open and his bottle of cold tea in his left hand pocket clashed ominously with the door knob.

"This lad 'ere. I'm not teking him, I'm not teking that train to York wi' him as mi fireman. He's too young. He don't know the arse end o' shovel from t' blade. You know it's blackout, poor coal an' bombings at York. 'E's only a kid. What ye thinking of?" The tirade paused briefly." Gi'me a fireman wi' some experience."

"Just a minute Bob" replied Jack Franker leaning back from his work on his desk and settling into the low wooden chair. "I know your concern. Bill Clarke's just telephoned me, said you were coming up."

"Did he tell you why?" Bob tipped his cap back on his head as a gesture of impatience.

"Yes he said you won't take Joe Wade with you to York to bring back that troop train."

"You bet I won't." Bob thumped his fist on Franker's desk.

"But you'll have to Bob," Franker asserted as he leaned back in his chair and looked up at the angry Bob. "There's no one else."

"There is if you look hard enough."

"Look Bob, I know your argument but you've been out with young lads as firemen before."

"He's sixteen," he exploded. "Just a Spotty kid. Only bin at the shed a few weeks." Bob was adamant. He slammed his fist on the desk again. Joe looked on merely awaiting the outcome, not expecting to be able to influence the dispute.

Jack Franker turned his face towards Joe dressed in clean overalls, a new black serge uniform jacket and a shiny peaked cap. The back of Joe's neck displayed a surgical plaster which covered a lanced boil. "Do you want to go son?" questioned Franker.

"Yes." Joe replied eagerly, glad of the chance to influence the course of the argument. "I want to go very much."

"He wants to go - course he wants to go. I don't want to tek him. He's too young. I've said so" Bob blurted angrily. "You could find an older fireman."

"Who? Can you tell me?" The shedmaster parried Bob with a defensive question.

Bob knew, or at least he thought he knew. "I'll tell you. There's Debb on the station pilot and Fisher taking a light engine to Brid. Give me one of them."

"Bob you know that I can't. You know the rules. They've both got to be finished by nine tonight so that they get enough rest for the early shift tomorrow. You've got to take young Wade."

Bob was adamant. "I'm not teking him. He's only sixteen. You can't mek mi tek him." He paused as if to gather strength for a new verbal assault. "The Union agreement says I can't be forced to tek a fireman under eighteen."

Jack Franker gave Joe a defeated look and leaned forwards over his desk. He was a big man with a balding head and a thick neck, used to arguing with difficult engine drivers and not giving way, but he knew that Bob Laker was correct. "You're right Bob. I can't make you take young Wade if you don't want to."

Bob's mood changed. His aggressive look softened. "Well that's it. You see my point."

"Yes Bob, but there's still nobody else to be your fireman. So what are you going to do?"

"It's 'Hobson's Choice' isn't it. Can't say, 'I'm not bringing a troop train back from York.' Can I? There's a war on." Clearly Bob's attitude was changing. Joe felt a little more hopeful. "Tell ye what Mr Franker, you gi'me a better engine than that load of crap that Clarkey's gi' me an' Ill tek young Wade."

"Well I could sort something out but you'll have to pick up another engine at York for your trip back."

"Yes, there's a point. We'll have to take our chance on what we get back over." He paused and smiled." Thanks Mr Franker. At least I know you understand my point of view" He turned towards Joe. "Come on Son. Let's go and pick up our engine and go to the station. We've got the four-fifteen York to work with the other engine that Mr Franker's going to give us"

A little while later Joe, feeling ten feet tall, climbed up the side of express passenger locomotive number 2726. He pulled himself into the cab, placed his bottle of cold tea and his haversack on the fireman's seat and then looked around.

The boiler front with its maze of pipes and gauges towered above him. He did not feel daunted, proud, yes. He was about to work an express passenger train to York. Fortune had indeed smiled upon him early in his new found career and Bob Laker was now quite friendly and relaxed.

Bob had been pleased to be given engine 2726, a fine Hunt Class D49 locomotive called 'The Meynell.' It was a Castlebrough engine and known to be very good. Within the hour they were backing their locomotive into platform one at Castlebrough Station to couple up to the four-fifteen express to York.

Castlebrough was a popular holiday resort on the North Eastern coast of Yorkshire; it boasted two beautiful bays and a Norman castle on a prominent headland which jutted out into the North Sea. The hotels which once catered for thousands of holiday makers were now billets for armed forces personnel and for evacuees from nearby large towns; the seafront promenades and cliffs were fortified or mined as a precaution against invasion by German forces. Castlebrough had a substantial railway terminus which served the town's forty thousand inhabitants and diversified small industry. The train to which Bob and Joe were to attach their locomotive was a regular service passenger train from Castlebrough to Leeds.

Bob's loco' buffered up to his train. Joe dropped down from the platform and between the tender and the first carriage to attach the engine's screw coupling and vacuum brake hose to the train. He felt proud and adult. The fact that the platform was occupied by a considerable number of uniformed W.A.A.F's and W.R.N's, who observed him working, swelled his pride. He scrambled out from beneath his engine.

The platform was buzzing with people jostling anxiously to obtain a seat or standing room. Each 'was going on leave,' 'coming back from leave,' or 'going to or from work or business' but none were going on holiday. The practice of holiday travel had virtually ceased as the war imposed it rigours on Britain. The poster campaign asking 'Is your journey really necessary?' and other factors had helped stop holiday travel. But journeys were very necessary, in huge numbers they were necessary and the great crowd on Platform One bore witness to that fact.

Bob Laker instructed Joe to go down the platform to the first guard's van and examine the guard's brake pipe guage reading. "We want twenty-one inches, not twenty and a half or twenty," Bob emphasised, "Or the brake 'll drag."

On the way to the van Joe, his cap tipped rakishly, his face already quite black, exchanged interested glances with the blue uniformed members of the 'Women's Auxiliary Air Force.' They in turn paid attention to him. Some winked at him or clicked their tongues. One asked him why he was looking black; another said "Are you coming out tonight fireman?" Joe grinned shyly but inwardly his masculinity surged and mild erotic thoughts fluttered through his mind in response to their feminine charms. After checking the brake pipe guage reading he returned to his engine and reported to Bob. He now felt much more important than before he had paraded in front of the train's passengers.

"We can go Bob." Joe shouted out urgently to his driver. "The guard's waving his flag and blowing his whistle." Bob checked the signal and then pulled open the steam regulator valve, the engine coughed at the chimney head and the one hundred and twenty ton locomotive heaved into motion. The couplings along the train tightened and slowly the three hundred tons of carriages and passengers eased forwards. Exhaust steam and black smoke belched from the chimney to an even rythmical beat, sending a thrill vibrating through Joe's young frame. "Keep ye eye open for any accidents or emergency stop signals," Bob instructed him.

Excitement stimulated Joe's imagination. His snorting, heaving locomotive took on the apple green livery of the pre-war L.N.E.R. locomotives. As his shovel swept coal into the firebox his mental eye witnessed green 2726, with its gleaming locomotive name plate 'The Meynell,' heading out from Castlebrough Station under the long signal gantry on the up main line towards Sander and York. His temples pulsated with emotion at the sight of his colourful express train urging on to York. His imagination flowered; his train was on its way to Kings Cross, London, 240 miles away, a large train name plate 'Castlebrough Flyer' high on the engine smokebox. There it was, the pre-war 'Flyer' and he was its fireman.

"Look out at your side son when we pass Washbeck." Bob's hand fell heavily on Joe's shoulder and rudely shattered his thoughts. "Keep yer eye on all signal cabins as we pass." Joe's vision of his 'Castlebrough Flyer' fell from his shocked mind. He threw down his shovel and looked out.

Two minutes into the journey the train was passing the locomotive sheds and the gasworks on Sander Road. Joe straightened from his labours in front of the hungry firebox and moved towards the cab doorway. He was eager to see who might be standing in the loco' yard to view his passage.

The cleaner chargeman Bill Clarke, stood cloth capped and blue overalled at the corner of the shed closest to the mainline. He displayed a rude 'up yah' sign with vee shaped fingers and grinned. His clean blue overalls - the sign, it was said "that he did nowt" marked his figure out against the shadow of the massive eight laned engine shed. Behind him an A8 tank locomotive stood blowing off, shooting a fountain of noisy excess steam skywards from its safety valves. Nearby hot fire was being shovelled by a shadowy labouring fireman from the cab of a 'Green Arrow' V2 class locomotive that was bathed in wisps of steam leaking from various joints and glands.

Joe's locomotive thundered on. Steam squeaked from its piston glands as a heavy torrent of exhaust steam gushed upwards from the chimney pushing a huge column of black smoke and billowing steam into the grey sky. The crack and groan of steel in relentless motion and the thump of the locomotive's big ends pulsating through the frame of the black locomotive excited every fibre in Joe's body.

On past the 'Mere'; on past Caxton's factory which still showed signs of the fire damage caused by the blitz some time ago; on with gathering speed to cover the remaining forty miles of track that lay between them and York. Joe laboured on, slicing his coal laden shovel through the tiny firehole doorway. As he did he was conscious of Bob's watchful eye on the steam pressure gauge needle, so he resolved to maintain maximum steam pressure and avoid Bob's criticism.

The fields stretched away from either side of the slight railway embankment which struck out across the broad glaciated Vale of Pickering. The bright greens of the landscape and the budding hedgerows promised the new life of spring. Rabbits with their tails flashing alarm tore away from the roar of Bob Laker's express train as it intruded on the quiet March countryside. The train moved like a creeping giant heading West across the level vale towards Malton the well known market town of Yorkshire.

"Fine engine, lad, good rider." Bob shouted across the engine cab to the sweating blackened Joe. "She's running on twenty per cent cut off with this load." His broad white face grinned in accompaniment with his remarks. He had already explained to Joe that, 'running on twenty per cent cut off is very economical, it's a bit like being in top gear on a good bike.' Like most steam engine drivers Bob was part of his engine and he could stroke her into new effort when the mood was upon him or kick her angrily when it was not.

"Like a good woman, son, that's what an engine's like," Bob yelled in the youngster's ear. "Look after her and she'll look after you." He bent his young mate's head to make him look out through the front window in the loco's cab. "See that smoke. It's just falling out, we're hardly using enough steam to lift the smoke, an' wi' twelve bogies on too." He put a warm friendly hand on his sixteen year old mate's shoulder. "That's good driving even if it's me saying so" he boasted with a grin into Joe's coal blackened ear. He was pleased, his home, the problems of tomorrow's roster and the distant depressing war news had briefly left his mind.

The engine rocked and rolled noisily at great speed, milepost after milepost slipped by. Joe's thoughts began to wander from his task; he became engrossed in the thrill of rolling steam, iron and fire. He was doing what he had always wanted to do, he was the fireman on an express train. They sped on through Ganton Station; then Weaverthorpe's distant signal loomed up and dashed past them. The signal post shuddered in the ground as the four hundred ton train crashed by noisily at sixty miles per hour; it's yellow and black semaphore arm with its vee-cut end hung downwards in salute and silently sanctioned 'all clear' to Bob Laker. Suddenly Joe was jolted from his day dreams; the steam gauge exhibiting a worrying drop in steam pressure.

"Do something about that" Bob yelled. "Turn yer watter injector off. That'll get her back up a few pounds." Joe obeyed without question. He balanced himself on the swaying footplate and slotted a few shovels of coal carefully to the front end. Then he jumped to the cab side window to view the colour of the smoke discharging from the chimney stack. He was disappointed, and so was Bob who was also looking.

The expected smoke discolourisation at the chimney top had not taken place. A clear white exhaust was being punched up into the sky to fall lazily in a billowing trail along the length of the train. Joe knew that his few shovels of coal should have caused the loco' to smoke heavily. Worry gripped his stomach. He eyed the half empty boiler gauge glasses and the falling steam pressure with growing anxiety.

Bob Laker's hand fell on Joe's shoulder and pulled Joe's head towards his own. "Let me have a look at what ye doing?" he yelled into his ear. He directed Joe towards the driver's seat. "Sit here keep yer eye on the road while I look at yer fire. She should steam better than this."

Joe assumed the driver's position by sitting on the driver's seat and pulling his legs up in front of the reversing screw. Obediently, but a little unhappily and with a feeling of failure, he gazed out attentively at the steel rails which stretched out endlessly before him. Once again he thought of the colossal magnitude of things on the railways; endless railway lines, huge bridges and viaducts and above all steam giants like his own 2726 that was getting the best of him.

Bob balanced his squat figure expertly on the swaying footplate and used the blade of the fireman's shovel to enable him view the white hot firebed. Within seconds he was standing on the step alongside the seated Joe.

"You've got a bloody camel's hump in the middle," Bob yelled at Joe.

"What's that?," mouthed the perplexed Joe.

"A big heap of coal in the middle of the firebox" shouted Bob. He climbed onto the driver's step, put his hand on Joe's shoulders, taking care not to catch the surgical plaster on the nape of Joe's neck, and spoke into his ear. "Get the long pricker down off the tender." Then as Joe started Bob added a note of caution, "Mind the passing trains, - and the telegraph wires."

Joe felt alarmed now. "Oh! bloody hell," he spoke audibly but addressed himself. "A camel's hump on my first mainline trip. I'll never hear the end of this if the lads at the shed get to know." He clambered up the front of the tender to reach amongst the long fire irons stacked along the top of the left side. True to the bit of training he had undergone with Bill Clarke on stationary engines he stood on the tender and got the iron down without putting his head above the cab roof of the hurtling and swaying loco.' As he worked, Bill's recalled words echoed in his mind. "Stick yer head above the roof when yer goin' under a bridge at sixty - do me a favour, knock some soddin' sense into your thick skull."

Joe steadied himself with the water chute handle as he balanced on the swaying tender. Methodically he struggled with the twelve foot long pricker that lay horizontally on the tender top. When in the cab he carefully threaded it through the narrow firehole door. Bob took over instructing him to occupy the driver's seat and "Keep a look out."

Before Joe had settled into the driving position black smoke was pouring from the chimney and throwing a shadow onto the fields over which it drifted. Sixty-three year old Bob handled the long pricker skilfully inside the ten foot long fire box moving with an agility that his stiff dumpy figure suggested was impossible. After a few moments of heavy pushing and pulling he withdrew the fire-iron, holding it carefully in his cloth protected hands.

He took his seat from Joe. "She'll steam better now. There was nowt at the front end and a bloody big hill in the middle."

Sure enough she did steam better. The steam pressure gauge needle popped up smartly to the one hundred and seventy-five pounds pressure mark. Even though Joe turned on his cold water injector to fill the boiler a thunderous clap of escaping steam told the crew that she was 'blowing off.' The loco' and train surged forwards faster now that the engine had a full head of steam.

Signal boards on posts appeared and flashed by; level crossings were crossed and stations went by in a blur as the train sped on. Joe enjoyed the ride now that he experienced no anxiety about his fire's performance. Though his left hand hurt, seared by the hot pricker he had just replaced on the top of the tender, and his lanced boil on the back of his neck smarted with renewed vigour, nothing spoilt his pleasure now that the engine steamed efficiently.

Bob brought his express to a halt in Malton Station exactly where he wanted it. He explained his skill to Joe. "That's mi mark son," he said proudly. "With a tender engine like this, stop with the cab door opposite that flagstone and you'll know all twelve bogies are on the platform." He was either boasting of his prowess or he was giving Joe an elementary lesson in driving and train control. Joe accepted all of Bob's morsels of train knowledge imparted in order to help him prepare for the day when he would be an engine driver.

"Keep yer eyes skinned for the flag. Look down the platform for the signal." Joe had been dreaming and Bob's sharp remark pulled him into action. "We only have two minutes here and if you miss the flag when Charley's waving it he'll have yer guts fer garters - his wife's garters - and that's a fate worse than death."

Joe acted accordingly and made a silent vow that he would not have to be told to look out for the flag ever again. He shuddered at the thought of being the garters at the top of Charley's wife's leg. He had seen her, "A sort of female camel" Bill Clarke had said in his description of her.

Charley raised his green flag and blew his whistle. "Right away mate, signal off," snapped Joe with an urgency that indicated that every second mattered. Bob with the same urgency wrenched the vertically hanging steam regulator handle into open position. The engine coughed at the chimney head as the superheated steam flowed through the valves to the cylinders. For the second time in Joe's day his engine gave a blast on its whistle and heaved energetically on the couplings and moved the train into life.

Joe rose from the fireman's seat when the train was clear of the platform. He bent down to adjust his bicycle clips around the ankle ends of his overall trousers. They were there to stop the coal dust from getting up his trouser legs. He pledged to himself as he started to fire, "I'll not get another camel's hump in the fire." He shovelled coal expertly into the firebox with the correct flexing of his wrists as he mused to himself, "Camels, why camels? What have they got to do with the railways and railwaymen's wives. I aint never seen one 'cept on the pictures. Bikes have got more to do with railways than camels have. All the blokes at the shed come to work on bikes not camels." His thoughts continued, "All of the enginemen, or nearly all of them wear bike clips around their ankles, and Johnny runs a bike repair shop in his spare time. Ye, bikes not camels 'ave more to do with railways."

The idle useless thoughts continued percolating his mind as he clenched the steam slaker pipe in his hand. With a turn of the pipe's control valve he blasted the dancing coal dust off the floorboards of the cab and the tender with a hot jet of water and steam. "Funny what goes on in the privacy of yer mind," he thought, "Camels and bikes - nowt to do with the railways really. Glad Bob can't read mi mind. I wonder what rubbish he's thinking on."

Joe bent to his task determined to manage without Bob's help. The train devoured the miles; it snaked on around the bends in the pair of tracks that accompanied the flowing River Derwent for many of the miles on the way to York. The journey was good, the loco functioned with efficiency. Bob was pleased. Joe was pleased, in spite of the camel's hump he felt responsible for the success. He did not now care about the plaster and wool on the back of his sore neck, or the grit in his left eye, or the burn on his hand.

* * * * * *

3
THE MAZE AND THE BLACKOUT.

Joe was moderately nervous as his train approached the vast railway junction at York where trains from the East, West, North and South converged. York played an important part in the railway communications system which straddled Britain. 1941 and 1942 had seen York and its railway facilities attacked by German bombers many times but now in 1943 air attacks were infrequent and less likely.

The train, beginning to slow as it approached York, clattered on through the railway cutting which was hedged by roads and houses; it passed under busy road bridges then out onto the railway bridge over the River Ouse. A confusing mass of shiny rails spread out before them as they left the bridge and rolled on into York Station. Water towers, water columns, signal gantries, station canopies, ground signals, points, signal dollies; a welter of railway paraphernalia intermingled with carriages, locomotives and smoke. Bob's passage was clear and prepared. his train rolled on unhindered Bob picked out his signalled instructions from the maze that confronted the train.

'How does he know what to do and when to do it?' thought Joe as he looked at Bob seated in front of the reversing screw with head and shoulders outside of the cab window.

The train coasted on, clanking over the innumerable rail crossings and points, carried forward by its own free motion. The steam regulator valve was shut, the engine gears were in neutral position and Bob was slowly depressing the vacuum brake handle and applying the train's brakes. The train entered number eight platform north and clamorously invaded the darkened space under the vast station roof. It swept on around the bend of the platform and underneath the main passenger footbridge to come to rest at the south end of platform eight.

"We've made good time Bob," Joe said as Bob turned away from the driving controls. "It's only five-fifteen. An hour from Castlebrough to York."

Carriage doors swung open before the train had stopped. Some passengers alighted while the train was still in motion, but as it settled to a halt it disgorged humanity in a torrent. Joe gazed out on the pouring mass. His acne pock marked face was as black as the coal in the tender. His habit of touching his itching spots with his dirty hands transferred to his youthful face more black filth than he desired or was healthy for him. He was engrossed in the clamour of the railway station, the loco's, the signal gantries and the people.

"Like bees in a beehive," he thought as he looked at the people and up and around the roofed station. They poured around the platforms, a torrent of individual journeys, of hopes, desires and fates; going this way once together, never again to be re-assembled as they were now.

Joe fell deep into thought about them and the beehive analogy until a "Howdy Bob" remark drew his attention to a big grimy clothed fellow who had moved up the platform to the cab side of Bob's engine.

"Hi Claude, you cum fer this?" Bob responded and questioned.

"Ye - didn't want to. Missus kicked me out of bed this afternoon. 'Can't lay in bed all day an' all night lazy bugger,' she said, 'Get to work an' I'll keep the bed warm fer yuh to cum back to'."

Claude, who was a large fellow with a big beer belly, replied to Bob whom he knew quite well as a result of his working trains to Castlebrough. He wore a cloth cap caked in the grease of a thousand loco's and a similarly oil caked jacket that had started life as a blue suit and had not been issued by the London and North Eastern Railway Company. His top pocket was stuffed with a pipe and a screwed up tobacco pouch. Behind his right ear was a half smoked 'tab.'

Claude grabbed the cab handrails, raised his heavy studded boots onto the engine cab footplate and heaved himself up. Joe had to back away from the cab doorway as the bulky replacement fireman - a man of twenty-five years - entered the cab. The fellow's half shaven chin and untrimmed 'tash' were slightly offensive to Joe even though he understood the footplate practice followed by some of the young loco' men of not shaving when they were doing a week on late shift.

Claude's driver pushed into the cab after him. 'What a contrast' mused Joe as he viewed the pair from his position on the wooden step at the firemen's side. The driver an 'old Yorky' known to Bob, was diminutive by comparison with Claude. His soft topped L.N.E.R. locoman's cap was crumpled forwards onto the peak and left its back-end standing up. Alongside him Claude was a big bulging brute.

"Are the lamps lit young un? Claude asked Joe.

Bob answered. "No - better light the headlamps Joe, and the gauge lamp. It'll be dark in half an hour. An' nip up and put the tarpaulin anti-glare sheet across when yuh come back." Then to the driver who was taking over from him. "There's plenty of water in the tender to get you through to Leeds. The coal's good and she's steaming well. This left hand injector's a bit dicky - but play with it and it'll come on."

The new driver took in all the information while he was stowing his jacket, his 'snap' tin, a bottle of cold tea, a railway rule book and his hand signal lamp in the locker on the tender front. He could be seen probing the contents of the locker and checking that the regulation detonators and red flags were present for use in case of emergency. His careful concern to check that all was in order on the loco' just being handed over to him seemed unexpected to one who might have judged his work abilities by reference to his tatty, soiled and somewhat eccentric appearance.

When the tasks were completed Joe extracted his belongings from the locker on the tender and from within the seat lockers.

"Don't pinch mi snap, mate," Claude said to Joe who was poking about in the locker looking for his own belongings. "I put mi snap in there an' I don't want you taking it. It took our lass a bloody week to pack me up. One day she put me up some eggs and bacon to fry on the shovel. She'd screwed 'em out a butcher on the black market and some bugger went and pinched 'em off of me when we were changing over like this."

Joe assured him quite seriously that he had only got his own possessions and "I've never took nowt that weren't mine."

"You don't put any coal on the bloody fire either do yuh? Look at that back end. What yer been doin'? Running the fire down so's yer could chuck it out?" Claude grumbled incessantly in a half jocular manner at Joe about all manner of things wrong with the loco.'

Joe and Bob descended onto the platform and waited for a few moments until the guard blew his whistle and displayed a green hand lamp through the falling gloom. The new crew responded with a blast on the engine whistle and a visual check to see that the signal board was off. Then with a yank on the heavy steam regulator valve the engine barked and the train's mass once again moved into life as steam surged into the cylinders.

The train passed them and they saw the flickering flame of the red paraffin tail lamp as the train disappeared into the forest of signal gantries and the maze of steel rails. Dusk was descending rapidly and the little red amber and green signal lights were beginning to appear like sparkling jewels on a darkening backcloth.

"Come on Joe, lets report at Control and find out where we pick up our engine and train for back." Bob turned his dumpy figure northwards up the platform.

They threaded their way through passengers, bags and cases all waiting for departing trains. Station porters moved in a variety of directions with huge flat barrows stacked with parcels, fish boxes, mail and luggage. Smoke drifted across the platform from a tank engine standing in the bay platform alongside Platform Eight. The ornate iron footbridge, joining Platforms Eight and Nine, carried a stream of walking people over the station's main lines. The large station clock hanging above Platform Eight showed the time to be five-twenty-five.

"Over the bridge we're going," Bob said to Joe. "To Central Control just back o' nine platform. They keep in touch with the signal boxes and other parts of the system and control all train movements. They'll tell us where to go for our engine and train."

"I'm ready to eat, Bob. Do you think we'll get a chance soon?" returned Joe with a smack of his lips and a tap on his stomach.

"Maybe - after Control tells us where to go. All I know is that we have to pick up Special twenty-forty-three at York and take it back to Castlebrough. Don't know what time we'll leave."

Joe looked around the grubby control room which they had just entered. It reminded him of an 'ops' room he had seen in a film about the Royal Air Force bombing Germany. Six men and a woman were manning telephones, consulting papers and operating electronic switch gear. They were observing lights on a large wall diagram which suggested to Joe that it was a diagram of the railway network at York. Earlier he had learned that the electrification of York Station signalling had been started just before the outbreak of war but had been suspended. Clearly this room was part of that electrification plan.

"Aye. What can we do for you?" A bespectacled man seated at the desk close to the door asked Bob.

"We're Castlebrough men here to pick up the Special Twenty-forty-three for Castlebrough. Just brought the four-fifteen Castlebrough-Leeds and changed o'er in Eight South. Do yuh have any information for us?"

"Try Sid o'er there. He's dealing wi' specials."

"Twenty-forty-three," said Sid a rotund, waistcoated middle-aged railwayman who had overheard in part. "Where are yuh from?" He paused and reached for a clipboard of papers and then continued, "What yer brought in or did yer come on the cushions?"

"The four-fifteen Castlebrough to Leeds," repeated Bob. "Just handed her over to a York crew Platform Eight South."

Sid sorted his way through his clipboard of papers while he ribbed away at Joe. "Can see that you haven't come on the cushions by the muck on your face. What they done wi' yuh son? Used yuh fer sweeping the tubes? Yuh must be blacker than coal in tender."

"There's a lot a muck on a footplate. Not like bein' sat on your arse in 'ere," rejoined Joe with appreciative amusement. His reply was ignored. Sid, with reference to his papers, continued. "There it is, Leeman Road Shed. Pick up your engine and leave platform nine wi' ten bogies on at seven-forty-five. Express straight through to Castlebrough. No stops son." He strengthened his message for Joe with a look. "You've got the road to yer sen until the regular eight-thirty express leaves for Castlebrough."

Joe and Bob departed when they had the necessary information and were soon in the blacked-out night outside of the railway station picking their way over railway lines and signal wires in the direction of Leeman Road Shed. Only with difficulty could Joe remain at Bob Laker's heels as Bob, quite remarkably and seemingly unerringly, picked out a path across the confusing mass of rails and sleepers. Bob's only aid was his carefully shielded electric torch. It picked out, with its tiny circle of light, a secure piece of ground for Bob's following feet. Joe wished that his feet could be so securely guided but he had to be content with blindly lunging into the darkness vacated by Bob's feet as he moved forward so surely into the bobbing circle of light.

The heavy black damp night hung like a close fitting shroud. Not even a distant shadow stood against the faint skyline. Only the dim station platform lights could be seen behind them for a while; soon even that indistinct vision of reality was gone and the only lights visible were the tiny subdued signal lights on the gantries and on the ground. The rolling clank of a working pilot engine only a few lines away reminded Joe of the dangers railmen faced as they walked along the railbed. It was not the all pervading blanket of darkness which bothered Joe, he was used to the lonely blackness of the blackout after three years of war; it was the imminent danger of being left behind by Bob amidst an obscured tangle of lines and wires. Bob seemed to press on unknowing of Joe's groping behind for the path picked out for him by the light. No murmur of complaint ushered forth from Joe, he did not even think of making one. He just pressed on obediently in the company of his old but very experienced 'mate' in whom he had total confidence.

The sheds at Leeman Road towered suddenly in the shape of a huge steam filled doorway. Between the pair of rails that stretched from their feet into the shed interior were the obscure lines of a deep inspection pit.

"Don't step in there," Bob motioned with his shaft of light. "They're sods in the blackout. Many a man's stepped in there thinking it were firm ground."

The interior of the shed stretched expansively upwards like a tall smokey witch's cavern. A dim gas light fell eerily from half blacked out lamps which hung from somewhere in the tall unseen heights.

Big wooden smoke stacks positioned above each set of rails and the intervening inspection pit, displayed years of caked soot.

As Joe's eyes became accustomed to the gloom and the drifting smoke and steam he could see that he was in part of a locomotive roundhouse with a large manually operated turntable at its centre. Spurs of railroad on which locomotives stood, radiated outwards from the turntable at the centre. Some of the roads were vacated, some housed loco's that were in various stages of dying or coming to life.

A group of women engine cleaners, all with turbanned heads and boilersuited figures, were standing by a piston and connecting rod which were part of a London Midland Railway locomotive - the like of which Joe had never seen before. They gossiped and smoked with paraffin cans, scrapers and cotton waste around their feet.

"C'mon daisies, get that con rod and big end cleaned. I've got to have it up in a couple of hours," Joe could hear the middle aged engine fitter saying to them as he passed. He heard also the repartee from the women about "Your big end" and "what we'll do with it."

"A rough looking lot," Joe said to Bob as he compared them in his mind with the bright, clean young girls he would see congregated outside of the 'Odeon Cinema' at six o' clock on a Sunday evening at Castlebrough. "Bet they're as hard as the fellers say," he continued and recalled a messroom tale about how York's women engine cleaners had once waylaid a young green male cleaner in the pits ripped off his trousers and coated his manhood with a liberal quantity of hot black superheat oil. Joe could not stop an involuntary shudder at the sight of the unfeminine, dirty, oily, overalled women engine cleaners.

"Up here son." Bob's voice broke into Joe's reverie. By 'up here' Bob had meant up the five stone steps to the door marked 'Running Foreman.' But he continued, "No, on second thoughts you stay here an' I'll go an' see Geordie an' ask the whereabouts of our engine an' then we'll go and eat."

Joe hung around the doorway and waited. With some anticipation he opened his 'snap' tin to see what his Mother had packed up for him. Six neat square slices of brown war-time 'white bread' neatly filled his tin. He lifted a slice to see what his Mother had prepared for him. He approved of the well fried dried egg which lay before him and was liberally spread with Yorkshire Relish. Dried egg was a regular 'pack up' for Joe but he didn't object especially as his Mother now complied with his demands and always coated each slab of dried egg with sauce.

Bob's voice broke into his thoughts. "We've time to eat before we pick up the engine. It's only six-fifteen now," he said with his watch cover flipped open. "C'mon."

Joe followed. Bob was not a talkative soul when there was nothing special to please him so Joe just drifted on silently and obediently behind him further into the sooty gloom of the huge dilapidated shed. When they passed through a brick doorway into the spacious messroom Joe realised that he would soon be eating his sandwiches. The floor of the enginemen's messroom was strewn with dry sand that produced a neat but gritty carpet when it was clean but a filthy one when it became oilcaked and littered. The floor of this messroom was dirty and littered with discarded matches, cigarette ends, bits of paper and quantities of grease from enginemen's boots. A roaring coal fire in a large cast iron grate heated a large iron kettle. The wooden benches and tables were oilcaked too in spite of the signs that daily cleaning efforts were undertaken.

"Not like Castlebrough messroom," Bob said quietly to Joe as they seated themselves close by a school of domino players. "Our tables are spotless at five in the morning after Len's scrubbed them with sand and soap. Len always teks a delight, don't he, in keeping our messroom spotless. I alus said it must brek his heart when he comes on again at ten p.m. and has it all to scrub again. This lot here is bloody scruffy" he whispered on. "York men's a scruffy lot at side o' Castlebrough men." With that he deposited his tin and bottle on the long table occupied by the domino players and then made off into the nearby stone sinked washroom to wash his hands. Joe followed him, unwrapping as he went, a large piece of regulation soap which he kept wrapped in a sponge cloth in his jacket pocket. The ability to wash in a greasy engine bucket, or in antiquated railway facilities, or under a village pump were necessary skills for a steam engineman in nineteen-forties Britain. The issued sponge cloths and soap were the London North Eastern's recognition of that fact.

Chatter, smoking, eating, reading and game playing were the activities of the twenty or so men in the messroom. An assortment of clothes and caps in various degrees of cleanliness or dirtiness attired them. Some displayed their London North Eastern Railway Servant badges on lapels or on caps. Some wore the badges of other railway companies or maybe an A.S.L.E.F. or N.U.R. trade union badge. In general there was an appearance that somehow or other these men were a uniformed body of enginemen or shedmen.

"Sandwiches look good son, a bit o' blackmarket traffic eh?" One of the domino school threw out a verbal aside to Joe as he extracted a bulky sandwich from the lidded buscuit tin in which he always carried his 'pack up.'

"Just dried egg , fried up, on the ration I think. Certainly not blackmarket."

"Go on! Yer ole mam'll get a bit of under counter stuff don't she?"

"Everybody does," retorted Joe. "But that aint blackmarket. Just favours from the shopkeeper or butcher. Anyway Co-ops don't mix in the blackmarket."

"Sixes up. That's me out. The kitty's mine lads," said the cloth capped steam raiser to the other three men in the domino school. "I'm off now I've taken your money. You guys shouldn't play against superior intelligence," he chuckled as he counted the kitty proceeds into a little leather purse. "Twelve and sixpence ha'penny - for tekin you pigeon brains on at dominoes. Hope yer kids aint goin' to have to starve now cos of yer mad gambling urges."

A suitable range of grunts, curses and responsive remarks greeted his gleeful boasts. "You're going now?" queried an aggrieved sharp faced young engine cleaner who was sitting in on the school and still held a handful of dominoes.

"Yes, got to go round twenty engines, check the watter levels and fires before I hand o'er to the night shift feller."

"Put a good back-end on that black five in three road, will yer?" grunted another man, in the domino school, who was obviously a fireman from his age and his A.S.L.E.F. trade union badge." I'm tekin' that out on the coal train to Darlington at nine-thirty an' I'll be shovelling all the time wi' the load they'll hang on to us at Gascoigne Wood."

"I don't put back-ends on for nobody," retorted the steam raiser. "If you keeps off yer fat ass when yer on the footplate yuh won't want someone to fix the back-end." He then chortled off rattling the coins in his pigskin satchel purse muttering "I'll buy miself a drink tonight out of this little lot if the Jerries don't close the pubs wi' a raid."

Bob and Joe declined to join in the next round of 'Five and Threes' and contented themselves with their own conversation, their sandwiches and tea and later with a couple of Woodbines. "Coffin nails" Bob would say on almost every occasion he lit a cigarette. He would say it with a wide grin on his face as he peered at the glowing end of the cigarette after his first heavy drag. When they had closed their tins and bottles Joe took from his pocket a copy of the 'Socialist Leader' which he persisted in reading in spite of jocular interfering verbal asides from the members of the newly re-formed domino school. "Politics is for ole fellers son," was one remark made to Joe but which he chose to ignore. Bob picked up a tattered copy of the

Daily Mirror from the bench seat and caught up on the day's reporting of the activities from the war fronts and the air-raids against Britain.

After a while, Bob said, "Let's go an' find our engine." He started collecting his belongings and continued, "That's if someone aint pinched her while we've been sat here."

With a "What have we got?" Joe replied and prepared to leave.

"Seven-four-five, a B16 in 'C' shed."

Their engine was in a totally neglected state, without most of its equipment. "She's been stripped," said Bob and then went on to explain that although the engine had been prepared for the road by other enginemen its tools had been stolen because there was no engine crew present to protect them. "What a mucky mess she is," Bob grumbled as he climbed up onto the footplate. Thick fluffy soot hung in a half-inch coat on the big circular boiler front. Smoke and flames from the fire licked gently back into the cab.

Their only light was the little circle of illumination thrown by the Bob's electric torch. His first action was to take a clean paraffin fuelled torch lamp from his haversack and instruct Joe.

"Go off and get some paraffin. Then we'll square this engine up. You'll have to sit on her and guard the belongings when we get some. We need headlamps, gauge lamps, pricker, clinker shovel, firing shovel ," he paused, "The whole lot it seems."

Joe set off into the bowels of the dimly lit confusing network of linked sheds. When he returned with the lighted paraffin torch lamp Bob settled him into various tasks.

"I'm off on a raiding mission. We've got to do what all the other fellers do; steal our tools off any unmanned engine we can find. You get on with your work while I come back."

Soon, thanks to Bob's efforts, their engine was equipped and ready to depart. Bob got a shedman to throw the points and to set the road for them to the water crane and the towering concrete electric coal cracker. He could not ask Joe to set the road, partly because of the blackness of the night and the complexity of the loco' yard, but above all because of Joe's inexperience.

They topped up the tank at the water crane and sampled the quality of coal from the chute at the electric coal cracker. As the coal tumbled down Bob complained "The coal's nowt but a load of shit, lad. Look at that slate there - all over the tender. God I sigh for the old Yorkshire Main we alus coaled up with at York shed before the war." He continued after a pause, "We're ready to go to the station. Stick yer head out son. Keep yer eyes skinned. It aint Blackpool illuminations. It's as black as a pit out there"

The big black loco' coughed at the chimney top and eased slowly forwards as the crew's eyes scoured the night across Leeman Road Shed Yard. Even though the firescreen was closed to eliminate the glare from the firebox there was still enough firelight in the cab to make looking out into the night a difficult task.

'Carrots that's what you need on a night like this.' The thought went through Joe's mind as he stared into the black overcast night to see the meshed railway network of the loco-yard lighted faintly by shaded gas light standards. He strained out through his locomotive cab side window. The further he got away from the firelight, he reasoned, the clearer his vision would become. His engine clanked noisily over the junctions, only occasionally puffing at the chimney head as Bob piped a little steam through to the cylinders. 'Yes, carrots, mebbe that's what we need. Night fighter pilots eat a lot of carrots to help them see Nazi planes at night.' Joe's thoughts mused on and he imagined he was a fighter pilot who had just sighted a Messerschmitt aircraft on a black night hundreds of feet up in the sky. His Hawker Hurricane was diving at three hundred miles per hour with its guns blazing to strike the Messerschmitt from the sky.

"Ay ! Are yuh bloody well asleep? That bloody light up there's for us." Bob's voice shouted irritably in Joe's ear. He'd crossed the cab and shattered Joe's fantasy. Bob's head was right behind Joe's.

"Oh! that light that's swinging from side to side?" Joe queried apologetically as Bob stepped back to his side and pulled open the steam regulator.

"Yes, yell out if you see any red lights," was Bob's clearly impatient response.

Joe smarted away consciously. He knew that he had been day-dreaming. He knew also that the green light up ahead swinging slowly from side to side was a green handlamp signal telling them to proceed. Joe knew that he should have seen that green light and called out to Bob. He swore to himself that he would not be caught napping again.

"Clear away. Get mobile. Dolly's off," a shadowy figure down in the darkness on a nearby line shouted up to Joe.

"Okay! Dolly signal's off Bob, a feller's shouting down here," echoed Joe in the direction of his mate who was leaning out probing the darkness with his eyes.

Bob straightened up, pulled his steam regulator sharply open and the B16 locomotive noisily gathered speed, pouring out a long white exhaust steam blanket into the dark night. Bob was master of his engine, and of the myriad of signal lights on the gantries and on the ground. That was Joe's confirmed view since he had not the slightest idea where they were going or what they were doing. Bob's dumpy figure showed no hesitation, his face no concern as he propelled his engine noisily at speed into the blackness of the night towards York Station. Even the sudden passing scream of a north bound express on the nearby down main line did not un-nerve him although it made Joe jump suddenly.

Within a few minutes they had covered the distance to the station and were coupled up to ten carriages in Platform Nine. The platform was relatively quiet with only a few khaki clad passengers hanging around close to the train.

"Straight through to Castlebrough, pal," the smart little guard of the troop special said to Bob. The guard was standing on the platform just below Bob Laker's engine cab window. He talked about the night's weather, synchronised his watch with Bob's and informed him that "The lads on the train are Green Howards from Africa - tired out - been on this train since Southampton."

"Bloody fool," Bob responded to his mate Joe when the guard was out of earshot. "Must know he shouldn't talk about troop movements. Don't he know about careless talk. For all he knows you've got a radio transmitter and the first thing you'll do at home is tinkle Lord Haw Haw in Berlin and tell him that the Green Howards are here and not in North Africa." Bob yarned on to Joe while they waited for the guard's green light and the raising of the semaphore signal at the head of the platform.

Joe spotted the guard's green light signal while Bob was nervously checking the boiler water level and the condition of the fire. "Right away mate," he shouted. "Board off too." He felt pleased to have been alert enough to spot the away signal while Bob was not looking out.

With a blast on the whistle in response to the guard's signal, and as a warning to all who may be connected with the train, he jerked open the regulator and put a full head of steam behind the engine's pistons. The powerful mixed traffic locomotive heaved the ten coaches easily into forward motion. The engine had been designed for hauling heavy trains and it found the three hundred ton train of little challenge. They left the platform quickly and smoothly with the heavy thump of exhausting steam beating its way up through the chimney to slowly merge into a roar as the engine and train started its journey to Castlebrough.

The faint blue shaded lights of the railway station merged into the void of the night as the train left York. The well blacked out houses on either side of the track presented a faint ghostly profile against the night sky. Only the firelight, contained largely within the tarpaulin shrouded cab, and the occasional glowing coal spouting skywards from the chimney broke the monotony of the almost black sky. Above the racket of the engine Bob and Joe could hear the distant wail of an air-raid siren drifting across the night sky.

"Keep yer fire screen down as often as yer can and don't open yer side windows. If Jerry's overhead we don't want him spotting us and tekin' pot shots at us," Bob yelled in Joe's ear. Within minutes they were out of sight of the dim silhouettes of York's buildings and were rapidly gathering speed.

Joe heeded Bob's warning: he drew his blacked-out cab side windows tightly shut, tied the anti-glare tarpaulin sheet down over the gaps on either side of the cab. He settled with his legs apart on the rocking cab floor to patiently feed the engine's white hot furnace with coal. His legs ached and dust found its way into his eyes; the heat scorched his left hand as the shovel slotted rhythmically through the small firehole doorway.

They were in a little world of their own; a dusty, rocking, hot, firelit, little world. The blackness of the night sped past and carried with it the occasional signal light which Bob's trained eyes picked out without difficulty. Bob's head protruded into the night from his partly open, black painted, sliding side window; his eyes searched diligently for the pin-prick, paraffin fuelled, lights of the signals. The steam regulator valve was in almost fully open position. The roaring exhaust tore from the engine chimney into the overcast night to form a billowing blanket of smoke and steam trailing back along the length of the train. The large B16 locomotive rode the track roughly and made standing difficult. Joe, with feet apart seeking to maintain a sufficiently steady balance, bent to the task of delivering each load of coal through the swaying firehole doorway.

Bob's hand grabbed Joe's shoulder. "Have yuh got a hole in yer firebed?" He pulled Joe up onto the driver's step and directed his gaze through the small front cab window. "See the sparks coming out. Must be a thin patch in the firebed. Look at yer fire, see if it's got hills an' hollers in it. I can't look cos it'll blind me, an' I won't be able to see out," Bob shouted into Joe's ear and pressed his hand onto Joe's painful neck. "Yer watter level's getting low. Put some watter in t' boiler."

Joe gesticulated with his mouth and nodded. Secretly he was worried. He was keeping a full head of steam; one hundred and eighty pounds pressure showed on the white circular gauge clock but he could not keep his water injector on for long without the steam pressure falling. Obediently Joe did as Bob instructed. Using his firing shovel blade as a shield he inserted it into the firebox to enable him view the firebed. He was disturbed by what he saw. Not only was there a pile of black coal three quarters of the way down the length of the ten foot firebox but there was a white hot dancing thin patch in the left hand front corner. From this white hot embers were being picked up by the blast on the fire and whisked away through the flue tubes and up the chimney.

'Oh! bloody hell, another camel's hump,' said Joe to himself with an internal whisper. He looked at Bob seated in the driver's bucket seat with his head stuck well out into the night. 'The boiler's half empty and the steam pressure's falling an' we haven't gone far yet.' Joe felt anxiety stricken. "Bob" he said weakly over Bob's shoulder. "You were right there's a hole in the fire."

"See them search lights." Bob remarked in return.

"Yes"

"They've caught a plane," he yelled at Joe who looked in the direction of the pencil like beams of light which poked skywards and crossed in an intersection which enclosed a moving spark of light. The search lights were sited in the distance behind a profile of trees that were barely discernible in the darkness of the night.

"Is it a bomber do yer think Bob?"

"A Jerry, yes," Bob replied. " See them flashes. Guns firing at it. He's real high though. Keep yer fire screen down. Don't want him spotting us."

Joe steadied himself against the tender and the back of Bob's bucket seat and looked back along the train they were trailing. His vision was not very clear. He was still blinded by the brightness of the firebox which he had just examined. He could however see that not a twinkle of light escaped from the carriages. Only the firelight that escaped from the engine cab and probed up onto the trailing smoke and steam and the ear shattering racket which their train made betrayed their presence in the night.

Joe did not care about the plane high in the sky. It might just as well be a milk cart standing at a railway crossing for all he cared. He had greater worries. "Got to put the fire right somehow," he muttered to himself worried stiff that Bob would discern the plight that he was in. "Oh! crike, this is the second time in a day that I've got a camel's hump in the fire," he said audibly and angrily to himself. "I'm in the wrong job. Tomorrow I'll go and join the bloody army." He saw Bob's head and shoulders pull in from the darkness and saw his eyes flash in the direction of the water guage columns and the boiler water level.

"Coming up to Kirkham Abbey's distant signal in a minute," Bob yelled quite distinctly towards Joe's concerned young face. "Forty-five miles per hour round there. I'll shut off an' give yuh a rally. Put yer water on." He then heaved on the long handle of the steam regulator and clanked it shut.

Joe had been at the shed for only few weeks but he certainly knew what 'a rally' was. Having a rally when hard up for steam was talked about and joked about by locomotive firemen at all times. They had 'rallies' during fast card games or when they stopped to stoke themselves up with food, or even, they claimed 'rallies' during long sexual encounters. Well, Joe was ready for a rally. He breathed heavily with obvious relief and put both of the engine's water injectors into action.

Bob's head disappeared into the darkness and he drew the blacked out cab side window up to his chest to shield his gaze from the firelight. His concern was to sight the signal lights at Kirkham Abbey. Joe turned the steam jet blower on full blast. The fire roared under its influence and the steam pressure and the water level rallied. Joe determined to use this breathing space to put things right in the firebox. 'Bob need never know' he thought. He turned towards the tender intent on seizing the long pricker iron and inserting it into the firebox as Bob had done on their previous engine. But how? access to the long pricker fire-iron on the tender top was blocked by the heavy tarpaulin sheet which draped from the cab roof onto the tender. He dare not move it when there was a German aircraft about. "Blooming snookered," he muttered audibly, "I'll have to use the short fire iron instead."

The short iron pricker which lay across the tender front end was not long enough to reach the front end of the firebox but Joe was desperate. He threw back the folding firescreen and latched open the hinged big iron fire door. With his hands hastily wrapped in cloths for some protection against the glaring heat, he plunged the short fire iron as far into the roaring heat as possible. He churned the uneven piles of burning coals; but there was nothing he could do to push the burning coals into the bare bouncing patch at the front end.

In desperation he withdrew the glowing hot fire iron and laid it gingerly but carefully across the front end of the tender. He seized his firing shovel and while Bob's head was still out in the blackness of the night he fed large lumps of coal with great speed to the front end of the firebox. The large open door made his task easier. The heat burnt his knuckles as he swept his coal load forwards from the tender. The white hot glare of the fire lit up the cab with a surprising intensity. He worried about Bob's eyes; he worried about the enemy plane in the sky, but he worried even more about his fire and the hole in the firebed at the front end.

He balanced a large coal on his shovel, balanced himself so as to absorb the rocking swing of the speeding locomotive, took the measure of his target, and swung to make a determined delivery. The coal took off towards the front end of the fire but to Joe's horrified amazement so did his shovel. With the speed of a twinkling eye he saw his wooden handled, steel bladed shovel sail straight through the open firehole door into the bright hot roaring flames.

"Christ!" he uttered loudly. His heart fell into his boots, straight through his bicycle clips. "Bloody hell!" He staggered with amazement. Without reasoning out his actions he reached forward and slammed shut the heavy fire-hole door and dropped the firescreen into position. He looked in shocked anticipation in Bob's direction.

* * * * * *

4
THE LOST SHOVEL

'Bang!' a small explosion thudded through the crashing noisy frame of the speeding locomotive to be followed in rapid succession by two other similar explosions. Bob jerked back into the cab. His hand struck down the vacuum brake handle. A great rush of air poured into the train brake pipe through the open valve. All the train's brake blocks ground into the moving wheels and the forwards motion of the train slowed perceptively.

"Here," Bob shouted and gesticulated towards Joe; then he again stuck his head out into the night. Joe moved across the footplate to Bob's side with an uncomfortable sickness in his gut and a nervous anxiety trembling in every limb. "See here." Bob's head turned and yelled into Joe's ear as he looked into the darkness outside of the engine cab.

Joe held his cap firmly on his head as he felt the rush of night air. His vision was scarred by the bright glare of the fire but he looked as Bob indicated, forwards and past the long engine boiler. Somewhere ahead in the darkness Joe could see a small circular amber light swinging in an arc from side to side.. He picked out also the amber light of Kirkham Abbey's semaphore caution signal. He did not know that he was at Kirkham Abbey, ten miles away from York, but he knew enough about railway operating to know that the side to side swinging light was in the hands of a ground signalman and that it meant that they had to proceed cautiously and be ready to stop in an instant.

"Those three crackers meant stop instantly," Bob said to Joe.

"Crackers - what's them?"

"Detonators," came the shouted reply.

Joe needed no more explanation. He knew of the twelve explosive detonators which his engine carried in its lockers. He knew that each would explode if crushed under a moving engine wheel.

"Why?" he addressed Bob seeking a reason for the emergency stop.

"Duh know."

The speed of the train reduced dramatically. Bob raised the loco's brake handle to normal running position and the train brakes eased as vacuum was created again in the train pipe.

"I've got to proceed at four miles per hour," Bob said to his fireman as he adjusted his brake controls and looked upwards in the cab to the circular vacuum gauge clock.

Joe could make out the small shadowy figure of the ground signalman waving his, flickering, amber, hand lamp from side to side.

"Gan up to home signal," shouted the figure as the giant mass of steel and wood moved noisily past him, "Stop yuh thah." The message in Yorkshire moors dialect told Bob all he needed to know. Neither he nor Joe hesitated to comprehend the broad dialect. Many of the men of the permanent way spoke in a deep north country tongue. Bob and Joe understood with ease. With a yell of acknowledgement they let their train creep past him and they craned their necks in search for the small red light on the home signal post.

Joe edged nervously over to the other side of the loco' cab and looked out. He felt miserable. He experienced a misery and anxiety that compared only with the fear he had felt when forced to fight the shed thug Monker three weeks ago in the shed sand store. The anxiety about the shovel burnt deeply into his guts.

"Christ! I'll join the army on Monday," he vowed inwardly. 'How will I manage without a shovel?' The thought agitated him. He couldn't bare to think of the problem. Hundreds of soldiers on the train would learn that he had lost his shovel. Thank God that his Dad was away working in London. 'God it might get into the papers. On Movietone News maybe.' He tried hard to stop the thoughts. He put a woodbine between his lips and lit it hastily; the acrid sulphur from the match flame scorched down the paper tube to infuriate his lungs.

Joe dragged furiously on the burning woodbine. He became aware that he was staring aimlessly into the dark night in front of his creeping locomotive. All he could see was a 'Daily Mirror' headline:

'TROOPS MISS EMBARKATION TO FRONT LINE'
'FIREMAN LOSES SHOVEL'

He shook his head and tried to pull himself together. His eyes smarted. His neck was painful. His scorched hands agonised. He sought to remind himself of happier thoughts in an attempt to drive away his troubled panic stricken thoughts.

"Here kid, snap out of it. Bring yer bloody sen o'er here."

'God he's irritable,' thought Joe as he snapped to attention when Bob's urgent instruction broke through his anxiety. "Okay," he responded as he moved over to Bob's side.

"All this bloody trouble an' here I am wi' a sixteen year old kid." Bob was nattering now and it went on. He lit a fag, pulled Joe over towards the engine locker and instructed him to get the handlamp out. "Stick yer bloody head outside while I light the lamp. Keep a look out. Don't fall asleep." He was in a spitting mood. 'An' he dunt know I've lost mi shovel,' Joe cried inwardly to himself as the creeping train ground slowly to a halt at the tall signal post which displayed a barely visible red light.

"Do yer know Rule Fifty-five?" Bob snapped as his train settled.

"No. Er, yes," Joe flapped.

"Yer either knows it or yuh don't. Put yer bloody fag out and pay attention." He spoke with the tone of an angry schoolmaster.

"Yes I know. Train protection and all that."

"Not 'an all that,' just train protection. Here get this light." He thrust the lit handlamp into Joe's hands. "Get off the soddin' engine an' walk down this side o' the line to the signal cabin. It's just o'er the railway crossing past this signal post. Go on up into the signal cabin and say 'Rule fifty-five, on yer Down line, special for Castlebrough stood at yer home signal. Have yer got it protected?" Bob still sucking on his lighted cigarette repeated the instruction as the painful, miserable, anxiety stricken Joe eased himself out of the cab doorway and down the steps into the night.

Joe's handlamp threw a little circle of light onto the stone ballast beneath his feet. A signal wire, stretching from post to post about one foot above the ground, ran alongside the track. The tall trees of the nearby wood, intensified the darkness for Joe. The big signal post, topped by its faint red light, towered in front of him. To his right stood the lofty, wheezing and creaking B16 locomotive.

'My shovel' he thought, and the full extent of his misery swept over him again as he moved along the ballast. He pulled his overall jacket across his chest as the cold evening air cooled his sweating body. He trudged on in the direction of Kirkham Abbey's signal box worrying about the missing firing shovel. He thought of saying to Bob on his return to the engine, 'Aye Bob, what have yer done with mi firing shovel I can't find it?" But he dismissed that idea. He knew that he was not capable of maintaining that pretence. He thought next of just walking off into the night until he got back to Castlebrough and then joining the army as soon as the recruiting office opened on Monday morning. But he had to dismiss that idea too. He could not really walk back for thirty-five miles and leave Bob. His mind raked around in his crisis and he trudged on. He resolved to ask the signalman if by any chance he had a firing shovel. 'Who knows,' he reasoned, 'he might collect firing shovels that fall off engines.'

Joe felt his way in the blackness over the railway crossing and glanced back towards his engine. He could see its profile hovering domineeringly against the black sky; its two illuminated white headlamps, displaying the express train code. Forward he could see the outlines of the signal cabin with a red handlamp signal displayed by the signalman in his cabin window. Soon Joe's heavy nailed boots fell noisily upon the wooden steps as he climbed the stairway up to the cabin doorway. A small lean uniformed signalman opened it for him with a greeting.

"Oi. Things been okay for you out there tonight? Or have you seen any bombing?"

"Quiet really, seen only searchlights wi' a Jerry plane trapped in the beam bein' shot at," returned Joe, "Has owt happened that you know on?"

"Not seen nowt. Think Hull's copping it and Castlebrough from what I can learn on the line. You're Castlebrough men aren't you? Been nowt at York from what I can mek out."

Joe noticed the 'Castlebrough Men' with a pride which was suddenly dampened with renewed anxiety about his plight. "Yes" he replied and continued, "Why we stopped? What's the crackers for?" Then he remembered Bob's instructions. "Oh! Ye, Rule Fifty-Five, Castlebrough-York train stood at yon signal. Can yer see?" he gesticulated feeling a little mixed up and panicky. "Have yuh got us protected?"

"Yes, I've got the collar on the lever an' I aint cleared the section back to Barton Hill yet." The signalman paused briefly and operated a train control device on the rack above his frame of signals and points levers. "What's tha mean? Castlebrough-York? You're the York to Castlebrough special on the Down Line. Just in front of the eight-thirty from York." His face beamed a friendly amused smile in response to Joe's confusion.

"Yes. Sorry, that's what I meant. Is that the collar on that lever that I'm supposed to see?" Joe motioned clearly to an upright red signal lever handle which had a large steel washer over it to stop it being operated.

"Ye."

"What's a marrer then?" Joe pursued, again wanting to know why the crackers had been used to bring their train to an emergency halt.

"Ye, nowt much really. A light engine up front failed, dropped a big end key just when I was waiting for it to clear Castle Howard. Got a line blocked warning so I sent Charley up wi' the crackers to make sure that you stopped." He paused to take a bell signal. "Just heard from Castle Howard that the light engine's moving up to his home signal an' he'll be clear soon."

"That all then? Thought it'd have summat to do wi' the air-raid warning," Joe questioned.

"Nop."

"Have yer got a spare firing shovel?" Joe blurted out his request without thought or hesitation.

"Got one there, stuck in the coal bucket," he grinned in reply. The small coal shovel stood mockingly in the bucket. "What's up? Lost yours or summat?"

"No course not." Joe lied with sudden and surprising ease. "Mine's a bad un though. I'd like to change it."

"Can't oblige." The signalman paused and listened to the cabin's audible electronic signals that suddenly called for attention. "Shouldn't be here long. Just waiting for line clear bell from Castle Howard."

For a few moments Joe's anxieties about his firing shovel left him. The little country signalman in his tight sleeved railway waistcoat with its dangling watch and chain, looked at ease in his spacious signal cabin. The comfortable, cushioned, chair in front of the glowing coal stove made the cabin much more attractive and homely than an engine cab. Joe surveyed the cabin. The long iron frame of signal and point levers; the shelf above them carrying an incomprehensible quantity of bells, indicators and handles; even the small upright, one man, iron air-raid shelter standing in the corner, made the cabin an interesting and attractive place to him.

The thought occurred to Joe, 'Maybe I should transfer and become a signalman. Less worry in this job.' These thoughts caused his anxiety about his lost shovel to re-surface with new vigour. He dreaded having to mount his engine and set off for Castlebrough. As he continued wondering whether he could feed the firebox with his bare hands the cabin door opened and Charley entered.

"Wotcha think Thomas?" questioned Charley holding up a brace of dead rabbits by their hind legs. "Worth two an' six o' anybody's brass - each that is."

"Are they off Howard's Estate?" the slim little signalman asked with a wink in Joe's direction.

"Mine. Caught on mi own allotment. They aint never seen the sky o'er Howard's Estate," lied big Charley with ease and confidence always ready to demolish allegations about him ever doing any poaching.

Joe had to pause and drink in the impact of Charley's presence. Round faced, with a big neatly trimmed white moustache, a white stubbled chin, round merry eyes above wrinkled cheeks; all added to a twinkling merriment which exuded from Charley's ageing face. A grubby soft cap sat at an angle over his right ear. He was big bellied, strong limbed and adequately clothed in an old tweed jacket and black worsted trousers. The dress habit which struck Joe most of all was the way in which Charley wore his trouser legs. Just below each knee around the leg a cord was tied which gripped each trouser leg to its respective shin. This caused his trouser bottoms to flare out and to be raised above his heavy boots.

"Two an' six? Na, mek it two bob an' I'll have one," the signalman rejoined.

"To you okay," Charley answered the signalman. Then he turned towards Joe, "What 'bout you lad? You from the loco' there?"

"Yes." Joe was answering Charley's second question but Charley assumed that he meant 'Yes' he wanted a rabbit, so Charley swung the brace of rabbits over Joe's shoulder and Joe cringed noticeably. They were warm and soft. Only minutes before they had been struggling unsuccessfully for life in the throttling embraces of Charley's wire snares. Joe felt more than a touch of sympathy for the two dead creatures even though he had kept and killed his own rabbits at home.

"Gi' one to Thomas," said Charley as the two dead rabbits fell on Joe's shoulder.

Joe flustered and searched his pockets for coins. He knew that his mother and brothers at home would eat rabbit anytime to supplement the bareness of war-time rations.

"Yuh eye kid, looks sore, I tell yuh when yuh gets home rub it wi' the green end of a goose tod," chuckled Charley towards Joe.

"Where's he going to get a goose tod at home?" Asked the signalman seriously as his contribution to the small talk.

Thomas seemed to have forgotten his signal duties and the special troop train standing at his home signal while he lovingly, or was it greedily, acquired the best of the two rabbits from Joe.

Suddenly their conversation was interrupted by the tinkling of the 'line clear' signal. Thomas left them and took the call. On his return to them he said to Joe, "I'm going to wave your mate up. You can jump on the engine as it comes down the platform." He slid back his signal cabin window, and, after having subdued even further the flame of the paraffin lamp which illuminated the cabin interior, he plunged his head into the night. He waved a green handlamp signal in the direction of Bob's B16 loco' which had just started blowing off steam.

"You're thirty minutes in front of the eight-thirty from York, so if you get shovelling and keep yer arse off yer seat you'll be in Castlebrough before him."

Joe felt pained by the signalman's reference to shovelling but he just had to swallow hard, grip his rabbit and the handlamp and nip smartly down the darkened steps to the platform below. Bob responded with a blast on his engine whistle when he had sighted the green light signal. As soon as he received an answering green light signal from the guard he put a full head of steam behind the pistons.

As he moved his train forward the hard clean exhaust blast from the chimney shattered the quiet of the dark leafy night in the tree surrounded station. The engine and train pulled over the level crossing and drew down the platform to where Joe, rabbit in hand, was displaying the white light of his hand lamp.

'Oh blimey! How the hell? Without a shovel,' were Joe's panicky thoughts as he leapt carefully onto the moving engine in the darkness. He knew that he had to be sure footed. If he was not and he slipped, well, he would slip between the platform and the moving train to be mangled by the wheels. He was sure footed and he pulled himself up into the cab to the attention of Bob. "What was it then?" Bob demanded irritably of Joe as he ducked into the cab through the cab doorway and beneath the anti-glare sheet.

"There was a light engine up front that dropped a big end key the signalman says." Joe placed his rabbit in the fireman's seat and continued to inform Bob." "But he's clear of the section now and standing inside at Castle Howard," Joe informed his driver as casually as possible while the anxiety over the shovel raged through his mind. "We are half an hour in front of the eight-thirty from York he says."

"Yes I know." Bob was struggling with the big steam regulator handle. He pulled hard then grunted with satisfaction. "That's okay now - in second port."

Joe did not know what Bob meant by 'getting his regulator valve into second port' but he did not enquire further. His misery was too profound to permit him express any interest in engine mechanics, he was too tired and dispirited. The grit in his left eye, the burn on his hand, his scrubbed knuckles and the plastered boil on the back of his neck; all caused him greater pain and discomfort than he had suffered previously. He noticed how his pains were more severe when he was worried about his job. He lit another woodbine with his homemade cigarette lighter. He dragged heavily on the cigarette and looked at the steam pressure gauge. He wondered just how long the steam would stay at one hundred and eighty pounds pressure now that Bob was making great demands on it.

Bob addressed Joe urgently, "We've got to belt on. Don't want to get stopped and put behind the eight-thirty from York. I want a pint in the Railway Tavern before closing." He stopped talking and thrust his head into the darkness again only to return it a few seconds later.

"You keep yer end up son. We're at Castle Howard in a minute.

Then there's Huttons Ambo, then Malton. I'll shut her off at Malton and coast through at forty-five and give yuh a rally. Then it's straight through to Sander - cracking on without a let up." Bob had to shout now that his train was picking up speed. The blast at the chimney top was harsh and heavy. The big ends thumped rythmically and heavily in response to the effort Bob had placed in the cylinders. Joe strained his hearing and read Bob's lips. "You look after the fire and watter, son. I'll have to keep mi head out cos visibility's bad, a bit of fog about." With that Bob's head disappeared again. Only his short thick legs and his broad backside were in Joe's world. Bob's head and shoulders were out in the night.

Joe felt all alone and loaded with responsibility. The black engine cab, illuminated by firelight, bounded by its shuttered sides and the huge curved roof and the anti-glare sheet, rocked through the dark night. Joe looked at the huge circular front of the boiler with its network of pipes, fittings, controls and gauges. His world was small, lonely and yet very complex, it was his responsibility and he did not have a shovel. The straining blasting B16 locomotive could only carry on through the night with its load of troops if he made it possible, if he kept a full head of steam, and if he kept the boiler full of water.

The engine would not go very far if he remained seated and worrying. He moved towards the tender. 'I'll have to try to feed some big lumps into the fire by hand, but what a lot of crap this is. Not many lumps, I'll just have to find what I can and say my bloody prayers.' He knew that he had to try so he raised his youthful five feet seven inch frame into unenthusiastic action. His hand searched for lumps of coal in the blackness of the bunker.

"What the hell?" he spoke out loudly. He was balanced precariously on the moving, jumping, flapper plate that bridged the space between the engine cab and the coal filled tender. He reached down with one hand. His searching hand fell unbelievingly on the tee shaped end of the wooden handle of a firing shovel. He pulled on it as his thoughts quickly dwelt on his knowledge of mirages. The shovel emerged its full length from the coal into the firelight.

Across the front of the tender, from which Joe had to shovel, were three heavy wooden coal boards to stop the heaped coals from falling forwards into the cab. The shovel which Joe pulled out had been thrust so far into the pile of coal and under the boards that it had been barely noticeable in the shadows of the swaying engine cab. He straightened himself and felt the shovel incredously with his fingers.

"It's no bloody mirage, it's real," he uttered audibly. "Will it carry coal?" Hardly believing that he was doing what he was doing, he opened the firehole door and commenced to shovel small quantities of coal through the elliptically shaped firehole. 'It works.' His mind raced with solutions. 'I didn't throw the shovel into the fire. That was the mirage,' he thought. He felt unhappy. 'If that were a mirage I must be puddled and that's really summat to worry about.

"That's Castle Howard" yelled Bob, interrupting the thoughts of his struggling fireman, as they both felt the train surge past station buildings and platforms. Bob produced a 'toot a toot - toot a toot' on his engine whistle in response to a welcoming short blast by the disabled light engine in the siding. "That's 'im as dropped the big-end key. Bloody glad he's out of the way. Could have kept us all night if he'd not cleared," Bob yelled down a cupped hand in the direction of Joe's ear. Joe mouthed acknowledgement. "Huttons Ambo's next" Bob continued, " then Malton - an' that's half way to Castlebrough."

Never had Joe's back and legs ached like they did now as they struggled to cope with the motion and swing of the loco.' He felt weak. Sweat oozed from beneath his cap to run into his eyes. He was really beginning to flag and tire as the clock approached eight-thirty. He was wishing again that he had stayed at his previous job as a lad parcels porter. That had been boring but at least he did have his Saturday nights out down Newborough in the amusement arcade or in the badly lit, blacked out cafes or dance halls. He wiped his brow and eyes with dirty hands and cursed the coal dust that rose in the cab. Suddenly the engine lurched and rolled more than usual. The clop-er-clop of the racing wheels on the rails changed to a drawn out metallic whooshing sound as the train raced over a steelbridge spanning a river.

"That's Ambo's bridge o'er the Derwent," Bob shouted in recognition of the sudden change in the train's sounds. "When I see Malton South's distant signal I'll shut off an' we'll coast through Malton Station."

Joe straightened up from his bowed labouring position and received Bob's remarks. "Thank God" he breathed in recognition of the respite the closing of the hungry steam regulator would give him. He laid down his shovel and turned on the water feed injector. He slid open his cab window, seated himself and thrust his head out into the misty damp night air that rushed past the engine cab and threatened to rip his cap from his head.

He gazed out into the night. Through his glare scarred vision he witnessed the passing of numerous signal gantries, the glint of the nearby river, the roar of Malton's station buildings as the train thundered through the roofed in station; the clatter of the level crossing and the silhouettes of the two signal cabins. After what seemed only seconds of respite the blast of exhausting steam again ripped out aloft from the chimney stack as Bob wrenched open the heavy regulator handle. The white billowing blast of exhausting steam poured out into the misty dark night sky and fell along the length of the snaking train. Joe pulled his cab side window closed and sank, semi-exhausted, into the well of the engine cab to continue shovelling.

The struggle that followed for Joe was hard and anxiety ridden. Bob's eyes probed the misty wartime night for the precious little amber, red or green, signals perched high on their signal posts. He could not, or refused, to concern himself with Joe's efforts.

The water level in the boiler fell slowly. Joe fired like an artist; a bit to this side, a bit to that side, a bit to the front end. The task went on endlessly into the night. The circular boiler front towered menacingly and rocked above Joe's tiring figure. He tried every little trick to coax the fire to raise the steam pressure, managing to maintain the pressure only by neglecting to maintain the water level. He could not afford to cool the boiler down by adding hundreds of gallons of cold water. He knew that his fire was slowly clinkering up and that the fierce red glow of the once healthy fire-bed was becoming dulled.

The train careered on, crashing and banging, rolling and blasting; four hundred tons rushing through the night. Anxiety burrowed away in Joe's stomach as the boiler water level continued to fall. In desperation he sought solutions. He balanced on the dusty, coal strewn wooden floor, and with his shovel blade as a shield he looked down the length of the B16's firebed. His heart once again shot into his heavy studded boots. He spoke out audibly in response to what he saw. "Oh! Bloody hell, another camel's hump, an' worse than before." It was worse than before. The lump in the middle burnt with a blue haze; only around the edges of the large firebed did the fire burn brightly. "Lumme! two camel's humps an' a lost shovel in one day." Joe was talking to himself. He wiped sweat from his eyes with oil soaked, dust caked hands. "What can I do? We're a long way from Castlebrough."

The boiler water level bobbed about in the bottom of the two water gauge glasses. Joe watched; mesmerised. 'How low does it have to go before the boiler blows a plug?' he asked within the loneliness of his anxiety stricken world. He'd had the answer to that question many times. "If the water level falls to the top of the firebox for even a split second she'll blow a lead plug and the steam and water will gush into the firebox and put the fire out." Fantasy flared in his mind. 'Daily Mirror' headlines and 'Movietone' news flashes appeared again with crystal clarity and reality.

'SECOND FRONT DELAYED.' 'FIVE HUNDRED TROOPS LOST IN RAILWAY ACCIDENT.' 'LOCOMOTIVE BOILER BURSTS IN YORKSHIRE.'

He shuddered as his fantasy filled out the text of the horror.

Joe decided that he must act to improve the situation. He dropped his firescreen shut so as to darken the cab as much as possible, then he turned back the anti-glare sheet to enable him pull a long fire-iron from off the tender top. He did not know which one he had secured; the darkness of the night made it impossible to choose by sight. He found that he had chosen the long clinker shovel. He thrust its twelve feet length into the fire and he heaved and sweated as he manipulated the great iron shovel to disperse the coal and spread it about the firebox. His anxiety raged as he struggled.

He withdrew the long shovel. It glowed incandescently and threatened to bend out of shape. He scorched his hand again for good measure in spite of his cautious use of sponge cloths in each hand. With the firehole door tightly shut he sat down and prayed silently as he watched the steam needle hovering around the one hundred and sixty-five pounds pressure mark. He could do nothing now but sit on his swaying engine, smoke Woodbines and hope. He ached all over; he was filthy, he was burnt and he was miserable. The only hope in his worried mind was that Monday morning would see him in the army recruiting office and 'away from this bloody mess and worry.'

The steam pressure fell back as the cold water from the injector flowed in and stemmed the falling water level. There was no alternative for Joe, he had to maintain the water level which was already far too low; he could not shut off his water injector in order to maintain steam.

Bob jerked back into the cab. His eyes lifted to the gauge that was displaying only one hundred and fifty pounds steam pressure. "We're coming up to Ganton's distant signal in a moment," he shouted across to Joe loud enough to be heard above the racket. "If the board's off they'll be giving us a run through in front o' the eight-thirty an' I'll get mi pint." "If it's not they'll be shunting us across to clear the line." With that interjection into Joe's depressing thoughts he slammed shut the steam regulator, turned on the blower and let the engine coast out of gear. His head disappeared into the night air again.

The steam pressure rallied a little and so did Joe's spirits. 'Blow Bob's pint in the Tavern. I hope we get stopped and put across and then I can have a good rally.' Joe didn't say this to Bob but it thundered loudly through his thoughts. For a few seconds the special troop train coasted on noisily through the dank unclear night. The engine boiler stored up vital new energy slowly and Joe's spirits heightened in the same slow manner.

Suddenly Bob's cloth-capped figure slipped back into the cab and stood up straight on the driver's step. "We've got it. He's givin' us a run," Bob yelled in delight. With both hands he yanked open the regulator valve. "There we are. The distant's off, we're all clear now through to Castlebrough." Ganton Station, with its blacked-out, silhouetted signal cabin, loomed up like a shadowy ghost onto a dim unclear screen. A little white hand lamp light moved rapidly up and down in the hands of an unseen signalman from the window of the cabin. A yell from the same signalman could be heard faintly amid the great roaring noises of the accelerating train. Bob gave a responsive blast on the engine whistle and turned backwards to speak to Joe. "Dicky up there, Dicky Crouch, he's wavin' us on, 'Get to hell out of it' he'll be saying. He don't want us stuck across at Ganton waiting on the eight-thirty to pass us. He'll want to be down in the village pub as soon as we're through and clear of the section to Sander."

'Pints,' Joe thought, 'everybody wants a pint on the railway. Pints keeps the railways going. I want a bloody rest here to get some wapping steam. Blast their pints, gi'me pounds - pounds of steam.' He didn't utter these thoughts to Bob, he would like to have done, but all of Bob's concentration was outside and focussed on the signal lights; instead Joe turned with sinking heart towards the mysterious shovel. He set himself astride the swaying cab floor and selectively fired the loco's firebox.

His task was a race against time; a race against steam. He knew that he must not lose the race. If they had to stop the train and raise steam they would halt the eight-thirty York express at Ganton. Bob would then have to make out a written report to the shedmaster and of course he would have to blame the fireman. Joe didn't want that to happen. He felt as though he'd had enough for one day. He recalled how Bob had started the day by saying "I'm not taking this kid wi' me. He don't know the arse end of the shovel from the blade." He recalled also how he, Joe, had gone on to acquire two camel's humps, an empty boiler, then to destroy his shovel in the firebox and then mysteriously acquire another. 'God what a catalogue of disaster?' thought Joe. He certainly didn't want to see his train stop to raise steam and halt the passage of the York-Castlebrough express.

The steam pressure fell as the train devoured the miles. Joe again raked around the firebox with the long clinker shovel but slowly steam pressure fell to one hundred and twenty pounds as they rolled on towards Sander Junction. The water level in the glasses bobbed in and out of sight as the engine rolled. It was perilously low. Joe did not dare to shut off his injector water feed no matter how much the steam pressure fell. Strangely, Bob displayed little interest. His nonchalance had a calming effect on Joe. When Bob blasted on the engine whistle at the sight of Sander Station's distant signal only one hundred pounds pressure displayed on the pressure gauge and the train was still about four miles away from Castlebrough.

Joe prayed and worried, there was little else he could do. Suddenly without a word to Joe, Bob closed his steam regulator and turned on the blower. The train under its own momentum coasted on towards Castlebrough. She clanked on; her hundreds of tons plunging on without steam in her cylinders. Joe realised that they were within reach of Castlebrough and some relief poured into his tired anxious body.

"There's still a raid on at Castlebrough. Some fires burning." Bob shouted.

Joe looked out in the direction of Bob's indication, he could see the silhouetted skyline of Castlebrough with about five large fires burning. The familiar vague outline of Oliver's Mount in the wet cloudy sky pleased him. Relief flooded into his stomach and his thoughts, his heart picked itself up from his boots. Somewhere over to the left in the darkness up on the valley side his Mother would be waiting at home ready to feed him. Joyfully, and without asking Bob's permission he pulled the engine whistle cord as they blasted on past the council housing estate. "For mi Mam," he shouted at Bob who looked back into the cab a little startled.

"Keep off that!" Bob shouted at him irritably. "I'm the one that blows the whistle. What yer tryin' to do - attract a German bomber?"

Joe shrank from the reprimand. He did not reply or excuse himself. He placed his head out through the cab window and stared into the fire glow that bathed Castlebrough. Above the clanking din of his now slowly moving train his ear could faintly catch the welcome swaying drone of the 'all clear' siren drifting across the night air. At least they would not now be held under cover of the station roof while the raid finished.

Joe glanced anxiously at the steam and water gauges both of which were showing crisis levels. Bob was struggling to keep the train rolling forwards by using his large vacuum ejector to keep the train's brakes clear of the wheels. His efforts were rewarded and he was soon able to close the engine steam valve and let the long train coast in over the network of points and crossings into the roof covered Castlebrough Station and Platform Three. As they grated to a halt in the black unlit platform populated only by few shadowy figures of station staff, Joe felt relieved but braced himself for Bob's expected irritable onslaught.

But Bob just sat on the driver's seat smoking and relaxing. The roar of the fire and the singing of the steam operated water injectors working to fill the almost empty boiler, provided a comforting contrast to the commotion and clatter that they had endured all of the way from York. Bob was wiping his hands and his brow with a clean white sponge cloth.

"Is tha there Bob?" The voice from the darkened platform disturbed Bob's quiet moment. As he turned to look outwards onto the platform that was slowly being illuminated by station gas lamps being lighted now that the raid had ended, his eyes fell on Dave Bainton's long figure pushing itself in through the tiny cab doorway. A pipe dangled from the corner of Dave Bainton's mouth has he spoke. "We'll back the train down to Gas Up sidings an' leave her there Bob" said Dave the late shift station shunter. Joe marvelled at Dave's long, neat figure and recounted mentally how calm and well spoken he thought Dave was. He often wondered how Dave kept himself so prim and proper and still managed to heave oily couplings about and creep under carriages and locomotives.

"You've had a mucky time lad," Dave said quietly with the hint of a smile in the direction of Joe whose spotty face was well blacked with engine oil and coal dust. "Has it been a rough ride then?" he asked with a knowing glance at the steam pressure and the bobbing water level in the gauge glasses. Bob and Joe satisfied his curiosity with a brief account of the trip, the sirens, the 'three crackers' at Kirkham Abbey, and the rabbit that Joe had acquired. Dave offered "I'll gi' yer three bob for the rabbit and that's a bob profit for you."

Joe declined the offer and said that it was for his Mam who could well use it feeding him and his two brothers. He made a mental note that his account to Dave of the evening's events had successfully missed out the destruction in the firebox of his firing shovel and the mysterious appearance of another one. They learnt from Dave how Castlebrough had suffered an air-raid lasting nearly two hours and that dozens of incendiary bombs and high explosives had been dropped causing some major fires and bomb damage. Joe gathered that some incendiaries had dropped on Hastings Estate but the brunt of the raid had been borne by the old town and the main steet shopping area. Joe wondered about his family and friends.

Dave left them with their instructions for shunting their train and he threaded his way down Platform Three through the hundreds of troops who were assembling with kit bags on the platform ready to move off towards the army lorries just outside of the station.

"When we get to the shed son, we'll turn her, coal her an' watter her. Then when I've placed her o'er the pit you'll have to clean yer fire, an rake the ashpan out and clean yer smoke box", Bob instructed. "Tha's done all that before as'nt tha?" he questioned. Joe nodded affirmatively. "Well I'll be leaving yuh then, an' be going up to 'Railway Tavern.' There'll be a pint there now the raids finished. You leave the engine on the pit. I'll ask Jack the Steam Raiser to put her down fer the night in the shed."

Joe just said "Yes" or "No" in all the right places as Bob outlined his instructions. It occurred to Joe that he'd be working away until midnight with all of the work he still had to do.

"You've done a good job tonight Joey lad", Bob said quietly and kindly to his grubby, sweat streaked young mate. "It's been a rough un fer you tonight. That bloody coal was rubbish - half on it's muck, as you'll see when yuh chuck out yer fire later."

Joe kept nodding while he prepared to offer Bob a Woodbine cigarette.

"But what did yuh do wi' yer shovel at Kirkham son? I couldn't find it any bloody where while yuh were up in that signal cabin.

Joe was shattered by the sudden question. "The shovel?" he queried. "Oh! it were there" he lied pointing to the corner of the cab near the exit through which Dave had just passed. "It were standing there when I went up to Kirkham's Box." His mind was in a confusion of anxiety again but he never dreamed of telling the terrible truth about the fate of his shovel. He just blundered on into the confusion. "Here do yuh want a Woodbine, Bob?" and he proffered the packet of five. There was a short pause in the interrogation and investigation while Bob drew on the fag in his mouth.

"But what of this shovel Bob?" Joe plucked up his fireman's shovel from the coals. "I realised this one weren't mine when I came back from Kirkham's box."

"Ah couldn't find your shovel son," said Bob. "Tha must ah knocked it out o' cab when tha got down onto ballast at Kirkham, if tha'd left it stood there."

"Mebbe so, but I don't remember." said Joe wanting to avoid a detailed recollection.

"By the Lord in heaven. It were a good job I'd stashed a spare shovel up on top o' them boxes at York." Bob motioned up in the direction of the two big metal lockers on the front end of the tender.

After a pause he continued. "I alus believe in keeping a spare shovel handy since I threw mi own shovel in the firebox when I first started firing." He chuckled at the memory and grinned into Joe's attentive face.

The blast of the shunter's whistle drew their attention to Dave out on the platform. Bob reached for his engine's controls not knowing that he'd just saved Joe's credibility. Joe glowed with success; silence had been his best policy.

Soon they were backing their train down to the sidings and then off to the shed where Bob quickly departed for the Railway Tavern and his mandatory two pints of Moor and Robson's mild.

Joe clumped slowly up Sander Road. The heavy blackness of the night was eerily lonely and quiet after the thunder and heat of the B16 locomotive. A calm had settled after the all clear; the fires in the town now burned low and cast faint glows in the sky that were distant and unreal. None burned on Sander Road or Hastings Estate.

Joe's empty tea bottle leaned from his left pocket, the limp cold rabbit hung from his right hand. As he felt his way through the road gap in the stone anti-tank barricade that stretched across the road near the football field, a large fire engine with masked headlights came towards him. He could see the shadowy figures of some tired firemen standing at the rear of the vehicle. The hour was close on midnight.

Joe had been a long time completing all of the hard dirty tasks on his engine even though Jack the Steam Raiser had been kind enough to lend a hand with the worst, probably prompted by sympathy for Joe, who was worn through with fatigue and hurt, ached and smarted in more places on his body than he knew he had.

His Mother was not in bed when he arrived home. She'd been too worried by the raid to think of going to bed. Grandad Peace had been in his bed for the duration of the raid. Joe's Mother reported him as having said, "If they are going to get me, they'll have to get me in bed." Her account of the raid indicated that there hadn't been a lot of action or damage on the estate.

Joe stripped and washed at the stone sink in the scullery, and his Mother changed the dressing on the lanced cyst on the back of his neck. She laid his supper of sausage, fried potatoes and cold rice pudding on the table shelter in the living room and went off to bed with a promise that she'd "get Mr Young next door to skin the rabbit tomorrow."

Joe sat eating and reading in the sparsely furnished living room. Faint embers glowed in the fire grate. After a while he switched on the wireless and tuned in to 'Germany Calling.' Sure enough the quiet, taunting voice of 'Lord Haw Haw sailed into the room, "Germany Calling. Germany Calling. Germany Calling. Stations Calais One, Calais Two, Bremen and Friesland. From the Fuhrer's

Headquarters on Sunday March the Twenty-third, Nineteen-hundred and Forty-three. The German Supreme Command announces." There was a short, but ominous silence followed by the echoing toll of a ship's bell. Joe chewed his supper slowly while he quietly counted each of the following bell sounds. Seventeen he counted before 'Lord Haw Haw' spoke the fatal expected words. "Seventeen bells toll for seventeen British ships destroyed at sea by the glorious navy of the German Third Reich."

Joe reached forward to the radio set and eliminated the scoffing voice. He quietly determined not to join the army on Monday because he preferred his job on the railways.

1
DE-RAILED AT THE STARTING POST

"Right away mate! Tom's loosed off and waved us ahead." Joe turned towards Bill Ankler the driver and gave a nod in the forward direction. They were on the foot-plate of a C7 locomotive at the head of a stationary mixed goods train on the up main line at Heslerton station.

Tom Rittler, the fat, little train guard had descended from his brake van, walked the length of the train's thirty-two wagons, and uncoupled those he wished to shunt into the small goods yard.

Bill gave a grunt, folded the 'Daily Express' he was reading and turned on his driver's seat to look backwards in the direction of Tom Rittler. He peered over the reading glasses he'd donned a few minutes ago to snatch sight of the newspaper's sporting page. The spectacles, with broken frames, supported themselves crookedly and crazily on his thick, black-head sprinkled, stubby nose.

He growled in belated reply , "He's bloody woke up 'as he? 'bout time too. Bloody guards! They sits on their arses all day in them vans while we do all the work an' they wants the same money as us drivers." With his paper and glasses held in his left hand he operated the engine's controls.

The engine coughed at the chimney as the first exhaust blast woofed up through the blast pipe and exhausted into the sky. The four driving wheeled locomotive surged forward and yanked on the ten attached wagons. Tom was hung on the side of the last wagon as he waved them forwards.

The cab interior was neat and shiny, gleaming copper pipes fed the water injectors and numerous gauges. Even the brass tops and bottoms of the water gauge column protectors glistened brightly. Joe had spent a considerable time cleaning the brass and copper fittings on the boiler front aiming to bring a touch of comfort and brightness to the normally extremely dirty engine cab.

The train had left Castlebrough at eight-thirty that morning to journey towards York. It was scheduled to meet the York to Castlebrough Goods and Bill, Joe and Tom would then exchange trains with the York crew. They had to shunt all station yards on the 'Up' journey and then again on the return journey. Coal wagons, open wagons stacked with newly made flare and ammunition boxes from Caxton's factory, bailey bridges from Packards, parcel vans, wood wagons and fish vans comprised Joe's train this September morning in 1943.

The road to York in front was clear for them until the ten-fifteen Castlebrough-York express wanted to pass. When that happened they would have to stand their train in a siding somewhere while the express flew by. Bill Ankler was keen to finish shunting Heslerton goods yard and arrive at Knapton before the express came. He wanted to be stopped at Knapton for the express because he planned to visit the signalman in his cabin and obtain a confidential hot racing tip from their contact at Malton racing stables.

The engine moved forwards smartly and noisily; the wagons jerked and rattled; Tom hung precariously on the last of the ten wagons. Bill raced his engine and wagons forward as if all the devils in hell were after him.

With the same urgency he displayed when he had given her a full head of steam, he closed the steam regulator and slammed on the brakes. As the engine and wagons ground to a tortured halt little Tom leapt, with surprising alacrity, from where he hung on the side of the last wagon and let his dumpy legs find the moving ground with an agility which surprised the onlooking Joe.

Tom's cloth-capped, but otherwise uniformed figure, kept Bill Ankler busy at the controls of his locomotive. Tom uncoupled wagons, he 'belted them up,' he fly shunted them, he shot them into their various positions in the yard and the little goods shed. He coupled to empty and loaded wagons with an ease that kept Joe marvelling. 'How does an over weight fifty-five year old do a job like this?' queried Joe silently but seriously to himself. He did his share to help, he kept leaving his engine cab and ducking in between the wagons to 'loose off' one of the three chain-linked couplings so that Bill could 'belt up' a wagon at speed. As the 'loosed off ' wagons shot away, Tom in the far distance caught them and ran alongside while he applied the hand-brakes and stopped them in the required positions.

Joe knew he should not be ducking in and out between wagons in order to couple or uncouple them. He had heard enough gory stories about firemen and shunters having their legs amputated by moving wagon wheels or being crushed between big iron buffers to frighten off the faint hearted who might have little imagination and caution. However these things always happened to the other fellow and to the men from other sheds. He was safe; he was cautious and nimble footed. Anyway he was rule breaking to speed up their passage and get the train to Knapton in time to be 'put across on the down line' at ten-thirty when the express from Castlebrough would 'zip' by on the 'Up line' on its journey to York.

Bill had said that he wanted 'to interrogate that bloody signalman about a hot tip from Malton's racing stables.' The signalman at

Knapton was well known to that fraternity of enginemen and guards who couldn't resist backing the horses. Joe wanted Tom and Bill to succeed because they'd said, "We'll see you alright son if we scoops the kitty."

After having completed most of the work in the small country station goods yard they returned their engine to the remains of their stationary train on the up main line. Tom Rittler was riding on the engine's steps and hanging by one arm from the cab hand rails. He looked up at Joe who was leaning out of the engine cab. "We've got three 'pee o double yews' wi' steel girders on for yon slip road."

He pointed with the long shunting pole which he held in his free hand. "Will yer tek 'em for'ard Bill when we pick 'em up?" he queried?. "Knock 'em into the slip road in the yard. Gi' 'em a good belt in. The road into the slip's got a bad curve wi' check rails. Belt 'em hard Bill else they'll stop before they gets to the crane." He paused and added to Joe, "You lose 'em off son." Bill and Joe nodded their understanding and agreement.

The long C7 locomotive bumped clamorously up to the standing train. The sheep in the cattle wagons staggered about in a struggle to stay upright as the wagon floors beneath their feet swayed and jostled at the impact of the locomotive. The loosely stacked parcels in the parcel vans rocked or cascaded onto the floors. The bang of the one hundred and twenty ton locomotive, as it buffered back impatiently at the mercy of the urgent hands of Bill Ankler, shuddered and clattered down the whole length of the loose coupled goods train.

The din of the exhausting steam and the clattering railway wagons echoed noisily across the ripe cornfields and the rows of potatoes and turnips which covered the fruitful Vale of Pickering right up to the fences that skirted the railway lines. Joe noted with approval how even the grass verges alongside the railway tracks had been ploughed for the growing of potatoes and corn. Platelayers' allotments, neat and prolific, filled the lineside with fertility.

The 'Dig for Victory' slogan which shouted down from poster hoardings in every railway station could point to the bulging harvests in the fields and allotments around Heslerton Railway Station as evidence of its effectiveness. The surrounding Vale of Pickering was an important breadbasket for Britain during its life and death struggle with Hitler's Nazism. No one in this area need starve if they were prepared to consume the prosaic products of the land and abide by the rules of the ration books.

The long, black, grime covered locomotive, at Bill's command, heaved the three P.O.W.'s into forward motion. 'Pee oh double yews,' mused Joe to himself as he laboured with his shovel to prepare his fire and steam pressure for the forthcoming dash to Knapton in front of the ten-fifteen York express. For Bill Ankler, getting his hoped for racing tip and placing a consequent bet with Naggy Nockels the Bookmaker at Castlebrough were the most urgent things in his life at the moment.

'Pee oh double yews' Joe continued his muse. 'Prisoners of War' or 'Privately owned Wagons'. Who would know if they'd never been told?' He swung his shovel while Bill caused the locomotive to career forwards as fast as possible.

Joe would never forget the meaning if only because of the memorable time when he and a driver had been instructed to pick up a string of 'Pee oh double ewes' at Bridlington for Castlebrough. Joe imagined that they were going for hundreds of prisoners of war all shackled together to be taken to captivity in camps up on the Yorkshire Moors.

Joe had not discussed it with anyone - not even his driver. He had been looking forward to seeing Hitler's defeated soldiers marched off by British Army guards. Fortunately he had not demonstrated his wish and his ignorance had remained concealed. He had merely said, as they were backing their engine up to a string of wagons at Bridlington, "Where are the string of Pee Oh Double Yews?. The curt answer delivered by his driver was, "Here - these privately owned wagons. See the first one there - says on its side MALTON BRICK COMPANY not LONDON NORTH EASTERN RAILWAY COMPANY."

Ankler suddenly applied his engine's steam brake and halted their rapid forwards progress. The wagons protested noisily. "Shin down the steps son," Ankler snapped through his clenched false teeth. It seemed as though he spoke deliberately through his teeth as if he feared he might lose them, as had frequently happened to him when he opened his mouth too wide. "Loose off all the three wagons and I'll belt 'em in to the slip when the signal woman sets the points. Rittler'l catch 'em at the other end." Bill was fumbling with his one-armed spec's and his folded 'Daily Express' while he struggled with the steam regulator, reversing screw and steam brake handle. "Don't let grass grow under yer feet either. We want to get on to Knapton."

Joe received his instructions without protest. He did not mind doing the guard's job of shunting wagons even if it was against the rules. Anyway he would be able to rest at Knapton, read his 'War Weekly' and his railway rule book; and eat his dried egg sandwiches while Bill and Tom were ferreting out their hot tip and considering how to get it backed with Naggy Nockels at Castlebrough.

There was another reason why Joe was keen to work quickly and help Tom: the day was Saturday and he had a night out planned with his mate Johnny at the Olympia Ballroom.

The grass didn't grow under Joe's feet. He was between the engine and the wagons almost before the engine and its load had come to rest.

Ankler blasted the customary signal on his engine whistle to the signal box woman; he wanted her to know that he was ready for her to change the points and set the road for his engine to gain access from the mainline into the goods yard. He spoke out loudly to himself on the lonely footplate about the slowness of the signal woman's response. "C'mon signal tart. Stop combin' yer flippin' hair - pull the bloody board off." She didn't hear his abusive words but she changed the points and pulled the signal off and Joe, who was climbing up the side of his engine to join Bill in the cab, shouted to Bill "C'mon belt 'em in Bill!"

Bill belted 'em in alright. He was in the devil's own rush. He was after the two-fifteen at Pontefract and it seemed as though he had entered his own C7 locomotive in that very race and that the 'Off' had just been signalled. He still grasped his broken spectacles and his newspaper in his free hand. He had been studying racing form in his newspaper for the few moments when his engine had been at rest. Now, as he yanked open the steam regulator valve his mind was half on racing form and half on his shunting. Woof,woof, woof, whu whu whu whu whooze - - the heavy exhaust blast torrented from the chimney high into the sky as the engine quickly gathered speed and slipped its driving wheels. Bill closed the regulator rapidly in response to the slipping wheels and then opened it again quickly, he used both hands even though he had to grasp his spec's and his newspaper at the same time. But his grasp faltered and his spectacles slipped from his occupied hands and bounced upwards in the air. He lunged for them, caught them, but also accidently dragged at his engine whistle cord which made his engine produce an unexpected whistle blast.

"Damn it", Bill blurted out. "Keep yer eyes out there lad." Joe's head was already outside even though it had turned to witness Bill's antics. He returned his gaze towards the yard in the direction of the tiny distant figure of Tom. The engine and wagons were clattering quickly backwards over the junction points and crossings into the yard when without warning the engine and wagons lurched crazily and suddenly fell from the rails.

Bill's hand shot out and applied the steam brake with the speed of 'Billy the Kid' reaching for his six-shooter in an emergency. Too late; their engine toppled and its wheels bounced along the wooden railway sleepers behind the three careering 'Pee Oh Double Yews.'

* * * * * *

2
STOP THE EXPRESS!

"I'll never get me tip from bloody Knapton now," cursed Bill Ankler as his heavy bellied figure walked up and down surveying the many tons of rolling stock that stood on the sleepers and the stone ballast instead of on the rails. "What did yer do? Stupid pratt," he addressed the wondering Joe.

"Nowt!"

"Mebbe yer should 'ave been doing summat and this lot wouldn't 'ave happened."

"I was on the soddin footplate!" exasperated Joe. "Ow could I have derailed her?" Joe was mildly indignant but not really concerned because he knew that Bill Ankler could not blame him for this rather exciting mishap.

Ankler moaned on as if everyone but he were to blame. "Let's look at t'other side... Christ!," he suddenly exclaimed, "We might be fouling the other mainline." The thought that his leaning engine might be obstructing the passage of an oncoming train had just drifted into his mind. They both urgently ran around the end of their engine to view the other mainline. "God that's close," Ankler said immediately his eyes revealed the danger that his leaning loco' had created for the other main line.

"Don't yer think a train could get past there?" asked Joe.

"Now if it did it'd be too close. Can't risk it both lines are blocked."

"What do we do then Bill?"

Suddenly Ankler realised that they would have to do something. "Both lines blocked," he repeated. Then he acted; or more precisely he made Joe act. Bill Ankler never did anything if he could get someone else to do it. "Aye, get a dozen crackers an' a red flag an' skip up this line ready to stop owt that's coming."

Joe startled into action. Up the cab side of the leaning locomotive he climbed. He was up in two steps instead of the usual four. Into the cab he slipped. His hands searched inside the black oily depths of the steel locker on the tender front; they successfully found the crackers and the red flag. "Thank God that I checked that we'd got these." He spoke out loudly to himself.

"Better protect the train Bill." The shouting voice of Tom Rittler the guard pierced into Joe's ears as he prepared to leave the cab. Tom had walked up from the goods yard when he had seen the derailment. "I'll go back to the signal cabin and then protect the rear of the train."

"Okay." Bill's voice was heard to interject just before it was drowned suddenly in a roaring gush of steam from the safety valves as their engine boiler blew off.

Joe opened the lidded canister of explosive detonators. He knew that inside he would find a clean folded red flag and twelve 'crackers.' He took the flag and six of the detonators, stuffed them into his pockets and made off down the engine steps.

"Get up there like shit of a stick," shouted Bill with a right arm gesticulation in the direction of the facing mainline which needed protecting. "One at a quarter, one at half, an' three at three quarters, an' don't sit on yer arse scratchin' yer spots."

Joe nodded and pointed to the fountain of steam that shot skywards from the safety valves.

"Ye, I'll look after the boiler. Get crackin' in case a train's coming an' needs stopping."

Joe moved off. First he paced himself along the uniformly spaced railway sleepers but they were too closely positioned for his feet to fall evenly upon them so he chose to run on the fine ballast strip alongside the railway track. He ran along, loped along. 'Like a camel' he mused inwardly. 'I could do with a camel now. I'd soon cover a quarter of a mile, and then another quarter of a mile and soon be at three quarters where I would dismount and lay my three detonators, each three yards apart on the rail.' He trotted on and mused on: 'The camels are coming taratara, the camels are coming taratara, the camels are coming taratara.' The lilt of the playground ditty pounded through his mind as he loped on. 'Why camels? Why did we sing 'camels are coming' in the playground. Strange that. There aren't no camels in Britain, aint never seen none - not even in a zoo.' The sound of his engine's escaping steam receded further into the distance as he pounded on.

'Crike - how far is a quarter of a mile? I should have been counting my steps. One step equals one yard. One mile equals one thousand seven hundred and sixty yards.' The thoughts paced through Joe's mind. 'Good job I learnt that at school. Thought it would be no good to me ever.' The thoughts went on. 'What is a quarter of one thousand seven hundred and sixty. I should have learnt my division arithmetic but didn't.' He halted his run of the lonely camel and paused to look back along the tree skirted line.

"Must be far enough now." He afforded himself the luxury of speaking out loudly. No one could hear him. "Hastings Road to Falsgrave is a mile - I've run a quarter of that." He did a little bit of mental linear judgement as he compared the distance he had just run with a quarter of the remembered distance between Hastings

Road and Falsgrave at Castlebrough. "That must be it." He stopped to place the two inch sized detonator on the railhead and strap it on with the two little lead straps which hung down from it. He looked up the line, no train was coming so his engine was safe from that direction. He could see that all the approach signals at Heslerton Station were at danger, any approaching train would see those signals as well as having to run over and explode his detonator so his derailed loco' ought to be safe from collision now.

The sky was clear. The fields were either green or golden. There was just a hint of autumn in the countryside. Indeed the whole vale still bore the richness of summer and the fullness of crops. Joe ran on, keen to finish his task and get back to his engine. Hunger was gnawing at his stomach. He savoured the thoughts of his sandwiches and his hot bottle of sweet milkless tea which waited for him on his de-railed engine; he'd have plenty of time for eating and reading when he arrived back.

"Hi luv. Wotcher running fer?" Joe hadn't noticed the plump figure of the country woman at Parky Road gate crossing. She was aproned with a kerchief on her plaited head of hair. Her main job was to open the small gate at this little used country accommodation crossing. Her other activity was keeping hens and pigs on the big allotment that adjoined her crossing keeper's railway house.

Joe paused in his stride to pass the time of day. To be on the safe side while he talked he placed three of his explosive detonators on the rail at one yard intervals just in case a train at speed came along. He told her how both lines were blocked at Heslerton by his engine's derailment. Her fat creased face rippled as she chuckled, "Ah can leave mi gates open all time if no trains is coming. Good, I'll get on wi' some bakin.' Does tha want a cup o' tea lad." Joe wanted one, and the thoughts of new baking, well, but he'd got to get back to his engine after he'd put down all of his detonators. He was sorry but he would have to say no.

It didn't take Joe long to cover the rest of the three quarters of the mile and lay down all of his detonators. He was breathless now, his hobnailed boots were heavier, he was feeling a bit tired so he took his time walking back to Heslerton Station and his loco.'

The Heslerton Station Master was surveying the derailed railway stock when Joe arrived back on the scene. "Right mess you've made here son." he said in a non-condemnatory manner but at the same time not approvingly.

"Somebody has," returned Joe.

A ganger from the Heslerton-Weaverthorpe permanent way intervened, "No way your goner get this lot on wi' out the steam crane from York."

"Do they always use cranes to put 'em back on the road when they're off like this?" Joe directed his question to the stocky white-haired Ganger.

"Nope. We could pull these wagons on if we had an engine behind 'em in the yard but we aint. We couldn't pull your engine back on the track though cos it's got too many wheels off," the ganger replied.

"Ye," agreed Bill Ankler, "We could 'ave pulled ourselves on wi' some ramps if the driving wheels had been on the rails, but they aint." He stood there letting everyone know how angry he was about not getting on the way to Knapton, he could see his plans evaporating. He looked and sounded irritable, his broad round bellied figure of five feet nine inches suggested an intransigent personality. His oily uniformed cap sat well back on the crown of his head, no badge adorned it or his regulation jacket lapel. He did not sport a watch in his railway waistcoat like many locomotive drivers. "If they wants me to wear a watch they'd better buy one for me," he had said on many occasions as a one man protest against the railway company's refusal to buy watches for their drivers. He would point out, "They expect us to run to a timetable an' they won't gi' us a watch." His dirty uniformed appearance was not enhanced by his Daily Express standing in his right hand pocket, his untidily packed sandwiches sitting visibly in his left hand pocket, and the disabled spectacles poking from his top jacket pocket. He stood in soft well worn shoes which he had picked up at a jumble sale.

The Station Master agreed with Bill and the Ganger. " It's a crane job," he said, "A job for the York breakdown gang. And it will take them two hours to travel here from York." He spoke precisely befitting his neat uniformed station master's appearance.

"Yep, looks like a long job," added the Ganger.

That meant Joe and Bill would be very late arriving back in Castlebrough. Bill realised that his planned visit to the bookmaker's shop with the hot tip could not become a reality now. There was only one bright spot of relief in the situation; both mainlines were not totally blocked - only the Up Main to York was completely blocked by the derailed locomotive, the other could be open to trains if they came past at caution.

"We are putting single line working in operation." The station master informed. "The ten-fifteen from Castlebrough is at Weaverthorpe waiting for the Pilotman to bring him through when we get the system set up. Your fireman will be going to the cabin to carry out Rule Fifty-Five, won't he?"

"Send him up to the cabin?" questioned Bill energetically. "You've got a tart in there as the signalman. Yuh can't send him, he's randy, aint he Tom?" Bill showed a bit of twisted humour. His eyes sparkled and his teeth clacked as his mouth broke into a pot grin.

"Can't have that? Don't know what he'll get up to," retorted Tom with the same old man's sense of humour about a teenager.

The station master joined in the spirit of the repartee. "Watch it son - she's only nineteen but she's got a big feller in the army - coming home soon. Army boxing champion too."

"Nineteen eh? She'll be alright with me," Joe spirited in return. He'd seen the girl in the signal cabin on all of the previous days of the week.. He looked forwards to having the chance of a chat with her. "Anyway I'll go up there and put mi feet up and drink tea while you loafers look after this." With his tea, sandwiches and newspaper tucked away in his pockets ,and a "tara" he stretched his legs in the direction of the signal cabin.

'So she's got an army feller has she. Must be a mug of a bloke to be in the army when there's a war on an' when he could be doing an interesting job like this one' Joe thought as he skipped across the lines leaving Bill and Tom to scheme about a way to get the tip from Knapton and get it backed at the bookmaker's. Joe walked towards the level crossing with its big wooden gates and its overshadowing two storey brick built signal cabin. The station porter-clerk was unloading and checking goods out of the two box wagons onto an open horse drawn cart. Joe's train stood uselessly occupying the Up Main.

Joe had to step carefully over the 'four-foot' and the 'six-foot.' They were minefields of lumpy ballast, signal wires, point rods and railway lines. He kept his eyes on the ground and only occasionally lifted them to look at the signal cabin towards which he walked. The field alongside the blocked Up Main glowed with ripe upstanding wheat. There had been no hard winds or rains to flatten it. The summer had been gentle.

Joe's feet fell upon the wooden sleepers that formed a crossing for the road traffic between the gates which for the moment were closed to road traffic. He mounted the platform ramp and then the wooden stairway which rose up to the signal cabin. He had no cause to feel concerned; he knew that he hadn't derailed the loco' and the wagons. 'Anyway,' he thought, 'even if I had, why should I worry. Nobody seems to get steamed up about minor derailments like this. I've seen tons worse than this an' I aint been around five minutes yet.'

"Hello!" Joe's meandering thoughts were interrupted by a feminine voice. Joe had been watching the stairs and where he placed his feet, he'd not noticed the signal woman who was looking out of the cabin window. Her head protruded and she smiled, her hair was rolled up around a halo style stocking roller as was the fashion with women in war-time Britain.

"Hello," came Joe's warm but unimaginative reply as he returned her gaze with a smile and walked up the steps towards the cabin door at the top. A cast iron name-plate proclaiming 'Heslerton' in white letters on a black background adhered to the gable end of the red brick signal cabin just above the large viewing windows. The girl opened the door for Joe and he felt welcome.

"Rule Fifty-Five," he said and subconsciously put his soiled right hand up to an itch on his acne spotted cheek. He removed it quickly as soon as it touched his cheek, aware that he might only succeed in drawing attention to his pockmarked countenance.

"There's the train book," she paused in reply, "And there's a pencil in the desk draw." Her hand gesticulated towards the tall sloping desk on which the train book lay. Her hand looked as smooth as her eggshell like complexion; her nails were clean and personally manicured. Joe felt warmed by her easy friendly presence. He recorded his signature, the date and the time, and the words 'Rule Fifty-Five' on a line in the train book. 'She's slim, and pretty really, not tarted up at all,' he thought as she moved up and down the signal-cabin paying attention to her electric instruments on the rack above the lever frame.

"How did it happen?" Joe asked with barely a nod in the direction of the derailed engine and wagons.

"I don't know." she came back quickly and defensively. "It wasn't my doing. I didn't touch those points." She indicated with a flourish towards a black points lever locked in forward position. It controlled the points over which Joe's engine had been travelling.

Joe felt taken aback and apologetic. He hadn't meant to accuse her. 'Christ! I always put my foot in it with women,' the thought raced warningly through his mind. 'It's these spots, they make me self conscious, and make me say the wrong things.' He changed the subject. "How's your young man. Is he on leave or boxing?"

"I don't have a young man. How do you mean - boxing?"

'Those baskets down there' thought Joe, embarrassed but angry. 'They told me that she'd got a fellow in the army.' He paused in a panic and looked out of the window at the station master who was leaving his office and walking down the platform towards the cabin. Joe thought he'd better watch what he said or else they might blame him for causing the derailment.

"The station master's coming." Joe blurted out with some feeling of confusion. She did not reply. "I mixed you up wi' someone else.

Sorry, I was thinking of the signal-woman at Sander. These signal boxes are all the same to me."

"Oh!" she replied, "I didn't know there'd ever been a signal-woman at Sander box. My Uncle Will's one of the signalmen there, Joe Brown's the other one." She paused a while and then said, "There aren't many of us signal women, a special breed of women we are; few and far between."

'Oh! Gawd,' Joe almost muttered the thought out aloud. He couldn't say anything right, so he didn't say anything else, he just slunk towards the little wooden form close to the cold iron stove. After carefully ensuring that he wouldn't be sitting in 'her seat' he sat down with his back up against the coat that hung from a peg on the wall. He took out his tin of sandwiches, his bottle of tea and his 'War Weekly' and settled down quietly to keep out of trouble. He had hardly raised the hinged lid on his sandwich tin when the signal-woman was disturbing him in order to move her coat on which he was leaning. Joe settled down again to eat and read. His confidence was shattered. He found himself wishing that he was in the army away on some distant war front miles away from the nearest woman.

The door clicked open and in drifted the station master. "I've been on to Train Control at York. They're sending a breakdown gang and the steam crane. Be here about one o' clock with luck. I've put single line working into operation between Weaverthorpe and Knapton. The Pilot Man's leaving Weaverthorpe in about ten minutes." The station master had an air of authority about him. He checked the train and the signal instruments in the cabin and read the entries in the train book. Quite clearly he was checking on the young signal-woman. Joe wondered whether the station master would have checked in the same manner on an older, grumpy signalman.

The young signal woman busied about her homely signal cabin. Alongside of the cast iron coal stove a comfortable but tatty upholstered chair reclined. In the chair bottom was an open paper novel and a piece of knitting on two needles.

"We'll have to ascertain what happened," continued the station master. "Clearly the three wagon's and the engine jumped the rails on the points leading into the yard. But what caused it to happen?" He paused and looked questioningly at Joe and the signal woman.

Her name was Laura, the station master soon revealed in his conversation. She was unshaken and confident. "I don't know! Mr Silverwood. My point's are locked in 'on position.' There's no way that I could have moved those points and derailed him with the signal board off." She paused to respond to the bell signal on the train indicator machine. "You know that!" she emphasised, "So put that in your report and let them make of it what they can." She was confident and unflappable and Joe envied her quiet confident composure.

"Did you see anything? Joe lad. Did the driver mix up his whistle signals when he was blowing for the board into the yard?"

"I was on the engine. couldn't see nowt," was Joe's neutral reply. He looked unconcerned while he engaged in the activities of eating his sandwiches and reading an article about the Battle of Stalingrad in his 'War Weekly' Laura looked at him; a thought flittered through her mind. 'He doesn't care, typical footplate man, Silverwood'll get nowt out of him even if he's got owt to tell.'

"I just wondered," continued Mr Silverwood, his small, pleasant, clean shaven, face smiling affably," whether those points could have been pulled over quickly in between the wagon wheelbase in response to a whistle pop at the wrong time. There's no locking bar on those points so it could have happened."

"How could it Mr Silverwood. I was nowhere near that point lever when he was shunting back. I was looking out of the window to see his movements at the time." Laura answered firmly and without panic.

"We just jumped the points mister," interjected Joe. "The points weren't split, they're as tight now as they were when they were first pulled over. There's no explanation."

"Don't get me wrong Laura. I'm not blaming you or the driver or the guard. It's just one of them things." He continued, "There should be a locking bar on those points as you know. I've said so before."

"I know there isn't."

"They'll have to put one in."

"But I didn't move those points while the train was in motion." Laura smiled patiently and Joe marvelled at her equanimity. He marvelled more because he, like Bill and Tom, believed she must be the one to have caused the derailment. He was not going to make his belief public. She looked serene - attractive. Joe regretted getting off on the wrong foot with her. He would like to have flirted with her but the courage was lacking now. She looked shapely in her signal-woman's uniform trousers and waistcoat; her breasts were small and round but prominent, her waistcoat sported a watch chain that hung across a small flat stomach from a button hole. The other end of the chain disappeared into a small pocket where the presumed watch hid from sight but was easily accessible. Joe wondered for a moment whether the railway company had provided her with the watch or whether she'd had to buy her own.

Silence reigned in the cabin. Joe sat eating and reading. Mr

Silverwood, stood with his arms draped and hands clasped behind his back. He was looking out of the signal cabin window towards the derailed locomotive and the three wagons. Laura was seated with her knitting, patiently weaving her wool according to her pattern and politely indifferent to Mr Silverwood's questions and concern.

A bell signal broke the silence. "Ah! there he is on the line from Weaverthorpe," responded Mr Silverwood. "Hum! the ten-fifteen from Castlebrough." He looked at the signal cabin clock. "Forty-five minutes late. I'll bet some of the passengers are steamed up and worried about their connections at York and Leeds."

"Its all in a day's work on the railways," Laura mused. There was almost a hint of insubordination in her response. She had her feet on the half steel wagon-wheel fender that edged around the forepart of her small coal stove. She knitted in her relaxed manner while she prepared for her next signalling move.

"Yes it's all in a day's work I agree Laura," returned the station master in response to Laura's hinted insubordination. "But it's not often our day's work includes a de-railed locomotive and three wagons blocking the Up Main Line," he smiled.

"A sudden question occurred to the ever inquisitive sixteen year old Joe. "How do you decide which is the Up Main Line and which is the Down Main Line?"

"The Up Main goes to London - no matter where you are." Laura jumped in with a quick reply while the station master had merely turned on his heel slightly as if to reply. "And the Down Main goes away from London."

"That makes it easy," responded Joe appreciatively.

"Yes it does," Mr Silverwood agreed. "I'll go back to the office now - check the wagon returns and the booking office receipts," he said. "You don't need me here now Laura, not now that we've put single line into operation and the Pilotman's on his way with the passenger train from Castlebrough."

He looked at Laura's novel that laid on her chair seat. He turned a few pages briefly, put it down and walked over towards the doorway. "T'rah," he said as he departed, "I'll see you a bit later."

Joe sat hunched on the little wooden form, his heavy boots shuffled on the floor. Occasionally he adjusted his bicycle clips or touched his spots when they irritated him, but for the most part he read quietly or thought to himself.

Joe read about the war all of the time. It was always a principal topic of conversation with railwaymen and women, it had affected their lives dramatically. Men had gone into the armed forces in large numbers. In many cases their places had been filled by young lads like Joe having to do a full man's job much before they were physically developed or trained. "You young fellows are lucky," ran the regular conversations of the older firemen and drivers to the likes of Joe. "Firing at your age! Firing expresses and fast goods at sixteen! Did you know Simmy and Baker and all that crowd now driving on the workmen's trains and in the slow passenger link? - they cleaned engines for twenty years. Only the war promoted them and made them into firemen one day and drivers the next."

Joe knew all that. He knew also that Laura owed her job to the war. Here she was - only a little older than he was - and she was doing a man's job too. If the war had not happened she might have been in service at some farm house or some small country estate. She was glad to have been liberated from such drudgery even though she did not approve of the violence of war. The result of the war for her, for Joe and for thousands of young and middle-aged people had been to give them a job, promotion and responsibility.

"Your mate's coming," Laura said to Joe a few minutes after Mr Silverwood had departed. She was at the window looking in the direction of the leaning locomotive and the three wagons.

"Oh! he'll be asking to ring Knapton no doubt," responded Joe.

"What for?" came Laura's query.

"It's Charlie isn't it? - the signalman at Knapton I mean," Joe replied with a question and went on without waiting for an answer. "My mate Bill Ankler wants to talk to Charlie about a racing tip." Then he hastened with an anxious, "Don't let on to my mate Bill that I've spilt the beans to you about Charlie and the racing tip."

"Charlie Hunter you mean - he's on the two to six shift at Knapton. Yes, he's the tipster," she continued with a sly smile. "The man with his ear to the leak at Malton racing stables."

"Hi - that's it - Charlie Hunter. I remember our guard saying that name." Joe nodded his head in affirmation. Laura went on, "It's supposed to be secret about the tips from Malton but everyone on this line knows about them. There's not only Charlie who claims to be the bookies' terror - there's lots of Charlies on this line who can tell you what's going to win the two-thirty."

"Are they any good then?" came Joe's reply.

"Who, the Charlies or the tips?, responded the quick Laura. She was busy turning the four-foot iron wheel that operated the long wooden gates that could be swung across and cut the road passage off from the railway tracks. Laura was closing the gates to the road and preparing for the passage, on the single line, of the Castlebrough express which had just been accepted from Weaverthorpe. The gates were big and heavy; Joe was surprised by the ease with which the slight figure of Laura swung the iron wheel and closed the gates.

"The tips," Joe smarted a little at being caught out using a poorly constructed question. "Are the tips any good?"

"They say so. They tell tales about big wins. Cooper at Rillington's said to have cleaned up one hundred and fifty pounds on a tanner treble and two of his winners were from Malton."

"Hundred and fifty," whistled Joe, "an' I only gets two pound fifteen shillings a week for forty-eight hours work."

"You're getting more than me," she exerted slightly on the last swing of the wheel. The big wooden gates crashed to a close against the metal stops in the roadway. The tracks were opened for the train and the road was closed to traffic. "I'm not interested in backing horses, there are more losers than winners," she continued.

"Me too, but Bill my mate, he eats, and drinks and sleeps racing."

With that remark the cabin door opened and Bill Ankler swaggered in, his lightly shod feet fell on the floor of the cabin and the door clicked shut behind him. His broad shouldered, round-bellied figure, demonstrated a conscious swagger.

"Have yer got enough coal fer yer fire ducky?" Bill asked Laura. He was quite clearly offering to give her some coal for her cabin stove from his engine in preparation to his asking a favour.

'He's greasing round her,' thought Joe as his mind flitted over Bill's practice of giving away engine coals at every verse end in order to obtain favours. Bill could bring home a pheasant, a rabbit, flowers, vegetables, mushrooms, or a selection from a whole host of country products almost anytime he was working on a stopping goods train. If Joe acquired anything he took it home to help feed the family but Bill marketed all his gains in the local pub.

"I'm not a duck," Laura replied with a grimace that showed her distaste for Bill's address. "I've got enough coal. Anyway, I'm not burning the stove at this time of year, weather's warm enough."

Bill ignored her unproductive response and tried another tack. "Is everything workin' out then? Is single line in operation?"

"Yes, okay" said Laura as she reached for a green flag on a short staff which stuck in a holder near the window. "I'm just going to flag the Castlebrough express down the facing line. Maybe you want to be down near your engine to make sure that it's not fouling the line when the express comes by?"

"If the bloody driver of yon train can't see if the road's clear for 'im. I'm not going to do it fer him." Bill wasn't angry, just keen to show that he didn't take his duties too seriously. Joe looked up from his 'War Weekly' and exchanged glances with Laura. He was still munching his way through his mountain of sandwiches and tomatoes.

"Yes, but you know that some loco' driver's are blind even when they aren't reading papers instead of looking out," she teased in return. Joe marvelled at her spirit, no one could sit on her in spite of her youth.

"Joe, get off yer arse and go down and look at our engine. See if the boiler and fire's okay and go an' check that she's clear enough of the down main when that express comes by."

"Oh, hell! I'm having my dinner. You know I'm entitled to twenty minutes for eating."

"Go on," Bill jerked his thumb in the direction of the cabin door. "Go on - have yer twenty minutes as two ten minutes," Bill insisted moving up to Joe and peering at his 'War Weekly'.

"I'll see mi union first Bill," Joe returned more in a spirit of repartee than rebellion.

"The union aint here an' I'm captain on this ship and you's guilty of mutiny."

Joe began returning his uneaten sandwiches to his tin with an air of resignation. "An' what are you goin' to do while I foregoes mi meal break."

"Eatin' yer sandwiches if yer leaves 'em."

"I'm tekin' 'em." Joe was rising. He heard the distant whistle of the express making its way slowly down the facing main line from Weaverthorpe towards Heslerton. "I'll bet that you're after ringing Knapton to contact Charlie Hunter. He's on six-to-two shift, Laura says."

"Go on you get on to yon engine an' see if it's clear of this main line when that train comes by, - 'an keep yer head in the engine cab when it does. The passengers 'ill think it's a cattle train if they sees you lookin' out," Bill added insistently. He didn't say what his intentions were about ringing Charlie Hunter.

Regardless of his promise to take them, Joe left his sandwiches, his bottle of hot milkless tea and his 'War Weekly' on the wooden form. He winked at Laura as he made his way towards the cabin door. He was hoping that she would be difficult with Bill and tell him that he could not use the telephone.

* * * * * *

3
THE RACE TO THE BOOKMAKERS

The ten-fifteen from Castlebrough passed safely on its way through Heslerton. As it crept by the derailed engine and wagons, which were only six inches clear, Joe and the station master 'stood guard' and warned inquisitive passengers to "Keep your heads in." Joe then climbed onto the footplate of his derailed locomotive and carried out some essential tasks.

As he worked he wondered whether to spend his waiting time on the footplate instead of in the cabin. He always had plenty of reading matter with him; at the moment he had the 'Locomotive Man's Pocket Book' and a full copy of Robert Burn's poem 'Man was made to Mourn.' He hadn't been a good scholar at Gladstone Road School, a school which he maintained was more like a boy's reformatory than an institution of learning.

The railways had created in him a desire for learning. He had joined the National Union of Railwaymen and had become the minute-taker at local branch meetings, he had joined the loco' shed 'Mutual Improvement Class' in order to study railway operating and the mechanics of steam locomotives. He was stimulated by the politics of the World War which raged in Europe and the Far East. He was encouraged to read and educate himself by the politically and trade union conscious minority of enginemen who dominated the union branch and the mutual improvement class. Only that morning one of them had given Joe the copy of Burn's poem with the message, "Remember, 'Man's inhumanity to man makes countless thousands mourn.' You read Burn's poem o'er and o'er ag'in. Look around this cursed world and ponder on it." Yes, Joe liked to sit and read at work whenever the opportunity offered itself but at the moment it was the cool steady attraction of Laura that drew him away from the present chance to sit on his engine and read.

He slipped away from the engine and skipped across the sleepers and the rails under the late summer sunshine towards the country signal cabin. There he found that Tom Rittler had joined the conniving Bill.

Bill was grumbling about something to Tom; he sat hunched on the wooden form alongside Joe's sandwiches. he was thumbing his way through Joe's 'War Weekly' in a disinterested manner. "She took the phone off a mi, said I can't use it while there's a train in the section. Bloody whippersnapper - an' she aint stopped wetting her knickers yet," Bill grumbled quietly to Tom so that Joe could overhear but so that Laura could not. "Don't know what the world's comin' to, war's elevated women above their station," he continued while Laura stood at the open window looking out down the roadway.

"You'll be able to use the phone when the train's clear o' the section. She's got to be careful about who she let's use the telephone - it connects up to all the gatehouses and signal cabins from Weaverthorpe to Rillington." Tom answered by way of explanation rather than support for Laura. You don't know who's listening in on these signalmen's lines," he continued. Tom had a little white billy-can in one hand and a box of sandwiches in the other. He had come to the cabin hoping to get a quantity of boiling water in order to make some tea but the cabin didn't contain the usual hot stove and boiling kettle.

"There's a point Tom," Bill came back into the conversation. "Charlie won't be keen to talk on an open telephone line about his racing tips."

"True," Tom replied, "An' if yer get it from Charlie how are yer going to ring it through to Castlebrough Shed and Naggy Nockels." He paused and prepared to change the subject to a matter of greater concern to him. "How 'm I goin' to get some tea. She aint got a fire on to boil the keckle. Aint never been in a cabin like this before. No keckle on! That's women fer yuh." Tom's baggy eyes agitated concern. "How'm I going to get a mash of tea?"

"What do yer do fer a mash, luv?" Bill's loud voice came to Tom's aid and stretched across to Laura at the door end of the signal cabin.

"Oh! It's tea you want." She came towards them, her five-foot-six figure, lithe and shapely in her uniform waistcoat and trousers. Her hair style caught Joe's imagination, not that it was unique; it was similar to that worn by many other women in wartime Britain. Hidden in her hair was a stocking roll worn like a halo with her hair tucked in. At the front it was shaped and rolled in so that it stood up in two up swept waves. 'She's keen on her appearance,' Joe thought as he observed her.

Laura looked in Tom's direction, "You want a boiling kettle?" she asked.

Tom held out his can appealingly. "Yes, I always mashes mi tea in a cabin. There's always a keckle on a stove even in summer." He looked towards the cold unlit stove with the big iron kettle standing on it cold and empty.

"Yes there always is,- but not in this cabin in summer. There's a war on - or don't you know." Was she telling them off again? Joe wondered. He smiled at her nerve. Bill and Tom were a couple of hard bitten old railwaymen who pushed and scrounged their way through each working day. However, Laura was able to show that she was the boss in her signal cabin without having to say so. "We are supposed to save coal to help the war effort." She smiled in Joe's direction, "They know that don't they?"

"But what do yer do when yer want a brew o' tea," Tom returned insistently.

"I go home," she teased.

"Well I can't blooming well go home to Castlebrough. I want a cup o' tea now to drink wi' mi sandwiches."

"Yer can always get a cup 'o tea in a proper cabin." Bill joined the verbal affray, his chest puffed out aggressively and his top lip curled back slightly up his false teeth.

"I'll get you a cup o' tea soon," Laura demurred gently bringing the verbal affray to a close. "Look, we've got the York express on offer now from Knapton. He should've been in Castlebrough for eleven-thirty-five, see it's nearly twelve o' clock now." Her signalling bells had just announced the offer of the train from Knapton but they also touched a chord in Bill's memory.

"I want to ring Charlie Hunter at Knapton!" exclaimed Bill as he rose from his seat and moved across to her as she prepared to swing the big iron gate wheel into action and close the crossing to road traffic. "It'll only tek a minute. Charlie was expecting me at Knapton at this time so he'll have the information ready."

"We'll see. Mr Silverwood's got to be out of the way. He's a stickler. Works by the rule book at all times," she paused. "You shouldn't all be in this cabin, never mind using my phones for private business." She smiled as she uttered these remarks in Bill's direction.

Tom Rittler was seated on the form alongside Joe, his empty billy can, with lid off, stood, pathetically, close by his open sandwich box. Joe's sandwiches had vanished, his warm tea bottle was empty; his head was stuck once again into his opened copy of the 'War Weekly.'

"How can I get a cup o' tea?" Tom asked plaintively.

"Lucy's coming in a minute with my dinner," replied Laura as the big crossing gates clanked shut and the ratchets on the wheel fell silent as the wheel ceased to turn. "She'll take you to a boiling kettle when she arrives," Laura continued as she heaved the signal levers into new positions. The rattling wires and rods underneath the cabin floor carried her instructions to the cabin's signals and points.

"But how long's that goner be?" Tom's round face expressed impatience.

"She brings my dinner at twelve so she'll be here soon."

Tom accepted the situation and settled down to wait, he refused to eat his sandwiches until he had obtained a can of hot tea. He and Bill discussed how best to back the tip when they got it. Clearly today was going to be a big day in their sporting lives, they had been led to expect a very important tip from Charlie for the Pontefract meeting on this present Saturday afternoon.

Bill had been told at an earlier time by Charlie Hunter that the stables had been planning to enter a horse in each of the four races at Pontefract and that one of them was an unknown that would win at long odds. Tom and Bill had left a jointly owned five pound note with Bill Clarke, the Cleaner-Chargeman, at Castlebrough Shed, just in case they didn't get home in time to place the bet themselves. Bill Clarke was to be trusted to place their bet if they rang him up from Malton with a request and an instruction. They knew that he would proceed up the road to Naggy Nockel's and do as Bill Ankler had requested and also have his own little flutter on the 'hot tip' just in case. According to Bill Ankler's train time-table he and his train should be at Malton by eleven and back in Castlebrough for two o' clock but that was not to be, they were grounded at Heslerton waiting for the breakdown gang and the steam crane to arrive from York.

The time showing on the cabin clock was just passed twelve noon when the cabin door opened and a long skirted, short young woman carrying a cloth covered dinner plate entered. A bland smile covered her broad mongoloid face. There was something slow and deliberate about her every movement. Joe recognised her as a person who suffered from a mental handicap.

"Hello Lucy, I was just telling these three gentlemen that you would be arriving with my dinner soon."

Tom raised his head and showed interest. Lucy! wasn't this the person who would get some boiling water for him. He sized her up and wasn't impressed. She carried a tray on which a cloth covered dinner resided along with a tea-pot full of hot tea. She shuffled across the cabin with an innocent childish look on her face and placed the tray on the small bamboo table next to Laura's chair. She didn't answer Laura with words; only with a smile.

"Will you take this gentleman guard back to Mam's and get some boiling water for him in his tea can?"

"No!" The answer did not surprise Laura. She knew how her handicapped sister Lucy responded to unfamiliar requests.

"Will you take Mr Guard's can back and fill it from Mam's kettle?"

Lucy shook her head sheepishly like a shy child.

"Oh look! the tin's mine now. I've taken it off Mr Guard. That was clever wasn't it?" Lucy laughed and agreed to her sister's request.

Laura continued, "Run home now and ask Mam to give me some boiling water in this can. I want some more tea. Go on - good girl."

Lucy agreed readily and was soon gone from the cabin. Tom watched only half believingly as the sixteen year old mongoloid girl disappeared through the doorway of the signal cabin clutching his white enamelled billy can.

"Well that's one thing out of the way. How about my call to Knapton? The racing at Pontefract starts at two-fifteen." Bill Ankler started to show renewed concern for his problem.

"Laura didn't answer immediately; she was attracted by a voice outside of the cabin. She moved across to the open cabin window before she responded. She leaned out of the large open window and carried on a muted conversation with the station master who stood beneath the cabin window. The conversation did not carry to Joe, Bill and Tom, seated in the cabin. Laura re-appeared and answered Bill. "I can't let you use the telephones while there's a train in either the Knapton section or the Weaverthorpe section."

Bill grunted disapprovingly but Laura continued, "Mr Silverwood says that the steam crane has just left York and it's expected to get here for about two o' clock. There's not much traffic on the line between here and York so that'll help. Your change-over goods is at Malton and they'll have to hold him till the line's cleared."

"An' there'll be Castlebrough coal train between here and York; an' the twelve thirty-five passenger from Castlebrough, An' the Malton Workmen's train, an' others we don't know about. This bloody line - single line's going to be busier than Kings Cross Station on a pre-war bank holiday Monday," grumbled Bill, his sandwiches still uneaten and leaning, roughly packaged, in his jacket pocket. "Not goner get on that telephone. I can see."

"You can get on that telephone as soon as this fellow clears Weaverthorpe." She cocked her ear at the sound of a distant engine whistle blast. "That's the eleven-thirty Castlebrough blowing for my distant signal. When he clears Weaverthorpe, the next one through will be from Castlebrough on the facing line from Weaverthorpe."

"We'll never get on the bloody phone," grumbled Bill to Tom Rittler. "Charlie said yesterday that today's tip would be the killing of a lifetime. The stable has been saving this one for a big win, Charlie wouldn't know if it wasn't for the fact that is daughter's husband is the horse's trainer. I couldn't wait to come to work this morning and now look what's bloody happened."

Tom was equally despondent. "Ye, I was hoping too. Wanted to get some special things for our lass's birthday. There's plenty on the black market in Castlebrough since them Yanks came to Burniston

Barracks. Nylon stockings and fags galore. By gawd our lass wad go balmy wi' three pair of nylon stockings and a big packet of American fags. She won't get them if this bet don't come off." Bill was nodding agreement from the spare chair that he occupied. Tom was seated with Joe on the little bench. Laura's chair was unoccupied, she was standing at the cabin window with a green flag in her hand ready to signal the cautioned express past her cabin.

"How do you think you are going to place the bet Bill?" Joe asked. He had finished reading and was seated on the bench with the palms of his hands pressed down onto the bench at each side of his figure. His shoulders were hunched up with the pressure he had placed upon them. "We're not going to get home for a long time are we?"

"We'll be lucky to be home by six tonight," replied Tom. He had removed his uniform cap to expose his short greying hair and central bald patch. "Our lass wanted to go out fer a drink tonight an' likes to be back home in the house for nine o' clock in case o' air raids. It's goner be tight tonight if I don't leave work while six."

"We won't be home in time to place our bets our sens, especially if the tip's for the two-fifteen," Bill frowned. "Can't phone it through to Bill Clarke on these signal cabin phones. This cabin can only get back as far as Weaverthorpe by phone, Weaverthorpe can only get back as far as Sander West Cabin who can ring Bill Clarke's store. I've been sizing things up while you were stuck here with yer friggin' head in a book." He was addressing Joe.

"Can't we ring through on an outside national phone - straight through to Naggy's?" Joe asked helpfully.

"There aint a phone nearby - a mile to the village. There's a phone in the station master's office but he won't agree to us using that. He aint an obligin' git. Don't approve of racing an' gambling," Bill answered acrimoniously. "Anyway there aint an' outside phone in Clarkey's store."

"What do yer think about asking Weaverthorpe's signalman to pass a message to Sander West signal cabin who'll pass it on to Bill Clarke?" That was Tom's idea and contribution to the discussion aimed at solving their problem.

"Can do. There aint no choice. Means trusting two signalmen. Les Abbott's on at Sander West after one o' clock. Don't know who's on the late shift at Weaverthorpe. Hope it aint a woman though." Bill never said a good thing about women. 'There's no wonder he's separated from his wife an' livin' in lodgings,' Joe reflected on Bill's remark.

Lucy had returned with Tom's full billy can. Bill responded to that by scrounging a cup o' tea off Tom in the signalwoman's spare cup whilst he was engaged in eating his badly packed sandwiches.

An engine whistle blast alerted them to the oncoming Castlebrough express. Laura leaned from her cabin window and waved it on with her green flag. It crept slowly by the derailed loco' and wagons under the watchful eyes of Mr Silverwood and the Ganger. It neared the cabin and as it passed, the express's big loco' shook the signal cabin with its raucous blast of exhausting steam shooting skywards and disturbing the quiet plotting of Bill and Tom.

Laura turned from her window and addressed Weaverthorpe on her train signal equipment. Bill addressed Tom on the question of the elusive bet. "Yes, that's what we'll have to do Tom. Get the tip from Charlie over the phone and try to pass it on to Clarkey via Weaverthorpe and Sander West signalman."

"That's going to take a bit of doing Bill. Means using the telephone to get through to Knapton and then using it again to get through to Weaverthorpe," Tom added between bites of his sandwiches.

"Means bein' on the right side of this madam," Bill confided quietly to Tom and Joe while Laura went about her signalbox duties. When the passenger train and its heavy V2 locomotive had cleared her station all of her signals had to be put back to their danger positions and the gates opened to road traffic.

"She'll be goin' off duty soon - she'll be on a five-to-one shift. Her relief 'l be here soon," Tom said with a hopeful look.

"Might be a fellow. That'll mek things easier," Bill said wishfully. He soon found out, however, that she was not due to be relieved until three o' clock by her late shift relief.

"Well! you'll just have to keep on the right side of Laura," Joe advised them, his oily coal dust besmirched face creased up with an amused smile. "An' I don't think she likes either of you two," he chuckled.

"The kid's right. She'll like a randy young kid like him better than a couple of middle aged codgers like us." Bill stood up. His greasy overalled figure rolled across to Laura at the big iron gate-wheel. "Can I ring Charlie at Knapton now please luv?"

"I'll just give him 'train out of section' bells and then you can get through before Mr Silverwood comes up."

Bill did what she suggested. He waited and at the right time with Laura's permission he gave the correctly coded ring on the telephone line to attract Charlie at Knapton. It all worked smoothly and Charlie answered as was hoped. In hurried tones the signalman at Knapton gave Bill the sought after tip. "Thistle Top, Two-fifteen at Pontefract, offered at ten-to-one just now. I've put my shirt on it but don't shout it around Bill or else the tips 'll stop." Bill knew all about 'Thistle

Top' from the form tables in the Daily Express. A two year old outsider with no newspaper tipsters shouting for it. It looked good - 'Ten-to-one with five pounds on it,' the thought excited Bill. He swaggered back to the bench seat and the empty tea cup. He placed his railway cap jauntily on the back of his head and took another look at his newspaper's racing form.

"Just what the doctor ordered," he said to Tom. "We'll see about getting the rest done wi' Joe's help. Eh!" He glanced meaningfully at Joe then he told them what Charlie had said to him.

Laura seated herself in her dilapidated easy chair and laid back for a few minutes with her knitting needles clacking away. Then she started the conversation going again. "The crane and the breakdown vans are making good time from York. Probably be here before two o'clock. Mr Silverwood says 'this is an emergency - they want the line cleared quickly.' Something about urgent traffic got to come up the line in the late afternoon." As always she looked calm and conveyed no sense of emergency. "Both main lines will have to be stopped while they pick up your engine and wagons. I reckon that'll be about a two hour job. Four o'clock it could be before the line's properly cleared for two way traffic again."

"We're goner luv yer and leave yer," said the suddenly friendly Bill. His eyes twinkled and he showed more of his false teeth than the dentist had intended. He was trying to present a warm friendly personality. "Tom an' me 'll have to go down to the engine. We'll leave Joey here. You can look after him, can't you, while he carries out Rule Fifty-Five?" Bill patted Joe's uniform capped head in a light friendly manner. "Keep him at arm's length though." Joe brushed Bill's hand and arm to one side. He blushed visibly, he hated attention being focussed on himself in this patronising but friendly fashion.

"Come down to the engine for a minute Joe," said Bill as he moved with Tom towards the cabin doorway, "Want yuh to check the middle big-end for oil for me."

Joe left his jacket, his bottle and his sandwich tin with his papers on the wooden form and followed Bill and Tom down the cabin stairs. As they all walked across the lines and the ballast towards their toppled engine, Bill gave instructions to Joe in no uncertain manner. He hadn't wanted him to inspect the engine's middle big-end. "You stay in the cabin while we looks after the engine, stay wi' her and use your winning ways. Get her to ring Weaverthorpe. Got it, are yuh listening? I want yuh to have yer mind on this matter; it's important, a matter of life an' death. My life when this hoss wins at ten-ter-one and your death if yer cock it up fer me."

"I know," Joe interrupted impatiently, "Don't rub it in. Ring Weaverthorpe ask him to ring Sander West wi' a message to ring Castlebrough Motive Power Department for Bill Clarke. Then give him the tip. Keep it quiet if I can. The horse is 'Thistle Top,' two-fifteen at Pontefract and the bet is a fiver." Joe knew what was expected of him but this did not stop Bill from driving it home.

"Just say 'Tell Bill Clarke - Chargeman at Castlebrough Shed that Bill Ankler says "back Thistle Top, two-fifteen at Pontefract; straight win." Bill emphasised it as they walked along.

The mid-day sun had disappeared behind a thin veil of watery clouds. Bill's engine stood leaning slightly, the only sign of life in her was a drifting thin haze of smoke from the chimney and wisps of steam around the glands of the main cylinders. The three men climbed aboard their engine and after a little further discussion and a few tasks performed Joe left them and made off towards Laura and the signal cabin.

Joe had no difficulty with Laura, she did not mind him using her telephone line discreetly and showed her relief at the departure of Tom and Bill. She revealed that they irritated her and put her on her guard. "With you I feel relaxed, I don't mind you being here. Anyway you came to carry out Rule Fifty-Five." Joe spoke on the telephone to the signalman at Weaverthorpe and gave him Bill's requests and clear message, "Thistle Top, two-fifteen at Pontefract. All on the nose to win." Later as he waited in Laura's cabin he received a call from Weaverthorpe signalman to the effect that Sander West had passed the message on to Bill Clarke at Castlebrough's motive power depot just before he went off duty.

* * * * * *

4
TO THE FINISHING POST

The steam crane and breakdown gang arrived just before two o' clock. They were headed by a dilapidated and dirty D20 locomotive with a monotonously pounding Westinghouse donkey engine providing compressed air for the train's air brake system. The engine's tall chimney and dome on a slim boiler provided adequate contrast between it and Bill's big C7 locomotive. An equally dirty driver and fireman looked out from the engine cab. They had been withdrawn abruptly from their 'dusthole duties' at York Shed where they were engaged on cleaning loco' fires and emptying ashpans; they had been instructed to proceed with the breakdown crane to Heslerton. The train their engine pulled was not long; it comprised; the mighty steam crane which had smoke curling away from its small chimney and steam wisping away from joints on its relatively small vertical boiler, two closed vans for tools and chocks and a blue accommodation van in which the breakdown gang travelled. The long jib of the crane lay horizontally along the train length resting on its own jib-wagon. The train came to rest on the down main line alongside the derailed C7 loco' and wagons.

Joe was on his locomotive's footplate. He had left Laura and the signal cabin now that both lines were completely closed to all traffic and adequately protected and would remain so until the breakdown gang and crane cleared the line. Joe busied himself cleaning the circular boiler front and the rest of the cab. Bill sat in the driver's corner on his wooden box seat with his eyes closed and his opened Daily Express laid alongside him, he was having his mid-day forty winks. He felt pleased and confident now about his bet which he felt certain Bill Clarke would have placed on 'Thistle Top' at Naggy Nockel's.

Joe finished his tasks in the cab when the breakdown crew started their work and seated himself on his fireman's seat looking on as the crew busied themselves. The Gang Foreman and a Locomotive Inspector were in charge. The inspector was trilby hatted and brown suited, his task looked more advisory and supervisory than physical. The gang foreman looked like a working foreman, he was flat capped and rough jacketed and had his trousers tied up at the knees. The driver of the steam crane was busy in his cab producing steam pressure in the crane's boiler. He kept testing the operating abilities of his crane by putting steam through the small pair of cylinders and making the small piston rods and flywheels rattle and rotate at high speed.

The gang and the steam crane driver appeared to be an experienced team. They halted the crane alongside the derailed wagons; big wooden blocks were inserted under the crane's crucial weight bearing parts and then it was jacked up so that the stone ballast and not the rails took the main weight and any load it might lift. The three derailed wagons were lifted easily by the crane and placed on the rails; they were pushed into the yard by the men and were examined by a Carriage and Wagon Inspector. The crane was then unjacked and moved into position alongside Bill Ankler's locomotive.

"It's our turn now Bill," Joe said loudly to the slumbering figure of Bill. "They're going to want us off the loco' inspector says." Bill grunted and stirred, pushed his cap back from his eyes and made to pocket his paper and his incomplete spectacles. "We should be on the rails by three o' clock says the inspector and be on our way to change over with the Castlebrough bound goods at Rillington before four o'clock. It's going to be a longer day than we expected," continued Joe to his stirring and stretching mate.

Soon the steam crane and the men commenced the task of re-railing the C7 locomotive and its tender. The crane's steel jib hung high in the afternoon sky above the loco.' Chains, hooks, tee pieces, and other paraphernalia dangled from the great jib arm. They were secured firmly to crucial strong points on the locomotive's frame and tender. One hundred and twenty tons had to be picked up firmly and steadily and slowly lowered onto the rails. The job was done with diligence and efficiency. Chains tightened, the Gang foreman called out instructions, whistle pop signals and the noise of scurrying pistons and heavy flywheels on the crane drifted across the countryside and startled the sheep in the cattle wagons of Tom's waiting goods train. Up she eased slowly. "This is an easy job," the locomotive inspector whispered in Joe's ear as he looked on. "Hardly worth coming out for." He continued, "We have 'em a lot more difficult than this."

The six-wheeled engine tender was completely derailed, its wheels had cut deep into the sleepers and wedged between the running rails and the check rails. Most of the locomotive section had been derailed; its pair of pony wheels beneath the engine cab and the four big six foot driving wheels were each settled on the sleepers and ballast and firmly lodged into the points which had been jumped during the shunt backwards.

How had it happened? Many were asking that question. Had Laura absent mindedly pulled the points and brought about the derailment or had Bill given one whistle too many to Laura causing her to pull the points and derail the wagons and the loco'? Maybe Bill had just been going too fast in his haste to finish his shunting and had caused the wagons to jump the rails. It didn't matter now, the questions were academic.

The engine needed lifting about twelve inches. With her front bogie wheels still in position on the rails she was swung, levered and pushed over, into position and lowered back on the rails. Slowly she sank down. Ankler, Rittler, Silverwood, the Ganger and the now 'off duty' Laura stood in an interested little crowd watching the day's drama evaporate before their eyes to be replaced by mundane railway operations.

The chocks, the chains, the ramps, the pinch bars and all of the assorted tools found themselves rapidly stowed away in the vans. The kettle was on the boil in the accommodation van and a long line of empty tea mugs stood on the van's tables with dominoes and cards awaiting the tea and the men. Soon the crane and the D20 locomotive with its panting donkey engine would be on their two hour journey back to York.

Joe and Bill climbed up onto their re-railed locomotive. Laura joined them; her handicapped sister Lucy stood on the grassed verge of the goods yard sidings watching with amazement. Laura sat on the fireman's seat talking and watching Joe and Bill making preparations to move as soon as the Permanent Way Inspector said that track was adequately repaired and secured.

"It's been a different day," said Laura with a smile; her slim uniformed figure reclining easily on Joe's fireman's seat.

"Yes, I've enjoyed it in an odd sort of way," laughed Joe, "But I had wanted to be home by the middle of this afternoon to go rabbiting near Forge Valley wi' me mate. Wo'nt be home now till six or seven tonight." Joe stooped to fire his engine firebox while Laura looked on and chatted.

"I hope your horse wins." Laura addressed herself to Bill, who stood fat and towering on the driver's step over and above the working figure of Joe.

"It'd better after all that."

"Let me know, wo'nt you?" Laura came back turning to Joe. "Are you on this train next week when I'm on late turn?"

Joe wasn't. "I'll pass here on the Gascoigne Wood coal train on Monday afternoon. I'll give you the thumbs up or the thumbs down sign as we pass to let you know the fate of the bet." Joe grinned and gesticulated with a wry twist of his face in the direction of Bill whose head was stuck out of the cab window. "Wish I could come up for a cup of tea on Monday but we are unlikely to stop here unless we get derailed," he chuckled.

They moved their engine carefully over the damaged rails and back onto to their waiting train. Tom coupled their engine to the train and then made off in the direction of his van ready to give the green flag indication 'go' when he was on board. They pulled off with the wagons rattling and jerking and the C7 locomotive's chimney pleasantly exhausting her beats in ever increasing tempo. Laura stood on the nearby station platform waving as they left. Joe felt pleased as he leaned out of the cab to give answering waves. 'A bit of alright' he thought, 'Pity she lives in this distant place and me in Castlebrough.'

The train gathered pace. Bill was in a hurry; his engine's gear lever was well down - on a low cut-off, he was exerting her so much that he made her spin her driving wheels and slip wildly on the rails. She gushed a column of black smoke skyward. Bill noted that all the signals were at clear and gave a long whistle blast of farewell to Heslerton and the breakdown Gang and their train. The D20 locomotive was preparing to run around its train and couple up and then make off at all speed after Joe and Bill towards York. It gave an answering friendly whistle blast to the C7. Bill Ankler made his way to Knapton as quickly as possible.

They wasted no time when they arrived, no tea or paper reading. They did not even do all of the work that was there to be done; they just put four cattle wagons loaded with sheep alongside the little cattle pen and left all other shunting work for the next goods train on Monday morning. They were in a rush to clear the road and let the breakdown train get on its way to York. If they didn't move smartly they knew that Train Control would order one of the station masters to hold them while the slow moving breakdown train passed them and went on its way to York. Bill didn't want that indignity, he wanted to get back to Castlebrough as soon as possible and obtain the results of the two-fifteen at Pontefract. They left Knapton as quickly as possible.

The sun was dipping well into the sky; its weak haze indicating its position as a light part of the thin cloudy sky. Beasts grazed in the fields, road traffic stood at the gate crossings. The C7 locomotive ripped on speedily straining its connecting rods on the driving wheels. The countryside was calm, disturbed only by the noise of the careering train, there was no hint of war, nor even of the derailment which they had just suffered.

At Rillington their change over crew and train from York stood patiently waiting for them on the down main line. Bill brought his train to a hurried halt alongside it; he and Joe grabbed their jackets, food tins, bottles and personal belongings and climbed across onto the waiting Castlebrough bound goods train.

"One perishable and two cattle wagons for Knapton. That's all that's urgent between here and Castlebrough," the York driver said to Bill as they changed over.

"Okay" was Bill's curt reply. "We're not doing anything that can be left until Monday. We're tekin' everything except perishables and livestock straight through to Castlebrough as quick as we can fly."

They saw Tom safely aboard his guard's van and away they went; their, newly acquired B16 engine's chimney exhausting hard into the atmosphere. Bill yanked open the steam regulator impatiently. He intended to get to Castlebrough quickly if he could get a clear road. He didn't, he couldn't. He had to take his turn. There was a huge volume of traffic that had been held up at both sides of Knapton and it had to pass along the recently cleared lines. Twice they were stopped and shunted aside while traffic passed by and all of Bill's complaints and curses could not alter the situation.

Joe laboured as was necessary, his task was not hard. The B16 locomotive handled the goods train with ease and steamed without difficulty. Only nineteen miles separated them from Castlebrough when they were at Rillington - not far for a big locomotive with forty-five assorted wagons but it still took them two hours of travel, shunting and standing aside to let others pass. Joe, Bill and Tom were ready for home when they arrived at Castlebrough and backed their train into Gallows Close Goods Yard at six-fifteen that Saturday evening. Joe and Bill were concluding a twelve hour shift. Tom was just in time to race home and 'take the missus down to the Working Men's Club.'

"What won the two-fifteen at Pontefract?" Bill addressed his urgent question to the goods yard shunter, Ken, at Gallow's Close Goods Yard as he reversed his train of forty-five wagons into the loop siding. Bill was leaning out of his engine cab window and Ken was just preparing to uncouple the loco' from the train with his eight foot hooked shunting pole. Joe, dirty and tired was leaning out at the same side of the engine as the anxious Bill. Joe wanted to hear Ken's reply. Ken paused, the whole train was slowly shuffling up and making a lot of noise, he pressed the nearby wagon brake down into the on position and secured it to hold the train still after the loco' had left.

"Two fifteen?" he replied. "That was the favourite at evens. 'Red Sunset.' One o' Richardson's."

Bill exploded with a mouthful of unrepeatable adjectives and curses. "Bloody Red Sunset!"

"Ye - romped home. T'others were nowhere, three lengths." The shunter replied clearly and almost happily.

"Where was 'Thistle Top? I backed the b...... wi a fiver." Bill spluttered uncontrollably. His false teeth threatened to evacuate his mouth. He took his cap off and with a show desperation wiped his craggy face with a sponge cloth. Joe felt a surge of sympathy.

"It were nowhere. Not in the fust three ony way." Ken the shunter came back a little less enthusiastically than when he had first answered Bill's question.

"Are you bloody sure?" Bill shouted down to the figure on the ground beneath his engine.

"Ye. I had it in a tanner treble wi' 'Pearly Queen' an' 'Early Bird.' 'Pearly Queen' won but 'Early Bird's' still runnin' or flyin'"

Bill's pain was permanent. He ceased to rebel and protest, he shrank into a pained silence in the corner of his cab. He drove his engine from the goods yard to Castlebrough locomotive shed with a speedy careless abandon. It shot past every signal that was in clear position and skated to a crazy halt up to every signal that stood in the danger position.

Joe was quiet, tucked away in the upper corner of his cab as they raced tender first home to the shed. What could he do to relieve Bill's suffering? He kept his eyes on the signals and the signal cabins past which they flew; he was as helpful and observant for Bill as he could be. He sympathised deeply. He knew that five pounds was more than a driver's weekly wage and that Bill and Tom had suffered a grievous financial blow. It had been their gamble and they couldn't blame anyone else for their misfortune.

Bill and Joe placed their locomotive on the outside pit on Number One Road of the eight-laned Castlebrough locomotive shed. The valley, down which Castlebrough was approached from the Vale of Picketing, was bathed in the light of the late summer evening. Blackout regulations were not due to be applied until eight-thirty. The time was approaching six-forty-five and a squad of home guards marched alongside the road railings and down Sander Road. A smoky haze drifted away from the busy gasworks' chimney towards the looming promontory of Oliver's Mount. Bill left with barely a word for anyone. Joe had a few words with the late shift cleaner chargeman before he prepared to make his way home.

"Bill's gone up to the Railway Tavern," the short bespectacled chargeman said to Joe about Ankler. "He's annoyed about something. Didn't say 'goodbye' or 'kiss me arse.' Just 'What a bloody day, Thank God the Tavern's open. Could just do wi' a couple o' pints.' Then he was off. Nowt else."

Joe with his empty tea bottle in his jacket pocket and his khaki haversack draped over his shoulder, stood for a few minutes in the

Chargeman's Time Office and Store. He told of the day's events and of the hot tip that had turned out to be cold.

The Chargeman was interested. "When I relieved Bill Clarke at two o' clock he said that he was going up to Naggy Nockel's wi' a big bet for Ankler. Yer - no wonder Ankler's like a bear wi' a sore arse. Five quid eh?" He gave an unsympathetic chuckle.

Joe nodded agreement. "Ye, lot o' money. Anyway I'm off. Hope to go out tonight to the Olympia dancing, after I've had summat to eat." With that he departed and made his way out through the shed gate onto Sander Road.

Meanwhile Bill Ankler, sore and depressed, had left the shed and gone in the other direction up Sander Road. His broad figure swaggering slightly as he walked, his light shoes giving him an uncaring casual look. His overalls were dirty after long service without a wash. In his round craggy face a lighted Park Drive cigarette burned away as he sauntered up Sander Road. Bill's goal was the Railway Tavern, a popular little local public house that served many locomotive men after their day on the footplate. Bill was sure of finding some railwaymen for company and maybe even a little commiseration.

The ornate double fronted Railway Tavern settled in a dip in the flow of Sander Road. Appropriately enough it looked out and over the moderately sized coal sidings known as Washbeck Yard. The Tavern witnessed the daily movement of hundreds of tons of coal from the Yard into the town and the nearby coal-fired electric generating station. Bill moved through the Tavern's portals gloomily, hoping for a sense of relief.

Bentwood chairs around circular wooden tables dominated the furnishing in the main bar. The ornate mirrored bar gave a Victorian air to the room that was adequate without boasting any finer comforts. There were no carpets and no upholstery. If such things had been provided they would soon have been soiled by the grease laden boots and overalls of the working men drinkers. Brassware, mirrors, polished woodwork and the odd poster broke the monotony of the 'fag-end' littered floors and wooden seating. About fifteen men drank, talked and smoked in the bar - most were in the uniforms of railway guards, footplatemen, shunters or porters. Card games and domino sessions were in agitated progress at three tables. A darts board was occupied by a four-some playing 'Five Hundred and One Up'.

Bill Ankler pulled up at the bar close to a shed labourer and a footplateman - both of whom he knew well.

"Pint o' mild Jack and some Park Drives if you've got any?" Bill addressed himself unsmilingly to the brawny, moustached barman who was pulling pints of Moor and Robson's ales from brass decorated hand pumps.

"No fags at all Bill, sorry." The barman answered that question indifferently. He said the same thing many times in the day to scores of customers. They all asked for cigarettes which were in short supply."Not seen you all week Bill. Thought you were on early turn."

"Ye. It's been a long day today, been derailed at Heslerton. Just back now. Have you got tonight's paper Jack?"

"The 'Castlebrough's' over there wi' Crocker in that domino school." The barman slid Bill's pint over the counter and indicated with his head the direction of the domino school around a circular table. Alf Crocker and three young locomen were engaged in a game of 'fives and threes.' One of the four had a folded newspaper pinned on the table beneath a leaning elbow. Bill Ankler received his pint of mild beer from Jack and moved over to Alf Crocker.

"Gi'me yer Castlebrough Evening News Alf? Fer a moment."

Alf lifted his arm and passed the publican's folded evening newspaper to Bill who seated himself on the nearby fixed oak bench seat. "Sure Bill. Do yer want a game cos Mike's leaving after this hand?."

Bill grunted his reply "Mebbe" and took a long drink from his pint of mild. He unfolded the 'Castlebrough Evening News and Daily Post.' The day's wartime headlines leaped out 'NEW SOVIET OFFENSIVE' 'Red Army Storms Svesk.' Most of the front page carried news from the various battle fronts of the world. A mere glance showed that the tide of war was turning against Hitler's armies but Bill's eyes were seeking other news. The long racing results column also nestled importantly on the front page. Bill maintained a casual chatter with Alf and the domino players while he urgently sought confirmation of Ken's news. Sure enough, there it was - the two-fifteen at Pontefract; 'Red Sunset' and in the also rans 'Thistle Top' at ten-to-one. The column etched itself miserably into his visual memory, he knew that he would not forget reading that day's racing results for as long as he lived.

A great sickness settled into his stomach. Misery blanketed his mental mood but he did not seek the commiseration of his immediate company. He confided nothing. He did not respond to the comments from the domino players about the day's racing results instead he talked more readily of the dominoes on the table or of the war news. Bill sought only to forget about racing and to drown his mood in mild beer but the sudden unannounced presence of Bill Clarke in the bar room brought his agony back sharply.

"Hello Bill." The blue suited figure of Bill Clarke, with anticipation displayed on his face, sought out Ankler and approached him urgently "Been a long day today for you. Eh?"

"Too long" returned the disinterested Ankler. "A rotten day."

"Well I backed it for you Bill. As yer said." His eyes widened "It really was summat, to see that betting shop stand still when 'Whistle Stop' pulled in at three-fifteen wi' your fiver and my ten bob on at twenty to one."

Bill's eyes fell down the racing column to the result of the three-fifteen at Pontefract and not a word uttered through his usually ready lips. He read the race result, then he read it again. A wave of relief, mixed with disbelief, flowed through his body from head to foot. Slowly he raised his gaze, his eyes clicked with the twinkle in Clarkey's eyes. The realisation struck home. Intense joy brought an uncontrollable grin across his face. "Whistle Stop! Yeh, sure. I knew it would win?"

1
A PIG'S BEEN KILLED

The hiss of steam drifted monotonously through the smoky, hot, gaslit darkness of Castlebrough Locomotive Shed; its pervading sound came from not just one sizzling pressure valve or squeaky gland but from many. The shed was full of engines; on each of its eight parallel railroads two or three locomotives 'in steam' were awaiting crews to take them out on carefully planned journeys. Smoke, steam and particles of soot drifted aimlessly on the warm currents of air to dissipate or cling to the walls, engines and brick paved roadways. A heavy early morning blackness still surrounded the shed.

Joe's hearing did not register the constant hissing of steam as he toiled boringly in the dirty, soot caked cab of the B16 locomotive. He and Driver Tom West were preparing the locomotive for another engine crew to work the Gasgoine Wood coal train at six a.m.

Joe had little interest in cleaning the soot caked boiler front, windows and seats, he wasn't doing it for himself, otherwise he would have been more enthusiastic. He was doing it for 'Jingo' Johnson and his 'oily' fireman 'Creeper' Cammish. These two were top of Joe's 'List of Nasty Characters.' It was his eternal hope that he would never be rostered to fire for Jingo who had an unsavoury reputation as a bully and whose rough driving caused a lot of hard work for his fireman. Joe knew Jingo would make a fuss if the engine wasn't clean for him and that thought created anxiety for Joe, though it did not make him keen to do a thorough job. So unwillingly he laboured in the light of the naked paraffin fuelled flame that danced on the end of his hand held torch lamp illuminating the dirty engine cab.

On the fireman's wooden seat a small heap of religious books and leaflets sat incongruously; Joe had just removed them from his overall pocket and placed them prominently where he would not overlook to repossess them when he left the engine. They triggered off thoughts about how he had come to acquire them the previous evening at the Methodist Young People's Bible Class, thoughts that were rudely interrupted by a shout from Tom somewhere in the deep pit beneath the engine.

"Tek care not to open yer damper Joseph, or move owt else," Tom West shouted. "I'm going to climb up behind the big-end to oil her and there ain't a lot of room."

Tom West was the father of Dan, Joe's closest friend and confidant. Tom was tall and blustery, he always talked extravagantly with his hands and said everything extremely loudly as if everyone else was hard of hearing. His son Dan lay at home in bed in the front room of a house not far from where Joe lived. At the age of fourteen Dan had fallen from a high tree and broken his back causing total paralysis from beneath his shoulders. Since the accident and a long period in the 'local workhouse hospital' Dan had never been off his back. He and Joe dreamed of a day when an operation would restore to him the use of his legs.

Joe currently and secretly entertained hopes of a divine inspired miracle that would restore Dan to the world of the walking and return them both to the scrapes and adventures they had known before Dan's accident. The tall elegantly featured, twenty year old, Catherine Hanson, who had taken Joe to the Bible class the night before, was the real source of the inspiration which had lit in Joe's mind the hope of divine intervention in the life of his friend Dan.

"You must give God a chance," she had said to him many times when they had talked quietly over the garden fence at the rear of Joe's home. "You only need to believe strongly enough and God can help in the most mysterious ways. You do believe, don't you?"

Joe had assured her that he did believe in God, indeed he stressed, "I read a portion of the New Testament every night and then say my prayers. I pray for Dan to walk again. What more can I do?"

"I can't tell you quickly and easily. The answer lies deep in your understanding, in your commitment to God. You have to commune with him closely, love him and spread his word. His love and his power will give you greater love and inspiration. He alone can make your friend walk again. It is true. It is true." She was so fervent in her mission, so inspiring and confident that she succeeded in obtaining Joe's ear and winning from him a promise that he would attend the Bible Class at least once before "Making up your mind against God and maybe stopping your friend from ever walking again."

Joe could not bear the possible responsibility that maybe an action of his might deprive his friend from walking and running again, but there was, in his mind, a suspicion that he was more attracted by the curves of Catherine's body than the promise of divine powers; he liked the fullness of her naturally very red lips and her serious deep blue penetrating eyes; he liked her because of her feminine company and, dare he think it about someone so holy, her 'sex appeal.'

He went with her, last evening, to the bible class and returned home with a secreted pile of religious literature which he cared not to leave at home in his bedroom for his family to mull over and surmise. He had brought the books and leaflets with him to work where he might have a chance to read some of their contents without any of the shed staff knowing of his interest in religion.

Joe's thoughts were again suddenly interrupted by his mate Tom who announced from his position on the roadway alongside the loco "I've finished Joseph, I'm going into the messroom for a cupper. Don't forgot, if you go off anywhere be back in time to leave the shed for six-fifteen, we've got to shunt the Gasworks for six-thirty."

"See yer in the mess-room mate, in a few minutes," replied Joe. His work of engine preparation was almost done and he intended to have a quiet private perusal of Catherine's divine literature in the unsteady light of his torch lamp before going into the messroom for his first breakfast. He pored over a leaflet entitled the 'Power of Christ,' he read avidly the claims of faith healing cures, looking desperately for a claim that a totally paralysed person had been made to walk; he studied the bible class syllabus, studied excerpts from the New Testament documenting early miracles and started on 'The Methodist Faith.'

"What yuh got there son? Today's racing form?" Joe was abruptly interrupted by the voice of Jack the Steamraiser who had climbed the side of the engine quietly. Joe exhibited a flustered embarrassment and bundled his books out of sight.

"No, just books, er, books on engines." Joe escaped quickly from the B16 loco. and crossed to his own little side-tank shunting engine number 9016; silently he stowed his books under his coat on the fireman's seat and went off to join his mate.

The messroom was cosy and clean in comparison with the rest of the shed; a fresh carpet of clean sand lay thinly but evenly spread over the whole of the rectangular concrete floor. A roaring coal fire about two feet deep filled the large cast iron fireplace; alongside the fire a big iron kettle nestled on the ledge formed by the now unused water boiler. The kettle simmered slowly; ever ready to service an engineman's billy can or tea mug. The ashes fell to the floor to be contained within the fender formed from a half wagon- wheel metal tyre. The two long tables were freshly scrubbed and scoured and left white and inviting. The four tall messroom windows were permanently blacked out by a coat of black paint to comply with wartime regulations, two gas lamps hanging from the ceiling cast their weak yellow light on the men seated on the built-in wooden seating that passed along two walls. Wall lockers and two wall desks with notice cases attached formed the only other 'furniture' in the room.

Joe joined Tom West who was cleaned up and sat eating and

drinking at one of the tables. The Night Foreman Bill Frobisher, Bill Ankler, engine cleaner Jeff Mason and night shift labourer Pusher Jackson were playing a game of 'Solo' for 'tanners' and 'coppers.' Two local policemen had visited the shed during the night and William Frobisher was explaining the purpose of their visit, while dealing the cards.

"Two hams missing; that were some cheeky sod fer you," the trilby hatted Frobisher was saying. "The nine-thirty last night hit an old sow as she was crossing from the gasworks allotments. How she got out on her sty I don't know. She were laid with her head smashed in on the Up Main an' both her hind quarters were cut out clean wi' a knife. Somebody's increased their rations unless they're going to put the hams on the black market."

"What did the police come for?" asked Joe taking an interest.

"Laker on the nine-thirty last night reported his train hitting something just outside the shed here. Saw blood on his bogie wheels when he stopped. Thought he'd hit a platelayer, felt proper sick he did. Station Foreman got police and an ambulance. Cos they found the old sow with her hams missing, it's a police job." He talked slowly and importantly as he dealt cards around the card school, aware that his story had an interested audience. " 'Must've been a butcher' I said to them. 'None of our lads would touch a warm carcass with a knife. They're enginemen not butchers'."

Joe listened as the story unfolded about police interviews with shedmen who had been on duty. He did not agee with Frobisher's claim that none of the shedmen would do such a thing; the chance to supplement family rations would be a big temptation to some of Joe's rabbiting and pig-keeping mates. As it happened the two police officers had departed during the early hours without their knowledge of the theft being increased. They had left with the intention of arranging for the disposal of the pig's carcass with the local abattoir, advising the Secretary of the Gasworks Allotment's Association about the pig's accidental slaughter and coming back later to interview the late shift shedmen and Bob Laker.

Joe left when the pig tale told by Frobisher had reached its climax. He made his way out through the messroom doorway leaving Ankler, Jackson, and Mason wrangling over the course of the game of solo which had just concluded with an unexpected win by engine cleaner Mason.

* * * * * *

2
THE TROUBLE WITH SLEEPERS

As Joe made his way towards his waiting engine on number one road at the mouth of the shed, early morning shafts of daylight entering the gaping doorways picked out the figure of his friend Johnny Marsay walking towards the time-keeper's office.

"Joe, you're on the early coal pilot today aren't you?" Johnny shouted across the intervening space and moved to join Joe.

"Sure," Joe replied.

"I'm on early shed dust-hole today and I've a little job I want you to help me with."

"What's that?" asked Joe with little alarm bells ringing.

"Move some sleepers for me an' our kid." Johnny was now close to Joe. "We've bought some old sleepers off Franker at firewood rate an' I want them moving from the top shed to our kid's allotment at Gas Down."

"How yuh goin' to do that?"

"I want you to do it for me with 9016."

Joe was staggered by his mate's confident demand. The sleepers were eight feet long and weighed about twelve stones each. "How the hell can I do that?"

"I want you to bring 9016 up from Gas Down when Tom West pop's home for his breakfast. Come up to the shed corner at about eight o' clock and me an' our kid'll join you and we'll go up to the top shed and between the three of us we'll load the sleepers on the front end of the engine and in the cab."

"That's crazy John. We'll need the signalman to give us the road, an' we wont have a driver on." Joe was used to his friend's unusual schemes, pastimes and activities but he thought this one a bit too risky to be involved in.

Johnny Marsay was about three years older than Joe and used the authority that his age and experience conferred upon him to lead, sometimes mislead, Joe into activities which he often wished he had avoided. Johnny had a broad, cheerful; even cheeky face with a pencil thin black moustache which he boasted made him very desirable to females.

"Can't you drive?" Johnny asked with a mock disbelief.

"Well of course I can. It's just - -." Joe's protesting remark was cut short by Tom West shouting to him from 9016

"Joe Wade, stop your bloody tongue wagging and get up here. We're due off the shed now."

Johnny added quickly, "Our kid's coming in specially on his way to work at eight just to give me a lift with the sleepers. He'll be with me at the bottom corner of the shed at about five to eight. You bring the engine up to this end of one road and wait for the signal to clear and then come up and collect me and our kid."

"I have to go Johnny" Joe uttered desperately.

"Okay I'll see you at eight, won't take us two minutes. I'll fix the signalman to give us the road, an,'" he paused, "I'll drive the engine so don't you worry."

Joe was worried. He rushed off towards 9016 and Tom West. Soon he was on board and directing his attention towards the expected pile of religious books he had left on his fireman's seat; but his seat was bare. His coat had been moved and the books were missing. He looked around all the possible places in which they might have been concealed; he asked Tom if he had seen the books on the seat, but without result; he had to forget about them and get on with his job of making his engine fit for its shunting task. While he worked he could not help thinking with anxiety about his excuses to Catherine Hanson for having lost her books. 'Why he wondered do things always go wrong for me?'

The shunter Bob Woodhouse joined them on their small sixty ton shunting engine as they left the push-bell exit of the shed. Soon they were busy shunting the empty wagons out of the nearby gasworks and replacing them with loaded coal wagons.

When the Gaswork's buzzer blew at seven-thirty Tom said to Joe, "We're goin' to shunt Collin's siding and then stop for our breakfast at about ten to eight. I'm goin' home for some egg and bacon, I'll be back for eight-thirty. You look after the engine while I'm gone."

Joe's agreement was taken for granted; of course he would, the remaining engineman always looked after the engine when one of them was away. The approach of breakfast time did more than make Joe's gastric juices flow in anticipation of the sandwiches he had left from his first breakfast; the approach of breakfast reminded him of Johnny's parting instruction. He worried about the decision he would have to take on the approach of eight o' clock; if he did not take the engine to meet Johnny then Johnny would come down to the engine and ask 'Why?' On the other hand if he moved the engine he might get a rattling from Tom West or, worse still, he might get into trouble with the railway authorities.

"Don't you clear off anywhere Joseph. I know your reputation for shootin' off for bread cakes an' newspapers and the like," Tom shouted as he stopped his shunting engine in Gasworks Down Sidings and screwed down the handbrake; he shouted at Joe as if Joe was at the other side of Sander Road.

Joe merely replied, "I'm getting mi head down when I've filled mi breadbasket." He thought he meant what he said because he had not yet made the decision to borrow the engine for Johnny's little haulage job.

Tom's long legs and bubbling vitality soon took him out of sight in the direction of his home a few hundred yards into the housing estate. Joe opened his sandwich tin and started giving some serious thought to Johnny Marsay's 'instructions.' As he ate the first of his remaining sandwiches he looked towards the locomotive shed a few hundred yards away; his eyes rested on the small red and white wooden semaphore signal which controlled the exit from the sidings; as he watched it fell slowly into its clear position. Further ahead Joe could see the broad figure of Johnny Marsay at the corner of the loco' shed wildly waving his right arm in the 'Come ahead' railway hand signal.

Joe looked and chewed, he didn't want to obey the signals; all his instincts warned him to stay and consume his sandwiches but instead he unscrewed the engine handbrake, put the shunting engine into forward gear and admitted enough steam into the cylinders to make her move forward slowly. The movement of the sixty ton loco' sent a pleasing shudder through his frame; he had often moved loco's in the shed yard but not outside where movements where governed by the signal cabins and strict regulations. His engine accelerated towards Johnny at the shed corner and towards the numerous signals which controlled movements along the increasingly complex track systems.

"Stop a minute Joe," Johnny's voice shouted up from the ground ballast. Johnny's hands grasped the engine handrails and hauled his black haired sturdy figure up the engine side. "Stop a minute and let Jacko get on."

"Jacko!" exclaimed Joe with some expressed surprise as he brought his engine to a steady halt. "I thought your kid was coming to help you."

"He was but he aint." Johnny paused and looked down the engine steps at the round, cloth-capped figure of shed labourer Pusher Jackson, who was endeavouring to climb up the engine steps into the cab. "You on now Pusher?" he directed towards Jackson as the labourer's weight was transferred from the ground to the engine. The grunted reply was enough for Johnny Marsay. "Come on Joe, give her some stick the signals are off up the side reception to the bell push cabin." He reached over the cab and grabbed the steam regulator handle from Joe's control and pulled it open urgently. The little tall chimneyed, locomotive went barking forward with a great spurt of acceleration. "We aint got all day Joe, stop scratchin' yerself, get crackin'."

"Where we going?" asked Joe looking completely relaxed and carefree. "We've only got until half eight when Westy comes back from breakfast."

"Loadsa time if we move."

"Where we going?" Joe repeated.

"To the top shed entrance, just outside Shed Master's office. Don't get worked up about that. He'll be just getting out of bed fer work. He wont be on 'til nine."

"Do you know all these signals Johnny? I don't." Joe did not know which signals applied to which lines and he felt a little nervous about the possibility of running past a signal at danger and causing an accident.

"There's nowt to know. Them two teks us right up alongside the boss's office. We stop just behind the ground dolly, gives a whistle to the signalman and pops back into the top siding behind the shed." He once more took the steam regulator handle from Joe's grasp and opened it wide. "Both signals is off. Let's get our skates on." The small engine scurried rapidly forwards and exhausted a noisy torrent from its tall chimney; it rocked unsteadily as only, small wheeled, light engines could. The three occupants in the small locomotive cab swayed with the engine as it gathered speed. Johnny had paused in his address to Joe; "Stop worrying Joe. Father John 'll look after yuh."

"I aint worrying. Get you're hands off the regulator, I'm driving."

"He's getting upperty, Pusher. Young upstarts, some of these yesterday's cleaners are." Joe ignored Johnny's teasing remarks.

Joe took confident control of the little engine: brushed Johnny's searching hand to one side, opened the regulator wide to make the engine scurry madly towards the point where they were going to halt and reverse into the top shed admission line. He knew the ground dolly behind which John meant they had to halt; he could see that they were approaching it rapidly so he applied the steam brake hard to arrest the engine's motion.

"Chrise sake! Yuh didn't tell me that it was bloody dangerous on here when yuh asked me to help," shouted the round bodied craggy faced Pusher Jackson. He swayed over crazily against the bunker as Joe brought the engine to a sliding, but abrupt halt behind the signal dolly on the ground close to Mr Franker's office.

"Stand on your feet, that's all you've got to do." Joe grinned back at the staggering Johnny and Pusher. "Nowt dangerous, not with yours truly at the brake and the regulator."

"That's what's worrying us," Johnny exclaimed. "Pop the whistle now for the points and the dolly."

The points and the dolly signal were soon moved in their favour and Joe commenced to back his engine slowly into the short siding that ended where two big wooden shed doors crossed the line and cut off admission to the top engine shed. "Go back slowly Joe. Don't want you to make her pick up her wheels and slide through those doors into the shed."

"Fer Christ's sake stop worrying," Joe answered light heartedly to Johnny; only to pause and find time for a mental reflection that he had just blasphemed against God by using the name of Jesus Christ in vain. His mental reference to God brought back his concern about Catherine's missing books.

"Bring her back steady. The sleepers are stood against that wall. Get as close up to the shed door as you can without touchin' up." Johnny was concerned that Joe might let the engine slide forwards and crash through the doors. "Steady. Steady."

"Stop worrying. You're getting quite nervous in your old age," Joe returned confidently with some expressed amusement.

The three jumped quickly from the engine when it came smoothly to a halt a few inches from the big closed shed doors. They soon had the heavy waste sleepers loaded quickly across the front end of the engine footplate and across the cab floor.

"Jump aboard you two" said Johnny, rubbing his hands at the success of his mission to acquire the waste sleepers. "The dolly's off for you to go out. When you get past the points stop and whistle for the dolly back over to be pulled off. Pick me up on the way back. I want to just leave those other sleepers a bit safer, they might fall over if I leave them as they are."

The J72 tank engine backed nippily out of the top shed inlet road, whistled, reversed and, when the ground signal moved into clear position, rolled back down the reception line towards the shed master's office and to pick up Johnny as it passed.

Joe and Pusher were on the footplate, raised to a somewhat elevated position because of the thick sleepers on the cab floor beneath their feet; they were looking out through the back windows in the bunker. Johnny was placing the four remaining upright standing sleepers as securely as possible against the red brick wall of the shed. He did not notice the small personnel door, in the larger wooden shed door, open slowly to reveal the stocky figure of Mr Franker, the Castlebrough Shedmaster.

"Christ," said Joe loudly. 'Blaspheming again,' he recorded to himself subconsciously, as he observed Franker emerge and move in the direction of Johnny Marsay. "The bloody gaffer. What's he doin' at work this early?" Pusher Jackson said nothing; he just ducked down out of sight below the door level. Joe had closed his steam regulator in preparation to halt and collect Johnny, he paused, wondering what he ought to do. Franker must not learn that the engine didn't have its authorised driver on board; Franker mustn't be allowed to know that Pusher Jackson and the unorthodox load of waste sleepers were aboard engine 9016. Joe did not hesitate, he could see that the small wooden signal on the signal gantry was in clear position and granting him safe access to the shed side reception line. He opened his steam regulator and made his engine roll as normally as possible past the place where Franker and Johnny were in ardent conversation. Within seconds Joe's engine was passed and rolling quickly down towards Gas Works Down Sidings.

"Christ, that was close Pusher. The gaffer nearly caught us." He wiped his acne spotted forehead with a dirty hand and left it grotesquely marked with dirty smears. He adjusted his engine controls and looked out for the signals which he knew were appropriate to his passage. He was surprised and pleased to realise that he did know which signals applied to the reception line down which his engine was passing on its way to the Gas Down Coal Sidings.

"What do you think Marsay 'll be saying to Franker right now?" asked Pusher Jackson.

"Johnny's got the wildest imagination, he'll tell Franker anything but the truth. He can't even tell you the truth if you asked him who his Mother is."

"We've got to get rid of these sleepers."

"Where did Johnny say he wanted them?" Joe asked with a sudden rush of concern. If he didn't look slippy he might still have them on board when Tom West returned from breakfast.

"On his brother's allotment." Pusher replied." Said he was going to get them picked up from there onto a lorry. Wants 'em at home for Christ knows what."

Joe noticed the further blasphemous remark by Jackson and for a moment wondered whether it was not in their best interests to avoid upsetting God because they both needed all the luck they could get. "Do you know which is the allotment Pusher?"

"Seen Johnny on one once. Think it's his brother's, I do, cos Johnny just said to me that its the one next but one to the last coal cell in Collins's yard. Its got a sleeper built shed on it."

The small six wheeled shunting engine rolled past the locomotive shed, where the clock pointed to eight-twenty, and on towards the coal sidings. "We've got ten minutes to get these off the engine before Westy gets back." Joe added, "We'll be alright if we find the allotment."

Joe didn't feel too concerned now that he had avoided Franker and brought the engine back safely into the coal sidings. His main concern now was to avoid his driver Tom West finding out that the engine had been used without permission for one of Marsay's hair-brained schemes. He was not too concerned about Franker finding out from Marsay that the engine had been used without Tom West on board because he was confident that Marsay would spin an authentic yarn and cover up the little escapade.

The engine clattered on past the coal cells in Collin's yard and drew up alongside the second allotment plot which quite rightly contained a shed made out of old railway sleepers. "Let's tip these off onto the path alongside the shed as quick as possible."

Pusher Jackson was a good help despite his habit of avoiding any task that could be described as work. He helped Joe to topple the sleepers from the engine to land with a thud and lie in a disordered pile alongside the shed on the allotment.

"Give me a run up to the shed now son. I want to catch Marsay as soon as possible. He promised me ten Park Drives for this job an' I'm right out o' smokes."

Joe did as Pusher wanted, the way to the shed was clear so he used his engine to provide the requested ride; soon he returned the engine to the spot where Tom West had left it when he had departed for home and breakfast. Joe now awaited the return of Tom West, passing the time by investigating the nearby allotment on which he and Pusher had just dumped the sleepers; it was neat and newly dug and planted with spring seeds and early vegetables. The shed, made of sleepers, had been recently tarred and glowed a smart black amongst the assortment of rubbish and water butts which surrounded it. On the door a large number 2 had been added in white paint. Alongside the door behind a piece of roughly framed glass the name and address of the owner was displayed in neat black printing on a white sheet. Out of idle interest Joe read the detail, PLOT 2, THOMAS WEST, CASTLEBROUGH LOCOMOTIVE DEPARTMENT.

The implications of the notice were slow in dawning on Joe. 'This must be Tom's allotment' he thought. 'Course it is. I might have known,' he almost spoke out aloud. 'There's the wireless aerial Dan's told me his dad had on his allotment shed.' He looked at the tall slender homemade aerial standing over the door and then he walked around to the sleepers they had dumped alongside the shed. 'Crike, what's he goin' to say about this lot. Don't think I'll tell him anything. Mum's got to be the word or else he'll get to know how they got here.'

Joe was beginning to feel more than a little worried. He poked around for a little while, disturbing bits of wood, brick and turf with his heavy leather boots. The large water butt drew his attention; water had been overflowing and one side was left wet and shiny. He idly lifted the lid and looked at the flooded surface, it was strangely marked, as if by an oily film; 'No. Its not oil,' his thoughts paused as if to work out the implications. 'Its blood!' He could not resist a wider exploration. He broke the misty surface of the water with a stick that came easily to hand; it shimmered and revealed a pig's foot just below the surface. He peered within the depths of the barrel. 'Christ sake. These are the two back legs of that sow. On Tom West's allotment. Bloody hell!'

Quickly, he re-covered the water butt and was away from the allotment and back to his engine as fast as his legs would carry him. He had been worrying about his find for about five minute when the sound of Tom West's loud clear tones carried up to him. Tom West was shouting a cheery query in the direction of the coalyard labourers who were loading the morning's coal delivery lorries when Joe heard him.

"Has the shunter come back from breakfast yet?" Tom asked as he started his climb up the engine side into the cab from which Joe leaned.

"Nope," Joe replied as he lifted the catch on the cab door and opened it to admit his mate. "He's just walking down from the direction of the shed now." Joe had seen the slim figure of Mike Thompson, their shunter, through the forward cab window.

"Good. Sorry I'm a bit later than I said. Went to pick a Daily Herald up an call at the butchers."

Joe's senses prickled at the mention of the butcher. "The butcher, Johnson's eh? Open at this time - eight-thirty? Didn't think he opened 'til nine."

"He don't. I went in the back way to get some bones for broth-making. I'm well in with Jack Johnson."

The suspicions in Joe's mind grew. 'He must have been arranging for those hams to be dressed,' he thought with some conviction. Joe was beginning to wish that he did not know so much about Tom West's involvement with the hams. Tom was his best friend's father; Joe did not want to be in possession of facts and evidence which could send his friend's father to prison, or at very least get him dismissed from the railway for stealing something found on railway property.

When the shunter joined them and instructed them to go to the distant Washbeck Coal Yard for shunting Joe felt relieved; he preferred to be away from the sleepers and the hams in the water butt. He was not sorry when they were relieved at twelve-thirty by a relief engine crew just outside of the shed.

* * * * * *

3
WHOSE BOOKS ARE THESE?

Tom West and Joe Wade, both with greasy enginemen's caps perched crookedly on the right hand sides of their heads and with khaki haversacks hanging from their shoulders, walked down the length of the shed towards the time-office. A few engines stood in the shadowy shed interior, most locomotives were out in the shed-yard in various stages of activity and movement. Outside of the time-office Joe recognised the firm, trilby hatted figure of Mr Franker talking to a very short round man. Both were in animated conversation together.

"They wont release it to me. Said they must have proof of ownership," the stranger exasperated with a strong show of impatience. His arms jerked as if to help him express anger. "How can anyone prove ownership of a pig's mutilated carcass?" Franker was nodding in sympathetic agreement. "You said I'll get compensation from the railway company. That's no good to me Mr Franker. She was piggin' too, an I was goin' to bring up the litter mi self."

"Oh. Tom, have you a minute?" Mr Franker diverted his sympathetic ear away from the complainant and called across to Tom and Joe as they walked close by. Joe worried immediately; his first flashing concern was that Franker was going to complain to Tom West about Marsay's possibly confessed use of the shunting engine, his second was that somehow the conversation between Franker and the stranger about the sow and its missing hams was going to involve Tom West.

"Always got a minute for you Jack," Tom exclaimed with a lively wave of his arm, without, Joe noted, any show of guilt or concern.

"Its an L.D.C. matter."

A Local Departmental matter! Joe had an idea what that meant. Even though his service at the shed was to be measured in months he had already learned that the shed L.D.C. was the joint shed committee of management and steam locomen. He knew also that Tom West was the Secretary of the men's side of the committee.

"Wont it wait while I can get the Chairman to join us."

Jack Franker shook his head. "No its a disciplinary matter. I just want your advice. Its a matter I want to settle quickly." He looked for understanding from his short fat conversationalist. "I wont be more than a minute with Mr Smith. Can I see you in the time office?"

Tom said "Yes" and Joe responded to his own growing concern

by moving with alacrity towards the mess-room door. The words 'disciplinary matter' etched themselves into Joe's mind.

The shed messroom was largely occupied by engine cleaners, who were either just finishing early turn or just starting late turn, when Joe entered to examine the roster for his next day's duty. Four 'foreign' enginemen were eating sandwiches, drinking tea and playing a fives and threes domino game. At the end of the second table, cleaners Smith and Mason were talking laughingly to Johnny Marsay about a number of booklets and leaflets laid out on the table. "Christ I would have expected french postcards in this place, not this crap; miracles and the like," said the crumpled, weedy Mason who appeared not to have strength enough to handle a firing shovel. "Whose is it all Mike?"

"Couldn't tell yuh. They were in Frobisher's time office this morning. Nobody wanted to admit to owning them when he was asking whose they were." Mike Smith replied. "Nobody 'll want to own up to havin' a sky pilot's instruction pack. It'll look like they're wanting to set up a ministry."

Joe was drawn inexorably towards the three. He said nothing, just placed his khaki haversack on the table and proceeded to examine the literature with a show of amazement.

"Bit cranky in't it Joe." Johnny Marsay expressed to his friend Joe. "Can't think who in this shed is this loony. Can you?"

"No" Joe found himself, quickly and involuntarily, saying while his mind tried to sort out the best way he ought to respond in this situation. "Can't really." He couldn't think of anything to contribute to the discussion about the literature so he just emphasised his one contribution, "No." He noticed that the books were becoming soiled from the hands that investigated them.

"Bet there's nobody in this list of miracles thats chucked a false leg away and got a proper one through a miracle." Johnny Marsay was a very determined atheist and always ridiculed religion. Joe sat down at the messroom table close to the books; through his mind the idea was coursing that he should sit with the books until he could secretly slip them into his haversack. There was no question in his mind that he should confess to being the owner and complain that they had been 'lifted' from the engine seat where he had left them.

"Thanks Joe for moving them sleepers for me while Westy was away. Pusher says you put 'em on our kid's allotment."

"Yes I did,"Joe replied. He said nothing about them being on Tom West's allotment. He hoped that the situation with the sleepers would correct itself without him being any further involved. His present hopes were that the worries in his mind did not show through and affect his behaviour.

"I meant to come with you but Franker turned up. You saw him didn't you? Good thing you cleared off quickly. Fancy him being at the shed at eight o' clock. Thought the bugger would still be in bed."

"What did yuh tell him Johnny when he came over to see you at the sleepers."

"Nowt really, I'd bought the firewood ticket off him yesterday. He saw me and came out to ask me if I wanted a job diggin' his garden this week-end." Johnny replied while he was piling the literature together. "I'll chuck this lot in the firebox on the next engine I get on."

"No!" Joe rose suddenly and intervened. "I'll chuck it on the steamraiser's fire as I pass. It was just being lit for tonight as I came in. It'll help it to burn and get started." Joe swept the books into a pile and picked them up. "I'll get away home now. I've a bird to see this afternoon," he lied unnecessarily as he rose and made his way out of the messroom.

As he passed the unattended steamraiser's newly lighted open furnace he looked quickly around the shed and slipped the religious literature into his haversack.

* * * * * *

4
A LESSON FROM THE SKY PILOT

"Is Joe in?" Jean Walton's strong voice sounded as the back door of the Wade's household opened inwardly.

Emily opened her sitting room door and saw Maisie Hanson and Jean entering.

"Just popped in with Mrs Hanson. Said to her that Joe might help," she continued as she entered the scullery.

"Mrs Hanson - are you alright? Is Mister?" Emily asked.

"I'm not bad," muttered Maisie without much life in her voice. "Not very happy though."

"Yes I know," Emily piped, expressing sympathy. " Fred said Jack's bad. Fred said Doctor Harker says that Jack hasn't much time left."

Maisie whimpered slightly, then pulled herself together. "Yes he's going to die. We've prayed, had a faith healer in, Jack's not religious but, me and Cathy is, so we've tried everything. Now Mr Cammish said 'God's willed it. Jack isn't for healing', so we're getting ready to give him up to God."

"Sometimes that's the best way," comforted Mrs Walton. "God's way of bringing peace."

"Shall I mek a cup o' tea for you both?" Emily put her hand soothingly on the small ill proportioned, lumpy Mrs Hanson.

"No thanks but I'll...." Mrs Hanson's reply was interrupted.

"Oh! here's our Joe." Emily gestured as the hall door opened. "You asked for Joe," she directed towards Jean.

"Yes! Joe. I said to Mrs Hanson that you might be able to help her get her money - seeing as you are well in with Mr West."

"What money?" Joe questioned urgently.

Jean and Emily waited while Mrs Hanson composed herself as she hesitatingly summarised her need to Joe. "I want to get Jack's Shed benevolent money off Mr West."

"How can I help?"

Jean came in with her suggestion. "Maisie needs someone Mr West knows to go and see him and collect Jack's benefit for this week. It's overdue. Mr West brings it on a Thursday."

"Main thing is getting some whisky and stout for Jack. I can't go, its the only pleasure Jack's getting from the pain. Needs a drink to get through the night. Can't have more morphine." She was tearfully uncertain in her speech.

"I'll go," said Joe eagerly. " I'll go to the Tavern for you. Stout and whisky! I'll lend you money for a drink. Buy it for Jack I would.

Jack's a good bloke. Good engine fitter. Allus do anything for you. He's missed at the shed."

"I'll lend you some money Maisie. Don't be stuck." echoed Emily.

Maisie Hanson came back guardedly. "I can't borrow. Never owed nothing in my life. I worry too much. If I can get Jack's shed money of one pound, ten shillings I'll manage."

"Okay I'll go for you, get yuh some stout and whisky. Just write down what Jack wants."

"Thanks you're a good lad."

"When I come back I'll bring it to your house. I've got some of Cathy's books to bring up too."

"There you are Maisie, said Joe would help. He'll do anything for anybody." Chipped in Jean. "Won't you Joe."

"Depends, depends wot it is," Joe uttered shyly, but his silent discourse within added without vocal expression, 'Do anything for you Jean, - you have'nt got a hubby to look after you.'

Joe's cycled off to visit the West's household. His arrival there revealed that Tom had forgotten to collect the Shed Sick Fund benefit from Alan Harker the shed coalman on late shift. Franker's L.D.C. meeting had taken from Tom's mind his intention to collect it at dinner time when he was relieved on the Coal Pilot.

"Can you go and see Alan now and collect it for me?" Tom requested. "Can't go meself, now. Got to take these ham sandwiches and biscuits down to the Mere Club. John French, you know him down the road from your house that escaped from a German prison camp and made it to Switzerland. He's home now, we've organised a welcome home do at eight. I'm late."

Ham! That word had a suggestive echo in Joe's mind as he left Tom to his task and set off on his bike to visit Alan Harker on the coal stage at Castlebrough Shed.

Alan was found filling a 2½cwt capacity iron barrow with coal. The evening was clear and carried only the sound of an unobtrusive loco puffing slowly about the loco yard. On the elevated coal stage rows of heaped two wheeled coal barrows stood in ordered lines on the iron paved stage. As Joe propped up his bike the loco for the 8pm Castlebrough - York express chugged off from the push bell cabin departure point and headed in the direction of the main passenger station.

"Howdy Joe, going somewhere?" Alan addressed Joe who was approaching him from the direction of the steps to Sander Road.

"Come to see you. Come from Tom West. Asks if I can collect the shed sick club money for Jack Hanson."

"Glad you've come. Tom should've picked up three lots for lads on Hastings. Expected him to call at dinner today. Forgot it yesterday, when he usually picks up his calls."

"Tom sez to tell you he forgot cos Franker called a meeting with him and the L.D.C. Chair."

The stocky little coal filler paused then slid his shovel blade along the wagon bottom to bite under the coal he was to transport into the wheeled tub. "Can you wait while I fill this tub. Its the last one today. I've only the nine-thirty to coal up then I can go."

"Tek yer time Alan. I can wait five minutes."

The coal stage was a high level structure constructed into the bankside; so placed as to enable loco's drive up beneath one of the three iron coal chutes and stock their bunkers.

"I'll sit in the cabin Alan and wait 'til you come in."

"Okay. You do. 'Creepers' in there doing the sick club books."

Joe almost cancelled his decision to enter the cabin. 'Creeper Cammish was on his 'list of nasty characters.' There was nothing really nasty about 'Creeper'; he just didn't talk the same language as the other shedmen. He talked with superiority about morality and piety; he played the pump organ at the Sander's Road Methodist Chapel; he sang solo hymns when someone else would accompany him with the organ. 'Creeper' wasn't nasty, he was 'one apart' from the rest; he never told or listened to 'mucky' jokes, talked sex, discussed politics; he never smoked or drank. He wasn't nasty, really just too good, Joe thought. They called him 'Creeper' because he crept about slowly in slouched position in soft soled shoes.

"Hi." Joe emitted as he entered the coal stage cabin.

"Hi." Creeper was totting up figures in note books and relating them to a penned balance sheet. After a period of silence he spoke to Joe. "Just doing a half year balance for the shed sick club."

Joe nodded. "I've just come for Jack Hanson's benefit from Alan."

"Jack's in a bad way. If you see him tell him Francis was asking about him and will be along to see him soon."

"Yes I will..." answered Joe, almost saying 'Francis?' He wasn't used to thinking of Creeper by his 'Sunday name.'

"Mrs Hanson says Jack can't have long. I'm taking her money to her tonight."

"I'd do it for you but I'm doing a job for the chapel tonight."

"Hope it's a good job. One you like."

"Oh. Its a duty. Jobs okay but I'm not keen on where I'm doing it."

"Where's that?"

'Mere Social club. All the estate's going to be there tonight. Celebration to welcome John French home. You know John, decorated in the North African campaign. You know John? - escaped from prison camp in Germany. Daring escape too, to Switzerland."

Creeper went on, aware he had an attentive audience. "He was a P.M. Sunday School teacher and also Mere Club Secretary. That's why there is a big do on for him tonight. That's why I've been asked to go with some Methodists and deliver a welcome address."

"I didn't know about the party tonight. Mebbe because I'm not old enough to drink."

"Course your not. Got to be eighteen. Catherine Hanson will be there with the P.M.ers. Mind she's a lot older than you."

"No! Not a lot! Not a lot, a bit." Joe emphasised, wondering what Creeper meant.

Alan Harker entered the coal cabin and the conversation changed. "Thanks for waiting, Joe. Will you take three lots to Tom? All in separate envelopes."

Joe nodded affirmatively and signed Alan's receipt book. Alan displayed the contents of the open envelopes before sealing the flaps. Joe stepped into the darkening night with, "Thanks" and "Ta rah" as his final expressions.

At the 'Railway Tavern' in the 'Bottle and Jug" out sales he had to open Jack Hanson's envelope to pay for six bottles of milk stout and a bottle of whisky. The barman wrote the prices on the envelope at Joe's request. Soon Joe was banging on Mrs Hanson's back door to make delivery of the money, drink, and of course return Cathy's books.

"She isn't in," Mrs Hanson informed. "She's down at the Mere Club 'do' with Mr Cammish."

Joe smarted without outward sign but inwardly his thoughts recorded, 'With Creeper Cammish. He's old enough to be her Grandad. And me not old enough to get in the club! We'll see! What's she doing with him anyway. I'll go and get round her. Older than me! Clever sod Cammish.' With Mrs Hanson's thanks ringing in his ears Joe set out eagerly for the 'Mere Club'

The blacked out club was bouncing and full. Joe signed in as an under aged visitor and was soon at Tom West's table with half a pint of Moor's mild when silence descended to permit "Mr Francis Cammish welcome John back on behalf of the P.M."

"Prime Minister?" Joe muttered questioningly in Tom's ear. "No! Primitive Methodist." Tom growled back through his teeth.

Cammish rose and commenced his address with a suggestion of confidence that Joe interpreted as arrogance. Joe's attention, however, turned to Cathy who was on her feet a few yards away from him. 'She looks womanly, tall, sexy in that floral cotton dress,' Joe mused.

He moved to join her, refusing to recognise the rapture on her face as she hung on every word that Francis broadcast from the platform.

Joe wasn't likewise occupied. He muttered in her ear, "I've took your books back to your Mam." Her eyes moved perceptively in the direction of his face. "I've took your Dad's money too." Her eyes moved again. He saw a hint of impatience but refused to recognise it. He threw all his cards on the table in a certain gamble. "Come and sit with me over there."

Her head moved sharply towards him, the hint became a clear expression. "Shut up Joe. Keep quiet. I'm listening to Francis." He smarted but added, "Okay, but will you come afterwards?"

"No! Keep quiet. I want to listen to Francis." Joe went quiet but Cathy didn't. "You should not be in here. You're under aged." She looked at him scornfully. "You're not properly dressed for a night out."

Joe sank into a deep silence, his self confidence crushed. A sickness settled down his chest and into his stomach. He felt that he would never recover. He stood in silence until 'Creeper' Cammish had embraced John French to the accompaniment of applause, cheering and foot stamping, then he melted into the crowd and made for the back exit. He brushed Johnny Marsay and his brother as he was about to leave.

"Didn't see you applauding our aspiring sky pilot." stated the grinning Johnny as he poised a full glass of mild in preparation for drinking.

"Sky pilot?" was Joe's forced query.

"Yes. Creeper the aspiring shed sky pilot. Didn't you know?"

Joe, forced to maintain the conversation, returned, "I know what the coal pilot is, an' the station pilot. But, What's sky pilot?"

"A vicar, pilots your soul to heaven. If you behave. Like keeping away from their women," grinned Johnny but then abruptly changed the subject. "Why did you drop the sleepers on Tom West's garden this morning? Played hell he did when I told him they were mine."

"Sorry," Joe replied almost sadly.

"Broke his edging, and some rhubarb crowns. Had to lie like hell, I did."

"Sorry."

"S alright Joe. Thanks."

Joe raised his eyes, nodded towards the door and the 'Mens,' held his stomach down and drifted out into the darkness behind the club adjacent to the main line. He sat despondently on a pile of old stacked timber and tried to find his heart.

The sky was a shining ebony canopy; stars twinkled piercingly and a full moon glowed majestically. Joe hung an unlit woodbine in the corner of his mouth and pensively mulled over his long list of inferiorities, his inadequacies, his hatred of women, and now aspiring sky pilots, - the list could go on. He would have extended it but the whistle blast of the incoming 9.30pm York express broke into his reverie.

It was a stirring demanding whistle; it was the express's audible communication to Gas Works Signal Cabin that a train was approaching Castlebrough.

The pierce of the blast echoed across the bowl of ebony; the stars and the moon glowed with extra brilliance in welcome. Poetry crept into Joe's lonely soul which rose up as the sight of the oncoming train joined its sounds.

Firelight shafted out from the cab, sparks shot aloft from the chimney; two white pin prick headlights displayed the express code and the ground began to shudder under Joe.

2726 and the nine-thirty express loomed up. As it passed Joe the roar at the chimney top ceased as the driver closed the steam regulator to let the train coast into Castlebrough. It tore past and under the Mere Bridge; its disappearing blacked out tail with its winking red tail lamp signalled a new silence.

The thrill of steam and motion visited Joe's spirit with welcome intensity. He recalled his 'camel's hump journey, and 2726, and how in a fit of imagined failure he'd nearly decided to join the army. He recalled Bob Laker's advice "An engine's like a good woman. Look after her and she'll look after you." He doubted that wisdom now after his spurning by Catherine. 'But' he mused, 'maybe I hadn't found a good woman and religion isn't for me.'

The nine-thirty produced another more distant whistle as it approached Castlebrough Station; it jogged Joe's memory. 'Hope there isn't a pig on the line tonight,' he thought as he rose to go and see his pal Dan for a game of draughts. Thoughts raced through his mind. It doesn't matter who got the hams. Jack Hansons going to die soon. John French would soon be in the army again and the war would continue. Maybe Dan would never walk again but life would go on, punctuated by death and uncertainty, brightened by hope and love. He kicked up a turf as he moved off into the darkness.

1
THE UNDERTAKER'S VISIT.

Wellington Road was quiet except for the noise of the horse and cart being driven up the incline by the coal delivery man. A hearse bearing a coffin had just come to a halt outside of semi-detached house number forty-three. A weak sunlight percolated through the thin mantle of cloud to fall on the council houses on Hastings Estate. Mr Cooper the Co-operative Undertaker's Manager left the hearse, opened the wooden garden gate to forty-three and climbed the eight steps through the garden to the green painted front door. He knocked lightly, almost gingerly, without using the cast iron knocker on the letter box.

The door was opened by a serious subdued Emily Wade. "Good morning Mrs Wade. You'll see we've brought Father home from hospital." His head turned slightly in the direction of the hearse as he spoke.

"Come in Mr Cooper." Mrs Wade replied." Fred's at home. I'll call him, he's upstairs." Her small thin black haired figure turned about to face into the shadowy hall and address the linoed interior towards the stairs. "Fred, it's Mr Cooper, he's brought me Dad home." Then to the black overcoated undertaker she said "Will you come in? I'll show you where we want Dad to lay." Mr Cooper looked back down the steps into the street and nodded to his three companions who sat in the waiting hearse with the occupied coffin, he indicated that they should await his orders. He entered the hall just as Fred Wade descended the stairs. Fred's strong medium height figure, with collarless shirt and rolled up shirt sleeves, was held tightly in the middle by a strong broad leather belt. Even though he wore strong black braces over his shoulders his belt was still relied upon to keep his coarse working trousers tight and secure. Thin framed horn-rimmed spectacles sat beneath a slightly receding black hairline on a broad clean shaven face.

"Come in Arthur. Nice to see you; just wish it were on a happier occasion, but then that's your job." Fred Wade knew the undertaker well; he had served with him as a Cooperative Director on the Management Board of Castlebrough Cooperative Society. "We'll have Dick's body resting in the parlour, it's the only place we can shut off."

"Didn't expect you to be at home Fred, knew you were working away."

"I'm working in Birmingham, but I came home last night for the funeral," he opened the door to the neat front parlour. "I've moved the furniture back to the walls so there's room for the coffin to stand."

The door to the nearby living room opened and Joe Wade, clean faced with ruffled hair and dressed in rough casual clothes, looked out into the hall to see who had called, he said "Hello," to Mr Cooper and then withdrew back into the living room. Mr Cooper and Fred Wade went out through the front door, a few minutes later the four Coop Funeral Services staff entered bearing the coffin and body of Richard Peace which they placed with care and concern in the parlour. When Joe's Mother saw the brass nameplate bearing the name and age of her father she wept quietly and withdrew into the living room; her husband Fred and Mr Cooper followed as soon as the coffin was safely laid on the trestles and the lid loosely positioned but easily removable.

Emily Wade was seated in the, easy fireside chair; she had inserted her darning mushroom into a woollen sock and was keeping her fingers busy while her shoulders shook with grief. Joe responded to the situation with silence, he did not know how to express his sorrow for, and his sympathy with, his grieving Mother; he and his younger brother Luke were busy operating a small, spirit fuelled, model stationary steam engine on the top of the table air-raid shelter. Only minutes before it had been in steam and busy rattling away before Joe's Mother had entered the room. Joe and Luke talked in whispers about the little brass engine which so fascinated them, they were contemplating a move into the kitchen while Mr Cooper and their parents talked about the coming funeral.

"Everything is arranged for tomorrow Fred. Three o'clock in the afternoon at St James' as we hoped and then up to Woodlands. I've been able to get the plot you wanted," He paused as he extracted some papers from an inside pocket. "There's only need for one car and the hearse, isn't there? One car for six persons to go to the cemetery."

"That's right," Fred Wade answered. "Mrs Wade, myself and the three lads. And one of Dick's friends."

"Mrs Walton, she's coming, she'll be the sixth," interjected the tearful Mrs Wade, her fingers busy with the needle and thread as she darned the heavy woollen working sock. "Don't start that thing up again Joe, my nerves won't stand it."

"It smells as well. Take it out of here, this is the living room," Joe's Father instructed the two brother's firmly. Luke acted on the instructions but Joe joined the conversation about the funeral while his brother withdrew.

"I'll be home from work about one tomorrow Mam, so I'll be

able to go to the funeral. Luke's off work he'll be alright for going but what about Tim?"

"He's coming home on leave today. There'll be five of us family and Mrs Walton," Fred spoke in the direction of his wife Emily." That's all for the taxi, and all that will be going to Woodlands." As Fred Wade talked a knock on the front door sounded and reached into the living room. "See who that is Joe."

Joe did so just as the red haired neighbour Jean Walton entered the back door with a shout "It's me. Can I come in?" Joe had to ignore the questioning shout of Jean Walton, he left the room and went down the passage to the front door where the figure of Len Bostock, the loco' shed messenger confronted him.

"Ticket for you Joe, for tomorrow. Want yuh to fire on early turn Whitby," said the diminutive, cloth capped messenger to Joe as the door opened.

"I was on early morning cleaning anyway tomorrow so that's alright."

"Yes I know, this brings you on at five-fifteen instead of six. Clarkey said you'd wanted to attend a funeral tomorrow and that you'd get away earlier on early Whitby than you would on early cleaning shift."

"Yes," said Joe with some thought. "I was going to leave a bit early tomorrow so's I could go to my Grandad's funeral for three o'clock. Ye, early Whitby'll be finished by quart to one so's I'll get home easy."

Ben handed over the little rectangular buff coloured ticket which instructed Joe about his duty time change for the following day, then he asked Joe to sign for the ticket in the ticket receipt book. "Another firing shift for you," Len commented, "Have you got far to go to get your first year in and get onto first year fireman's pay?"

"About another hundred, don't think that'll be long though with the rate that I keep getting called out." replied Joe as he signed for the ticket and the short bow legged shed labourer Len turned to go back to the shed. Joe returned to the living room where his father was examining some papers laid out for him by the undertaker. Mrs Walton was comforting Joe's mother and assuring her of help with anything that was required.

"Fred came home today so that he could go the registry office and take Dad's pension book in, and do anything else."

"How does Dad look? Is he peaceful?" Jean Walton asked her neighbour Emily in a quiet sympathetic voice.

"I have'nt seen him yet, they've only just brought him home from the hospital."

"The sooner you see him, the sooner you'll feel he's back home.

It's bad luck they say, to leave the coffin lid on when a body comes home. I believe it." Jean spoke with conviction, she was, like the older Emily, steeped in superstition; avoiding crossed knives, shoes on tables, visitors leaving the home by a door different from the one they entered, and a host of other like superstitions that gripped working class women. Emily didn't need any convincing, if she had not heard of and believed a superstition newly brought to her attention she soon took to it when told "its bad luck for so and so to happen." She placed her darning tools and sock on the buffet at the side of the low glowing fire and rose to go with Jean into the front room to take the necessary action and thus avoid bad luck.

"Will you come with me Jean?."

"Of course. Mr Cooper'll take the lid off and leave it off 'till tomorrow." She placed her hand on Emily's shoulder to comfort her as she rose from the chair.

"Yes, I'll take the lid off. It's not fastened, just laid on," said the smart, slim figured undertaker. He went into the front room before Jean and Emily entered, then he left as the two women passed through the doorway into the parlour where the coffin stood.

"Who was at the door Joe?" Joe's father asked the question belatedly.

"Just the shed messenger for me Dad. He was bringing me a ticket telling me to be on in the morning at five-fifteen for early Whitby. I'll still get home in time for the funeral, in fact I should get home a bit earlier."

Fred Wade just acknowledged the information and then turned to show Mr Cooper out of the house. Joe and Luke lounged on the buffets by the fire and awaited their Mother's return from the parlour. When they returned Mrs Walton said to Joe, "Make your Mother a cup of tea Joe. It'll help to compose her." She guided Joe's mother to the chair and left her weeping quietly while she followed Joe out and helped him prepare the drink. Emily Wade talked about her memories of her Father and Mother and commented on the hard lives they had led. Joe and Luke listened and when Mother said "He look's so peaceful now," Jean turned to Joe and Luke, "Are you going in to see your Grandad, It'll be good for you, you'll get used to having him in the house for tonight."

"Don't think I want to. I'm not very keen on seeing dead people," Joe's reply had a ring of certainty about it but Jean smiled comfortingly but persisted.

"Yes but your grandad isn't just dead people, he's Grandad, you know him well and you'll feel the need to say goodbye to him."

"Are you going Luke?" Joe asked his younger brother.

"Not really keen but I'll go if you want me to," Luke replied

Fred Wade entered the room as Jean asked Joe "Have'nt you ever seen anyone dead?"

"Not in a coffin though. I saw dead people at that rail crash at Castlebrough Station last year," he paused for a little reflection; "But that was different, I didn't know those soldiers, it seemed different. Now it's Grandad. I don't know really, I don't know what I mean." Joe felt flustered and confused; he collected the empty tea cups and carried them into the scullery to escape making a decision for a moment.

For some reason the buxom and attractive Jean Walton felt that it was her duty to see to it that the two lads, Joe and Luke, should have the courage to see their Grandfather in his coffin before much longer. However Fred Wade interrupted her campaign briefly.

"Where's your Jack now Jean? Did he hear anymore about going abroad like he expected when he was last home on leave."

"He's in Aldershot now, awaiting some orders. He thinks it's to do with getting ready for the Second Front. He doesn't want to go, says he had enough of the Italian landings. He's thinking of going on the Bevin Boy scheme down the pits."

"That might be better for him" replied Fred but Jean's overpowering need of the moment was to help the family come to terms with their grief and the presence of the dead Richard Peace in the front parlour. Her concern was genuine, she knew that the presence in a household of a dead member was a traumatic and worrying ordeal and the sooner it was faced, as a natural part of mourning, the better it would be for all concerned. She turned her attention to Emily.

"You are feeling better now, aren't you Emily?" Emily nodded, composed but sad, and she muttered her thanks and rose to collect those teacups which Joe had left. Jean continued,"I'll have to go in a minute, get some tea ready for the kids, they'll be coming home from school soon." She started to rise and continued her conversation in the direction of Joe and Luke. "Come on, you two lads, I'll just take you in to see your Grandad before I go, then your Mam and Dad won't have the worry." She moved to the hall doorway with the certainty that Joe and Luke would follow obediently; they did so without further question.

The oak coffin with brass handles stood length ways down the room, its padded interior with the shrouded body was visible on entering the room; the face of deceased Grandfather could not be seen immediately because it lay below the level of the coffin edge. The coffin lid with the name plate leaned securely against the side of the bureau bookcase. The room was in the gloom caused by the closed blinds. Jean Walton drew the blinds back slightly to admit enough light to permit viewing without using electric light. Joe and Luke drew close to the coffin with a feeling of trepidation. They could see the oval face of their Grandfather, clear and still; circled neatly by the silken cloth of the face shroud and the interior dressings of the coffin; a weeks growth of beard stubble lay on the usually clean shaven familiar face.

"I can't believe the change," said the wondering Joe, "He's like marble. So white."

Jean Walton placed her arms around the shoulders of the two brothers, her face warm and close to them as they paid their respects to the old man who had lived with them for the last four years. A sob broke from the chest of the younger Luke. "I'm sorry he's dead," he said.

"So am I," muttered Joe, feeling almost apologetic; he didn't know how he should feel, what he should say, whether he ought to cry. The big auburn haired Jean who was bowed to their levels pressed her cheek's onto the two heads she cradled in her arms and hands.

"We all have to say goodbye sometime. Now it's Grandad's time." She loosed her arms and hands from their task of cradling the heads of the two boys and reached to touch the marble like brow in the coffin. Her index fingers smoothed caringly across the lined cold forehead. Then she lifted Luke's hand, and then Joe's, and encouraged them to express their feelings of love and sorrow through gentle caresses on the brow and cheeks of their Grandfather.

Tears flowed easily for the younger Luke; Joe felt guilty, he just shook inwardly and wished that he could follow his younger brother's example but felt restrained by the warm embrace of the woman who sometimes stirred in him sexual feelings which he alternately encouraged or sought desperately to suppress. He was a mixture of manhood and boyhood; and at this moment he felt overwhelmed by boyhood confusions, so uncertain about the role he was playing that he could utter no expressions. Jean seemed to recognise his inability to cope, she placed her strong arm around his neck and pulled his head down to nestle just above her breast.

Joe felt the warmth of her body that had so aroused him at times. With his emotions in conflict he broke free; cupped his brow in his own hand and didn't halt the sob that rose and broke into the room.

"I don't think I've always been kind to Grandad," he blurted out. "I wish I had been." His tears fell profusely and his brother Luke joined the wave of emotion which had been unleashed. Mrs Walton held them both again tightly in a comforting embrace but Joe broke away with some feeling of self reproach.

"You haven't been unkind, don't be silly."

"No I don't mean unkind, I mean I've ignored him, I've made fun of him. I've took pocket money off him and not really thanked him. I've grumbled at him. I've told him he was old and couldn't understand. Oh! I don't know." Joe exasperated between his tears. "I just wish I'd treated him differently now he's gone. I just feel daft and mixed up now that he's dead." Joe touched Grandfather briefly on the cheek and then quickly moved away towards the door and started composing himself as he left; Luke followed quickly, more emotional than Joe and less able to articulate his feelings.

Joe decided to seek other surroundings. His Mother was working in the scullery as he approached, coat and flat cap in hand. "I'm going Mam, I'm going to West's to play draughts with Dan."

"You have'nt had any tea yet," his Mother said with some annoyance.

"I'll get some at Dan's." Joe with his hand on the back door knob paused for a moment. "Did I tell you Mam, I'm on at five-fifteen in the morning, not six. I'm firing to Whitby."

"No you didn't. I never know what you're on. At least when you were a porter you had regular times."

Joe's ears were receiving the usual complaints from his Mother about his job on the footplate. He interrupted her. "Don't get up in the morning Mam. You get some rest, I'll get my porridge ready and get off to work by myself. Just leave mi sandwiches ready." He left quickly and noisily through the back door into the afternoon quiet before his Mother could devise another reply.

* * * * * *

2
THE GIRL IN THE CAB.

"We'll turn the engine later on that turntable over there when that feller's left." Bert Woodley had just propelled his empty train out of the roofed railway station at Whitby Town. He intended to take his engine around the five carriages he had just brought from Castlebrough up the picturesque Yorkshire coast railway line and place them in number three platform. "We're not in a rush though cos we've got three hours here."

Joe was flabbergasted. "Three hours here? I thought we were taking the eleven-ten back to Castlebrough." Joe had walked across to Bert's side of the engine to address Bert and place more concerned emphasis on his question.

"Keep yer head out there, keep lookin' at the shunter."

Joe obeyed, conscious of the fact that he had neglected his look-out duty while the engine was in motion. He turned back from Bert and looked out of his side of the cab. "When are we going back?" he shouted his question across the cab.

"We're working the one o' clock special back. A Whitby crew are working our eleven-ten back. We'll get home about three."

The news dumbfounded Joe. He wondered why he had not been told about this when he had been called out for this shift. Joe was watching the shunter from his side of locomotive tank engine 9881 on which they had been since five-thirty that morning. When their engine was coupled to the five passenger bogies and given the signal to proceed back he addressed his next remark to Bert. "I thought that we'd a bin going up Sander Road on the way home by one o' clock. Mam'll have mi dinner ready then."

Bert eased his head back inside the cab as his engine slowly edged his train back up to the buffers in number three platform. "Your grub'll keep lad, unless your Ma feeds it to the cat." Bert showed no concern for Joe's missed dinner date. "I feeds meself when I get home, so I'll have to wait longer than you." He slowly squeezed his train up to the buffers and then stopped his engine with her handbrake screwed down tightly.

"Mi Grandad's funeral's at three o' clock. I wanted to get home, get mi dinner and then go to the service. When they sent me the ticket yesterday calling me out nobody told me that I'd not get back home until three o' clock."

"That's bloody railway for thee lad. Now yuh'll know what I means when I say I don't want to work every Sunday."

"I don't want to miss mi Grandad's funeral."

Bert's mouth rolled monotonously as he chewed a roll of black tobacco. His habit of spitting a long streak of spittle into the engine firebox with unerring accuracy irritated Joe and offended his standards of care and behaviour. "What church is the service at?" Bert asked.

"St James's"

"Well yuh'll just have to go straight up to the church from work won't yuh?" He paused and directed another well aimed ejection of tobacco stained spittle at the firehole door with every intention of it going straight into the fire. "You can go to the cemetery in one of the cars can't yuh? Yuh Grandad wouldn't want you to miss his funeral, he wouldn't care about you being mucky an' in yer workin' clothes."

"No he wouldn't." His thoughts turned sadly to yesterday's memory of his ex-miner Grandad lying in his coffin in the parlour at home. He just had to try to get to the funeral; that way he might pacify the guilt he felt about having neglected, even teased, Grandad, who had lived with Joe's family for his last few infirm years. "I'll have to go as soon as I get home, but Mam'll wonder what's matter cos she's expecting me home at one."

Bert turned his attention to the shunter who stood on the platform alongside of the engine and carried on a muted conversation which was too indistinct to reach Joe's ears. Bert then turned inwards. "We are leaving her tied down here until the twelve-five runs into platform one, then we shunt her and go and turn our engine and get ready for back over to Castlebrough."

"We can eat now can we?" asked Joe.

"Ye."

Joe extracted his bottle of milkless tea from the bucket of hot water where he had been reheating it. "What are you going to drink? Don't you ever bring a bottle of tea?" Joe addressed his questions to Bert. His mouthful of thick homemade bread with its slim slice of spam did not stop his continuous chatter.

"I'll get my drink when the pub opens at eleven. Tea aint no good to me - poisons mi stomach. I drink nowt but beer," he paused slightly, "An' water when I'm forced." He had stopped eating and was digging out the bowl of his pipe with a well worn pen knife. Periodically he blew fiercely down the pipe stem. "Baccy, beer and the occasional bit o' stuff keeps me going."

Joe had just extracted a book from his haversack. "Do you read much?"

Only mi payslip an' the shed roster. No time for papers, books an' the likes." He reached a long rolled paper taper into the firebox for a light for his pipe. "I goes to the pictures twice a week to see what's happening on the war news on Pathe or Movietone. I like to keep abreast o' what's happening at the fronts an' at sea. I was wi' Beatty at Jutland in the First World War an' saw lots o' ships and men lost. I've seen the blood an' guts side o' war an' I'm astounded at what the bloody scribes writes in the papers an' at the way they reports war as summat as is bloody heroic an' noble."

He drew heavily on his newly lighted pipe and stubbed out the lighted end of the long paper taper. "I likes to see for mi sen what's happening so I go to see the newsreels at the 'Odeon' and ' Capital.' Sometimes I goes to 'Londesbrough' if I can't get in at other two. But I comes out when news is oe'r. I don't stop fer films. I go on to the 'Commercial' or 'Ship' for mi refreshments after that. That's mi life - no books nor papers to twist mi mind."

Joe decided not to press on with the issue of reading and broadening his mind - even though he was convinced of its worthiness. He knew that when one was only nearly seventeen and not worldly-wise or war experienced it was foolhardy to speak to an old driver about knowledge gleaned from the world of print. Instead he often resorted to secret reading when in the company of most of his locomotive mates in order to avoid their disparaging remarks about reading. He changed the subject. "I think I'll get mi head down when you go for your 'walk' Bert. I'm a bit flaked out wi' not sleeping much lately. Glad it's Sunday tomorrow - won't be on early tomorrow."

"Bloody Sunday. I hate Sundays - havin' to work every Sunday. Dammit - it gets mi mad. I pay it all in tax. All this over-time is alright for the young uns and the married uns, but not me." Bert grumbled on. He was well known for his opposition to the enforced Sunday work brought about by the manpower shortage caused by the war.

Joe filled the engine fire-bucket with boiling hot water at Bert's request and then sat and watched him wash out some socks, handkerchiefs and a heavy dark blue working shirt then hung them to dry on a string washline which he'd stretched across the cab. The heat of the cab would dry them very quickly. "Saves mi havin' to wash them at home," he told Joe, "an' it saves me the expense of sendin' 'em to the laundry." He packed his pipe again and lit it with the long taper and then turning to go for his 'tea' he instructed, "Stay put lad. Don' t go anywhere til I get back."

Joe had no intention of going anywhere. He set about making a 'bed' for himself with the equipment at hand. He folded his jacket for use as a pillow; and spanned the gap between his fireman's seat and the shelf on the coal bunker end with his firing shovel, it would carry the weight of his legs while he slept horizontally on his seat. He balanced himself on his uncomfortable bed. Regardless of his squirming and discomfort, sleep began to creep across his tired limbs.

"Hello! Is there anyone there?" The quiet spoken female voice alerted Joe instantly. His cap fell from his eyes where it had created a 'mock' darkness, his legs turned outwards and fell down as his body raised up.

'Am I dreaming?' the thought was his first conscious response. He sat somewhat confused with one hand on the wooden fireman's seat and his hobnailed boots on the floor of the cab. His brain cleared quickly, he knew where the voiced query had come from, his subconscious had recorded its source before he was fully awake. The voice had echoed gently from the station platform at the other side of the metal hinged door through which Bert had earlier lowered himself onto the platform. Joe stretched upright and rose to cross the engine cab floor towards the voice. He looked over the metal hand rails on Bert's side. A small upturned female face greeted his questioning gaze.

"Hello." His voice had the softness and pleasantness that is usual in the vocal utterances of males when suddenly confronted with a pretty female face.

"Hello. I wondered if you could tell me whether this train here," her hand gesticulated with a flowing movement in the direction of the carriages standing behind Joe's engine, "is going to Castlebrough."

"I don't know. I'm sorry," he responded and stifled a yawn. "I'm going to Castlebrough with this engine at one o' clock," he volunteered. "But I don't know if these are our carriages or what platform we're going to leave from."

"I'm going on the ten past eleven."

"That was to have been our train back, but we're staying here and taking a one o' clock special back instead"

Her face was round and smooth, no acne spots or marks, Joe noted. Auburn hair topped off with a fairisle knitted tam he also noted approvingly. Her lips were round and full beneath a broad slightly upturned soft nose. Her hair blossomed out in natural curls around and beneath the circular tam with its loose bobble lolling in the centre. Joe liked what he saw and wondered how he could keep her talking. He lowered himself down onto the platform through the cab doorway. 'About sixteen or seventeen' he thought.

"Shall I go and ask at the booking office?" She asked and looked away in the direction of the main booking hall.

"You've no rush though" Joe said in the most relaxed manner he could muster. "It's only quart to ten now. You've time to hang about a bit" he said hopefully trusting that she would recognise his invitation.

"I like looking at steam engines." Her face swung towards the cab of the grimy A8 tank engine in its wartime coat of dull black paint. "Are you the driver?" She didn't wait for Joe's reply. "No you're too young aren't you?"

Joe wiped his hands on a white sponge cloth then raised his right boot onto the top engine step and leaned on it. "No not too young I can drive this, I do very often when my mate's not around." He was thinking of the times when he had driven light engines without authority. She was thinking about driving the engine at high speed with a train attached but she left her thoughts unspoken and pursued another line of conversation.

"I live close to Leeman Road Sheds at York. I see lots of loco's. I've often had a ride," she said with a bright friendly smile into Joe's face. He detected a hint of flirtation; it motivated his conversation.

"Climb aboard then," he said with light jocularity. "I'll take you up to the Ravenscar Peak and down to Castlebrough and back in time for you to catch the one o'clock to Castlebrough."

She caught the spirit of the conversation. "But I wouldn't need to come back to Whitby once I'd got to Castlebrough. Would I?"

"You would because I wouldn't be able to come back on my own. I'd need you to fire for me back over. Wouldn't I?"

"You'd expect me to do that?" She questioned with an impish grin that set Joe's heart off on a little flutter. "Yes, Why not?"

"Jump aboard then," he said with an equally impish grin and a flourish of his right hand reminiscent of the air of an old-time footman bidding that she mount the step of an ornate horse drawn coach and step inside.

"Thanks," she said. Much to Joe's surprise she placed her woollen gloved hand on the upright engine hand rail and hauled her small slim figure up through the open cab doorway. "I'm taking care not to get my coat dirty," she said out loudly for Joe to hear as her head disappeared into the cab interior.

Joe was, as he would later describe to his shed mates, 'proper gob smacked.' He looked up and down the platform hastily. There were no written instructions about not having females on locomotive footplates so far as he knew. He guessed logically enough that such an instruction would not need to be written; it was so obvious. He was relieved that no-one was nearby to see her climb aboard because, had there been, he would have had to ask her to get down again onto the platform.

"This is an A8 locomotive isn't it. Four-six-two wheelbase. It's steam superheated too isn't it. Not like the old 'Willies' that run up these coast road lines sometimes. They're hard work for a fireman, aren't they?"

"Yes." Joe was lost for words. He pulled himself into the cab alongside her. His cap was knocked off his head by the cab doorway top because of his flustered haste. He was clumsy and a bit embarrassed. 'Crike' he thought 'I didn't know about the old Willy class A6 loco's not being superheated.' He felt his confidence waning.

"Can I sit on your seat?" she motioned to the seat at Joe's side of the cab. "I'd sit at the driver's side but someone might see me."

'Blimey! She knows that she's not supposed to be on here. Should I try to get rid of her?.' His confidence had evaporated. He sat on the driver's seat and looked across the cab at her. 'Smashing.' The thought stretched out slowly in his mind. 'in better places and better times - wow' the thought lingered on and threatened to become fantasy. Her round hazel eyes were wide and friendly.

"Is that what makes it go?" She now asked a question with simplicity as she pointed to the steam regulator handle in the centre of the boiler front.

"Yes, that controls the flow of steam to the cylinders." Joe replied as a renewed feeling of confidence returned. "You seem to know a lot about engines. Did you learn it at Leeman Road Sheds?"

"Well not really. I wasn't supposed to go into the shed or on the engines. My uncle Jack's an engine driver and he has lots of models. He's talked to me for years about his engines."

A girl interested in railways was a new phenomenon to Joe. He didn't mind though, in fact he liked it. At least they had a common subject on which to discourse; a subject he liked and one on which he believed he was knowledgeable. His confidence had returned completely now. Indeed he felt 'Cock o' the midden.' There was some time to elapse before Bert Woodley came back so Joe felt quite relaxed. He took a small tarpaulin square out of the locker and attached it to the hooks around the opening of the cab on the fireman's side of the engine. It would shield her, them in fact, from the prying eyes on the train in the next platform.

They talked about railways just a little, more about schooldays and the jobs they would like to do in the future. They talked about the effects of the war on them. She had spent part of the war at school in Whitby where she lived with her Aunt at her parent's request. She'd become a sort of voluntary evacuee from enemy air-raids on York. 'She's a bright girl,' Joe thought as she talked of reading books and of wanting to act in Shakespearean plays. Her company pleased him. Never once did the thought of his expected late arrival in Castlebrough and his Grandad's funeral and the hot dinner he had yearned for enter his mind. He and the girl, engrossed in each other's company, sat on the locomotive footplate quite oblivious to the movements and activities within the surrounding Whitby Station.

If they had looked across the valley they would have viewed the estuary of the Esk as it opened out into the harbour and the sea. The buildings and streets of Whitby Town clothed the steep banks of the wide river valley. The tall stone ruin of the centuries old Whitby Abbey was silhouetted against the skyline and the drifting grey clouds above the high south bank of the valley. In the seawards direction, but far out of the vision of those on the engine, the comforting arms of Whitby's stone piers created a tranquil harbour at the mouth of the river as it spread out into the North Sea.

Back up the valley of the Esk, but just out of sight behind the high banks of the valley, in a south westerly direction towered the red bricked railway viaduct across which Bert and Joe had travelled when they had arrived from Castlebrough. The viaduct was a monument to the engineers of the nineteenth century, its twelve arches strode majestically across the wide valley and opened up an important rail route along the north Yorkshire coast. Joe would never have looked out from the exciting confines of his engine cab if he had not heard the sound of Bert's distant voice carry towards him on the gentle breeze.

Joe's capped head bobbed swiftly out through the sheeted side of the loco' cab. He peered down the platform towards the exit end in the direction of Bert's shout. The small stocky figure of Bert was standing at the foot of the signal post at the end of the platform on the clinker ballast on the track. His right arm was raised and signalling quite clearly the 'come forward' indication used by all railwaymen.

"I've got to take the engine forward, mi driver's out there waving mi forward." Joe addressed himself to his young lady companion while he busied himself unscrewing the engine handbrake, closing the steam cocks and generally getting ready to move forwards as Bert had instructed. "You'd better get off at this side quickly."

The auburn haired young lady rose to do as Joe had commanded. Joe popped his engine whistle as an indication that he was about to move the engine and looked out down both sides of his loco' before opening the steam regulator.

"Blimey! You can't get off here, the station inspector's standing on the platform." Joe restrained the girl who had been about to open the door and leave the engine cab. "We'll only be moving to another platform so you'd better come along for the ride. Keep out of sight." He opened the engine steam regulator valve just enough to make his engine move forwards with a gentle beat at the chimney head and a rattle of connecting rods and big-ends.

He glanced through the forward cab window and up to the signal arm that controlled the exit from his platform and he noted its clear position. Bert was further up the line waving Joe to move forward as quickly as possible. Joe did so feeling quite important to be driving the loco' with the attractive teenager on board. Bert grabbed hold of the engine handrails as the locomotive passed him at moderate speed. He looked up and commenced to drag himself up the three steps.

"Come on son," he shouted up to Joe who was leaning out of the cab, "Get cracking. The boards are all off all the way to Prospect Hill Junction." He stayed on the top step just outside of the loco's closed cab door as the engine gathered speed under Joe's control. Bert was leaning outwards from the engine preparing to catch a shouted message from a uniformed railman on the ground who was waving them forwards. Joe edged back into the cab to wind the reversing screw up onto a lower cut-off point.

"Blimey!" he said with a feeling of approaching anxiety as his eyes fell upon the girl's figure, part seated and part lounging on the fireman's seat, "I've got to get you off here somehow." She smiled at him, she looked soft against the hard outlines of the shadowy cab interior.

"Tell me when" she said, "I don't want to get you in trouble." Joe turned his attention to Bert outside of the cab door and to the controls of the engine. They were rapidly approaching the railman standing on the ballast waiting for them to pass. Joe heard him shout, "Don't waste any time Bert. She's lost an hour already."

Bert shouted his reply of "Okay" and raised himself up onto the top step as Joe moved to lift the latch on the door to admit Bert. "Give her a bit more steam lad. We're going up to Sandsend to poke one up through the Sandsend-Kettleness tunnel."

Joe worried. "We can't Bert. We've got to stop."

Bert heaved himself into the cab. "Well, I'll go tiv our house."

Joe had been anxiously waiting for it, now it had happened; Bert had seen his loco's unauthorised passenger.

"What have we got here?" He stepped across the cab footplate as the engine rolled on. "Where's he got you from, young lady?" He turned as if to enquire of Joe who sheepishly pushed open the regulator with a jerk; the resulting sudden acceleration caused Bert to stagger across the cab floor and arrest his bodily motion by grasping the handle of the engine handbrake. He looked at Joe with annoyance on his face, he was expecting a reply from Joe but it was their passenger who spoke.

"He asked me if I'd like to come aboard." She was shifting the blame onto Joe, she felt that he was more able to take the blame because he had some authority; she had none. "I've been on engines before," she said as if that would somehow excuse her for being present on Bert's engine.

"Mebbe! but not on ours." Bert put his pipe between his teeth and moved to take over the controls that Joe was vacating without instruction and with some feeling of embarrassment. "I'll bet you haven't even got a ticket, have you?" Joe was not certain whether his mate was reproving her or enjoying her presence.

Joe had expected Bert to blow a safety valve and give him a good rollicking but he was doing neither. "You'll have to get off at Whitby West Cliff station when we stop, an' take care no one's lookin." He paused. "You'll get us shot fer this, lad. They don't hand out medals for havin' lasses on board loco's, they hands out the sack." He was at the moving loco's controls with his head outside looking ahead.

"Joe! get yer sel' out o' this door and pick up the tablet from the signalman as we go through Bog Hall crossing."

Joe opened the door and took a firm grasp on the handrail and hung down the side of the now speeding loco' with his hooked arm out stretched ready to scoop the hooped tablet from the hands of the signalman who stood on the ground alongside where they were to pass.

"Couldn't she get off here Bert? You could stop couldn't you?"

"An' let all Whitby an' all who might be on that viaduct see 'er," exasperated Bert as he kept his eye forward for a clear road and signals. "If yer goin' to break the rules on the railways don't let anyone see yer doin' it or yer won't last long on the L.N.E.R." Bert lectured his fireman. "Sit her back well into that corner where nobody'll see her if she sits still."

* * * * * *

3
THE DIRECTORS' TRAIN

Joe scooped the tablet from the hands of the signalman at Bog Hall as the engine sped through gathering speed for the gentle climb ahead. Bert told Joe that they and their engine had been called on in emergency to proceed through Whitby West Cliff Station to Sandsend to help push a failed train with five bogies through the two uphill tunnels known as the Sandsend and Kettleness tunnels.

The tunnels occupied a legendary place in the folklore of North Eastern locomotivemen; there was an unending stream of stories of heroic struggles against suffocating smoke and fumes from engines valiantly struggling through the mile long uphill tunnel. Joe anticipated his first journey through the tunnels with some excitement.

Joe started to prepare his fire for the forthcoming journey, as he swung his shovel from the coal bunker to the firehole door and balanced precariously on the swaying footplate, he paid some discreet attention to his young female passenger. He was pleased by what he could see; she wore ankle socks which settled loosely around her ankles and the tops of her, neatly polished, laced shoes. Her legs were clothed in old, well repaired, silk stockings. Her legs hung invitingly down the side of the fireman's seat only feet away from his eyes and his stooped figure.

Only now as he shovelled coal into the firebox did he have an unobserved opportunity to consider her closely. She wore a green woollen worsted overcoat that had a faint braid pattern and a very broad collar and lapels. A silken scarf fluffed out under her chin which was small and round with the suggestion of a dimple. Then he noticed, and smiled inwardly, smudges of dirt on her cheeks, yes; on her chin; ah! and on her nose. 'There's not many as can escape the muck on a loco.' he thought. Her auburn hair, topped by her knitted woollen tam, ringed her face and added youth and vivacity to the harsh lines and shadows of the engine cab.

"Change the tablet at Prospect Hill Cabin an' don't let that lass show herself tiv anybody either. Keep that tarpaulin sheet closed oe'r that side." Bert reached for the hooped tablet that hung on the engine handbrake for safety and put it into Joe's outstretched hand.

Their engine ran on easily up the incline with only moderate steam pressure in her cylinders; she ran on towards the large wooden signal cabin that straddled the line as if on stilts. The cabin was over and above the line which ran directly from Whitby Town up to

Prospect Hill and on to Whitby West Cliff Station on the route to Sandsend and Kettleness. As the engine passed beneath the cabin Joe leaned out and exchanged tablets at speed with the signalman who stood on a specially constructed small platform designed to enable him exchange tablets with moving trains.

All signals were at clear and Bert Woodley opened his regulator wider in order to speed on to Whitby West Cliff. When he was satisfied that the controls were properly set he left them unattended and stepped across the cab to settle briefly in front of the engine's young female passenger. He warmed to her innocent presence; she was seated confidently in the corner as if she had travelled thousands of miles on the footplate. He removed his cap and wiped his thinning scalp with his sponge cloth. His pipe was in his teeth as he spoke. "Well, what's yer name young lady."

"Carol, Carol Blanchard," she returned. He paused and didn't reply immediately so she asked a question. "I'd like to know yours. I keep a diary and I like to record the names of all the interesting people I meet."

"Now," and his finger pointed and then wagged while he spoke. " I don't want to be in no young lady's diary, an' 'e don't neither."

"Well it isn't every day I get invited onto an engine and get taken for a ride." She pressed back into the seat corner she was occupying and her eyes laughed and her lids fell briefly as if to avoid Bert's, and Joe's gaze. Bert saw her as a mischievous school girl just taking a peek into womanly adolescence; Joe saw her as a female, with legs and things, and he warmed to her and admired her daring.

The engine rolled up the gradient to West Cliff Station which could be seen at the end of the shallow cutting. The smoke of a waiting locomotive could be seen drifting up into the sky. The outer-home signal board was displaying its stop position. Bert sounded his engine whistle requesting permission to approach the station and as the signal board moved into its clear position he stepped across the cab again and addressed Carol.

"Be ready to slip off the engine when we get into this station but I don't want nobody to see you getting off." He emphasised the instruction with a stab of his pipe stem in her direction. "Get off without being seen. I'll tell yuh when." He moved back to his engine controls and closed the steam regulator and then turned back to her and continued, "You'll have to find your own way back down to Whitby Town Station by road and join your train to Castlebrough."

Carol nodded, spent a few moments in thought, and then she left her seat and leaned over to Joe who was in the middle of the cab. "Will I manage to walk to Whitby in time for the eleven-ten train?"

She had to put her question loudly to Joe because she spoke as the engine rattled noisily over the points and check rails approaching the station.

"I don't know. I've never been to Whitby or West Cliff before. This is my first time." Joe looked out towards the station they were approaching. It was a station with two platforms and two main lines to enable trains pass each other and continue on their journeys up or down the single line route along the coast between Castlebrough and Middlesbrough.

One of the platforms was occupied by a two coach train which had just arrived from the Castlebrough direction; its engine was smoking lazily and dropping a haze over the station buildings and adding more gloom to the overcast day. The other platform was clear and Bert had just received a signal for his engine to proceed forwards at caution. The Whitby West Cliff Station Master was standing at the edge of the platform on the end closest to the slowly advancing A8 locomotive.

"Flipping heck, the station master's wanting to come aboard. He'll be after the tablet for the signalman. See if you can stop him." Bert Woodley was not an alarmist, he usually took every little emergency in his stride but his voice did carry a measure of concern.

Joe quickly reached for the hooped tablet on the handbrake handle and moved to the side of the locomotive closest to the platform on which the the small heavy figure of the station master was waiting. Joe had moved the tarpaulin sheet slightly to one side to enable him look out through the cab opening but still obscure Carol from view.

The station master's short, white-haired, figure brought memories of dead grandfather flooding back to Joe; there was some similarity between the stature of the dead ex-collier and the dumpy uniformed figure on the platform. For a moment his sadness at the prospect of the forthcoming funeral came back to him, but the imminence of the expected confrontation with the station master drove the memories away almost as soon as they had surfaced.

Bert brought his engine to a grinding halt close to the station master but short of the train standing in the adjacent platform. His head squeezed out alongside Joe's and the tarpaulin cover. "What Yer want then?" Bert asked with an aggressive tone of the station master whose hand reached up and grasped hold of the cab handrail.

"We want you to go on to Sandsend station and push a Middlesbrough train up through the tunnels to Kettleness."

"What for? Why us? You could've used the engine off that train standing there doin' nowt." Bert was keen to show his displeasure at the task which he was expected to carry out and the tone of his voice did just that. To some extent Joe felt startled, partly because he knew that he was to blame for the presence of Carol on their footplate and partly because Bert had not really shown any anger about the problem until now.

"Can't use that one. It's a Director's train, It'd be more than my job's worth to interfere with it; it's just pulled in in front of you. York Train Control gave the instruction that you had to be used because you were standing at Whitby." The station master's reply to Bert was almost apologetic.

"That train's full o' top brass, scrambled egg crowd?" queried Bert in search of confirmation of the news he had just received and understood quite clearly.

"Yes. They've been held up twenty minutes and they can't go on till you've helped the Middlesbrough man through the tunnels."

"Bloody good fortune for me today, aint it. I've been on since five-thirty this morning and I've bloody well," he emphasised his words angrily, "been held back to work a one o' clock special instead of our own. I'll be on ten hours today." He turned his head away and then back with a show of exasperation. "Oh! gi' him the tablet. Let's get on our way. No good me bloody rebelling. Not in this dictatorship we've got to work under." He turned away and let the sheet drape down over the space he had just occupied.

The wrinkled white moustached face of the station master looked closely into Joe's eyes and displayed discomforture. Joe raised his eyes in a returned expression of 'It's not my fault.' "Do we have to go then?" he questioned the station master.

"Course you have. You'd better tell yer mate to pick the Middlesbrough fireman up at the signal cabin. He's got the tablet - and take yourselves forward as soon as you can and clear the line." He lowered himself from the engine step onto the platform and paused for a moment. "Tell Bert Woodley I'm sorry, - he'll know I'm only giving him the orders I've been given."

Joe turned inwards to the waiting Bert and the station master strolled away in the direction of the other platform. Bert did not look as pleased as Joe had hoped he would be after he had successfully deterred the station master from boarding his engine.

"Thank God he's bloody gone. How do yuh think I'd 'ave explained her on mi engine?" He pulled his cloth cap firmly on his head, stuck his cold pipe in his jaw and grasped the engine's controls. Steam exhausted leisurely from the chimney head as the engine crept slowly past the 'Directors' Train' in the adjacent platform and towards the signal cabin. "We've got to get her off" Bert blurted out irritably as he conveyed his anxiety, and indeed some anger, in Joe's direction.

Joe turned away slightly as if to avert an expected onslaught. He looked at the soft figure, curled quietly in the corner on the fireman's seat but it did nothing to quench the erupting fire of concern in his breast and his intestines. "Get her off, either at this side or that. I don't care. Just get her off and don't let anyone see her."

"She'll have to get off when we stop at the cabin at the end o' the platform." Joe said it firmly as if there was no doubt about her coming expulsion from his engine footplate.

"But you can't leave me here." Carol had unfurled and slipped from the corner into the centre of the cab. Joe pushed her back suddenly to keep her out of view from the 'Director's Train' which was being passed slowly by their moving engine.

"Well we can't leave her here," Joe supplicated to Bert on her behalf. "She's only a kid."

The A8 loco' was moving forwards more rapidly and covering the distance to the signal cabin while the dramatic exchange developed. It had nearly travelled the length of the train in the next platform. "Get her ready to get off on the platform when we stop near the cabin. The Middlesbrough fireman's stood on the platform getting ready to jump on board. He's got the tablet and the signal's at clear." Bert was still in an angry mood.

"You've got to get off here," Joe said to the worried looking Carol with an air of finality and sorrow. She looked ready to protest. Bert halted the loco' close to where the dirty figure of the Middlebrough fireman stood. He looked at the facing platform on which the 'Director's Train' was standing. He could now view the platform opposite his engine. "Chrise sake! The bloody platform's swarming wi' scrambled egg and toffs from York." There was no doubt about his concern. "Get yer head down or you'll be seen from this side." Joe and Carol understood immediately.

Joe pulled Carol's arm as an indication to her to crouch down on the floor so that she was below the level of the cab door. He glanced in the direction of 'the scrambled egg crowd' and saw them idling their time away in conversation on the platform and viewing Bert's locomotive tank engine with interest. It was nothing short of a miracle that had enabled Carol to duck down out of sight and avert being seen by so many searching eyes. Joe felt a growing level of alarm as he realised that he quite certainly would not escape blame if Carol had been seen on the footplate.

A rattle at the cab door on the platform side of their standing locomotive drew Joe's alarmed attention from its focus on the crowd of London and North Eastern Railway Company managers. A hand was rattling away at the sheeted door sending a certain message that someone was trying to gain immediate entrance. The sheet was pushed aside and a very black, uniform capped, head pushed in and grinned.

"Okay mate, I'm aboard now.Yuh can get yer skates on as soon as yer can." The Middlesbrough fireman had mounted the steps and pushed his way in past the tarpaulin sheet that had given Carol some cover from prying eyes. "Let's get away from all these gaffers, they gives me the frights." His arm reached over the cab door and down to turn the handle which was situated inside of the door. He pushed the door open and inserted himself inside the cab. "My mate's stood at Sandsend tekin' some clinker out o' the fire. By the time we gets there he'll be ready to have another go at the holes."

"Put that sheet back in place." Bert pointed with the stem of his cold pipe. Joe rushed to do as he commanded. The newcomer to the cab looked around with an expression of surprise when his eyes alighted on the figure of the attractive young girl crouched down low in the centre of the cab with the heat and light of the fire falling on her.

Before he could speak Bert brushed past him, turned a corner of the sheet back, and looked out onto the platform and towards the signal cabin which stood on the end of the platform. He withdrew his head immediately, he had seen what he sought and feared; two neat, black suited figures from the 'Director's Train' were conversing leisurely only a few yards ahead of his standing locomotive. He pushed his way across the now crowded cab footplate to reach his engine controls.

"Gaffers on that side, gaffers on this side, gaffers all over the bloody place." He stood uncertain of his next action. Joe looked on and sympathised but felt extremely guilty.

* * * * * *

4
THE STRUGGLE IN THE TUNNEL

"You've got a woman fireman on here - eh? That's interesting. I alus said them women cleaners 'ud get our jobs." The most recent addition to the growing fraternity on the A8's cab interrupted Joe's deliberations.

The lanky figure was the strangest and dirtiest fireman they had ever seen - and Bert had considerable experience of strange and dirty firemen. A grease ladened uniformed cap sat perilously on one side of his head; that was the sole concession his dress made towards the standard regulation that 'Railway Servants shall at all times attire themselves in the appropriate uniform provided by the Company.'

A silken muffler circled his neck tightly; his face was almost totally blackened by soot, coal and oil; the only exceptions were the two eyes, surrounded by white sweat washed circles, that floated in his thin black face. He wore a well blackened, overall boiler suit held tightly around his waist by a twisted leather belt. His baggy trouser legs bloomed around poor weak shoes and were restrained from covering his shoes by the ubiquitous bicycle clips.

Bert still paused thoughtfully at his engine controls. Joe could see he was experiencing considerable uncertainty about his future actions. Never the less Bert replied to the Middlesbrough fireman with surprising lightness. "She's not a fireman, or firewoman. Can't yuh tell? We're on a family outing' to the seaside. What I want to know is where the cat dragged you from - not the soddin bath-house."

"Bath's is for mucky people. Why should I have one. Here, better tek the tablet for Kettleness." Joe took the tablet which authorised them to travel into the section ahead and draped it over his engine handbrake.

Bert left his controls again and looked out from the cab onto the platform. The two authoritative looking men were still there sauntering up the platform towards Bert's locomotive.

"We've had a rough time up there in yon 'ole mate. Three goes we've had to get through. Slippin' all the time we wus, short o' steam as well." The visiting fireman sank his five foot ten figure onto the fireman's seat and cast a quizzical look at Carol who was still crouched as low as was possible on her haunches in front of the firebox door. "What's the lass doin' here like? We want some at our shed if you've got 'em at Castlebrough." A grin cracked across his thin black face showing long uneven teeth.

Bert opened his engine steam regulator very slightly and made his engine move forwards. "They wouldn't trust you Middlesbrough fellers with cats, never mind young ladies," he said.

Joe wondered what Bert planned to do, clearly a decision had to be taken. Bert crossed and recrossed his engine cab and looked out onto both platforms in turn. He let his engine crawl slowly up to the end of the platform and stopped her while he surveyed the possibilities for Carol's departure but he concluded that too many curious eyes had his engine under constant serveilance. He popped his engine whistle and moved his engine forwards into the section of line which held the Middlesbrough train which was awaiting their assistance.

"We'd better be off. Too many busy bodies here." They were off to help rescue the failed train even though they still had their unauthorised female passenger on board. The engine gathered speed and rocked as it rattled across the last points and crossings, its chimney shot exhaust steam and smoke up into the overcast sky. A fine haze hung in the atmosphere and suggested the possibility of rain thus evoking a grumble from Bert about the rails being greasy.

"How did you get'er on board?" asked the Middlesbrough fireman quietly in Joe's ear. Joe told him in words spoken straight into the fellow's well blackened ear so that they could be received above the noise of the travelling loco.'

Carol raised herself without instruction and occupied her previous station on the fireman's seat and adopting the role of an innocent and somewhat smudged onlooker. Her little woolly hat still sat attractively above her ring of auburn curls. There was much grime on her face and on her clothes. The grime she had collected and continued to collect added a charming new dimension to her being in Joe's storehouse of fantasy. He was pleased by her presence on his locomotive; he was more than glad that fate had decreed the day's happenings. He chose not to recall the anxieties that had raged in his vital organs not many minutes before the present ones in which he admired her youthful being.

Their side tank locomotive stormed along the undulating single track, rocking and swaying in a manner which delighted Joe and played no part in alarming Carol. As the journey proceeded Bert learned from the Middlesbrough fireman that the five coach passenger train on line from Castlebrough to Middlesbrough was standing at Sandsend Station about two miles ahead of them.

"Why didn't your guard come back here for help instead of you. You could've been getting some clinker out of your fire?" asked Bert as the story unfolded.

"That's wot mi mate said, but we couldn't cos Chuck our guard had sprained 'is ankle when he were out rabbitin' yesterday an' he said that he couldn't walk this far back."The extremely dirty fireman talked as much with his black hands as he did with his pink mouth. "So my mate sez to me, 'get on back there wi' this tablet, tha'll be better at walkin' than firing.While tha's gone I'll get some muck out of this fire an' get a head o' steam in 'er ready for another go when you've got somebody to push us from behind.'We had three goes to get through that first hole, slippin' and fartin' we was. Bloody hell it fair cooked me. We were both laid on the floor tryin' to get some fresh air up through the floor boards. Even got Chuck in the van, spewin' up 'is ring 'e said he was. Sulphur gets on his stomach he sez."

As the fireman talked Bert kept an experienced eye on the single line ahead and on his engine's speed. They passed over the tubular metal viaducts carrying the line over little valleys that cut their ways down to the sandy beach from the higher land on the left side of the track. Joe and Carol talked quietly and looked out onto the great North Sea bay which occupied the right side of the line.

The rail track followed the coastline closely, the waves could be seen clearly washing the rough pebbled beaches. In the far distance under the shadow of the Kettleness Headland they could see the small Sandsend railway station nestled at the end of a steel viaduct just above the village of Sandsend and the small river which coursed down to the sea. In spite of the drizzle which slightly obscured their vision they could see the waiting Middlesbrough train.

Joe and Carol were suddenly joined at their side of the engine by the fireman from Middlesbrough. He eased himself in roughly alongside them without seeking permission, his dirty presence made Carol draw back. "Ha! mi mates gone and done it fer me. He's cleaned the fire and got her stoked up." He pointed to the waiting train at Sandsend station and the locomotive emitting a cloud of black smoke from the chimney to drift down onto the nearby beach. His enthusiasm, in spite of his un-attractiveness, was infectious.

Joe and Carol showed increased interest in the train ahead, especially when the Middlesbrough lad pointed out the route up the hillside to the tunnel mouth. High up on the rocky headland that towered above the breakers on the rocks below they could just discern the thin mark of the rail track as it disappeared into the rocky face.

The Middlesbrough youth anticipated the coming journey through the tunnel, "We'll soon be poking' up through there again. Two engines on this time, she'll go like shit off a end o' a piece o' stick" Joe felt annoyed on hearing the bad language in front of Carol.

"Anyone got a fag?" the Middlesbrough lad asked. "I could do wi' a smoke to put me on 'til we get into that tunnel."

No one offered him a cigarette so he produced his own Woodbine cigarette and used Bert's long paper taper to obtain a light from the firebox. It glowed in his black face and he dragged on it with great relish. Joe refused an offered cigarette, he had no desire to smoke a cigarette just before entering a tunnel which he expected to be full of smoke and heat. He tended his fire and damper controls to increase his engine's steam pressure, soon they would be pushing the five coaches through the tunnel and they would need all of the steam pressure Joe could muster.

The Castlebrough engine rattled over the tubular steel viaduct that approached the railway station and crossed the mouth of the small river on which Sandsend village nestled. Bert eased his brakes on and prepared to stop close behind the motionless train.

"Get your head in Carol." Bert's shouted instruction across the cab awoke Joe and Carol to the reality of her unauthorised presence on the footplate of the locomotive. Joe acted by closing off his side of the cab by securing the tarpaulin sheet back into its earlier position. He knew that Bert would insist on Carol being left at Sandsend station until they returned from Kettleness. The prospect displeased him but there was nothing he could do to avert that course of action.

"Slip down this side lad." Bert broke into Joe's thoughts as the engine bumped up to the five coaches. "Slip in between and hang on then get yer self back up here. Mek sure that no one sees yer girl friend when yer opens the door."

The guard of the Middlesbrough train approached the engine along the viaduct on which it was standing as Joe and the Middlesbrough fireman with the tablet in his possession descended to the ground. The guard looked up to Bert and grimaced in the direction of the lean black figure who was about to make off in the direction of the Middlesbrough locomotive at the other end of the train on which both engines were now attached. The train guard grumbled up into the face of Bert Woodley who was leaning out of the cab side. Joe walked into earshot. "This is what comes of putting young kids like Blackie on the footplate. Can't fire for toffee, his mate sez."

Joe listened as the conversation progressed; he didn't have any sympathy for the guard who had only been inconvenienced, he had more sympathy for the obviously inefficient Blackie. Joe knew that the footplate could be rough for anyone especially 'young kids.' he guessed that the mile long uphill trip through Kettleness tunnel with a bad engine would be tough even for an experienced fireman. What chance would the hair-brained Blackie have?

Joe climbed back aboard the loco' while the guard moaned on at Bert. Joe had to take great care not to open the cab door too wide when he entered; he must not let the guard see Carol on their footplate, Joe had enough worries just knowing that Blackie would tell his mates at Middlesbrough shed about 'the lass on the footplate of a Castlebrough engine.' He took great care when entering the cab, the guard saw nothing and soon moved off to Bert's relief.

"When we move our engine up to the platform I want her off wi' out anyone seeing her," he was sharp when he spoke to Joe. "She's been on too long. Don't yuh know how serious it is to have a member of the public on the footplate, especially women members." Joe nodded vigorously and punctuated Bert's complaints with apologetic, "Hmm's" and "Yes, I know." To Carol, Bert said, "I want you to slip off at this side wi' out anyone seeing you, then go and sit in the station waiting room. I'll pick yer up when we comes back and take yer to Whitby."

"Yes" Carol muttered and started to try saying that she was very sorry but the words were slow in forming and Bert had turned his attention to the outside off the engine with some show of impatience. His mind was full of the dangers to his job security that he faced if he was charged under disciplinary procedures. 'A woman on the footplate.' The charge echoed in his mind. The charge would carry with it more than just the implication that he had had a member of the public on his engine while it was in traffic. 'A woman's more than just a member of the travelling public, she's a woman, and that suggests something more than a simple interest she might have in engines.'

Bert's mind was increasingly absorbed in his worrying thoughts. He could hear his accusers, "How long was she on the footplate of your locomotive Woodley? Were You alone with her?" He could hear the emotion charged questions uttered by an accuser in a court like hearing in the York Headquarters of the London and North Eastern Railway Company. He would be appealing against an instant dismissal decision, his union representative would be fighting to save his job for him, they might force him to become a shed labourer.

Bert shuddered and struggled to halt the flood of thoughts. He knew that he would have to take great care to see that the story about Bert Woodley having a woman on board his locomotive did not become common currency on the tongues of North Eastern railmen. Their imaginative minds would embroider the incident to give it colourful details and conclusions.

Bert turned his attention to the practicality of getting rid of Carol as soon and safely as possible. "Joe, you run forward to the

Middlesbrough engine, give that scruffy kid these five Park Drives an' tell him that mums the word about this young woman. Make sure he knows he's got to keep quiet, our jobs, yours especially, depends on it." Bert handed the packet of five Park Drives to Joe.

"Then tell the driver that I'll give him a blast on the whistle when we're ready to start but tell him I want to crawl up the platform to let a pilot man get off. Tell him I'll blast him twice on the whistle when we are ready for off. Then we'll both get stuck in beltin' up yon hill an through the tunnels."

A deep disappointment settled on Joe. He listened to Carol protesting to Bert that she didn't want to be left on the platform waiting for them. "What" she asked "will happen to me if you have an accident and don't come back for me?"

"Course we'll come back," was Bert single response. Joe considered the wisdom of trying to influence his driver to follow another course of action; but what course? Clearly Joe dare not advocate that Carol should stay with them on the footplate and make the journey through the two tunnels. Bert was clearly agitated and was pushing Joe to get out of the cab and carry the message to the driver on the Middlesbrough engine.

The platform was being cleared of passengers as the station master and a porter signalman ushered them into the waiting carriages with announcements that 'the train will be leaving again in a few moments.' Joe threaded his way amongst the passengers in the direction of the foremost engine; his own engine suddenly blew off steam indicating her readiness for the exertions the coming journey would demand of her.

The Middlesbrough engine crew had an A8 side tank locomotive like Joe's, it was dull and very grease laden, its black livery was covered in the white ash deposited by the burning clinker and ash which the driver had withdrawn from the firebox and thrown out through the cab doorway onto the lineside.

Joe climbed in through the open cab door; his eyes settled on a much more inhospitable locomotive than the one he had just left. Ash and coal dust covered the whole of the cab floor and boiler front, there were none of the bright copper pipes, shiny brasses and nicely oiled boiler front paintwork that were features of his Castlebrough locomotive. The Middlesbrough engine's safety valves on the boiler top outside suddenly lifted with a great roar as surplus boiler pressure burst through and shot a tall white column of steam skywards.

The thin tall driver was washing his hands and face in hot water contained in a battered greasy engine water bucket. "She's ready now," he shouted through the dirty veil of soap suds circling his face. "Mebbe we could've managed without you now that we've cleaned the fire. Don't know though for sure cos the rails in the tunnels is quite slippy."

Joe looked into the firebox. "Not as good as my fire, still looks on the blue side."

"True, couldn't get all the clinker out," the driver interjected. "What's your engine steaming like?"

"Good. Best one I've been on, I kept her poppin' off all the way up the peak this morning." Joe remembered the packet of five Park Drives and his message for Blackie. The driver turned at the sound of a mouth blown whistle and gazed down the platform towards the rear as Joe whispered urgently into Blackie's attentive ear. "Let's be off now son." The driver added. "The guard's waggin' us away. Is your mate ready when you get aboard?"

"Yes," Joe replied quickly, interrupting his whispered instructions in Blackie's ear.

"Right, run back to your engine and let's be off. Give me a blast on your whistle when your aboard and ready. There's that nobs train waiting' to come on after us."

Joe nodded urgently as he sought to finish his whispered conversation with Blackie.

"Skip out here lad" the driver encouraged him, "They're waiting for us to leave."

Good at responding to orders, Joe reacted and was out through the cab door and down the steps in a flash."Tarah" he shouted up and turned on his heel to be off along the ballast and up onto the platform. Suddenly his mind returned to Carol; he wasn't dismayed at the recalled thought that reminded him of the duty he had neglected to perform for Bert when he was on the Middlesbrough footplate. He would just say 'Okay, Bert, gi' him yer whistle. He's ready, purging to be off.' Then unfortunately, or fortunately, he couldn't be sure which, Carol would get off their engine and they would do the job assigned to them.

He ran along the platform through the gazes of the passengers who looked out through the smoke grimed windows. The end of the platform was reached quickly and he was soon descending the sloped end down onto the viaduct where his engine stood attached to the rear of the train. Up the cabside steps he clambered and surprised Bert who had been looking out for him from the other side of the locomotive. Both engines were letting off surplus steam from their safety valves with blasts that shattered the calm of the sleepy little town of Sandsend. "Is he ready?" Bert shouted the question.

Joe closed the cab door behind him. "Yes. Gi' him a pop he sez." Carol sat demurely, if somewhat soiled in the corner of the fireman's seat. She knew that she would have to go; she showed her concern and lack of enthusiasm for the prospect. Joe said nothing further.

Bert looked out of his engine cab along the platform and took a flag waved signal from the guard of the train. He popped his engine whistle with a smart pull of the whistle cord that hung stretched from his side of the cab to the whistle control lever.

"Stop that racket a minute lad. Put some more watter in the boiler to cool 'er a bit." Joe did as he was instructed and as Bert opened his steam regulator and caused his engine to move forwards gently the blowing off from the safety valves ceased suddenly.

"Carol." Bert leaned across the cab and shouted above the engine noises. "Keep down, don't be seen but be ready to get off at this side when we pass the bend in the platform. I'll stop the train just for a split second when we're out of sight of the station master and the others on the platform. Get off quickly and just stand on the platform until we come back an' I'll find some way of picking you up and takin' you on to Whitby."

"But what if you don't manage to pick me up, what will I do?"

"We'll pick you up okay. Just get yerself off when I shout."

The two engines and the five passenger ladened coaches moved forwards along the line of the platform, a few figures, including the station master watched the progress as if they had nothing else in the world to do. Passengers heads protruded from carriage windows at both sides of the train, these were of concern to Bert; he knew that some of the passengers at least would see Carol leave the cab of his locomotive when he slowed to a halt at the end of the platform. That worried him, but he was determined to get Carol off his engine: he would just have to gamble on the fact that those people who saw her leave the engine would not report the fact to anyone in authority.

"He's goin' fast. Did yuh tell him about the pilotman we'd got to drop off on the platform?"

"Course I did," was Joe's only possible reply.

The train was gathering more speed than Bert had hoped; he closed the steam regulator valve because his train was now half way down the length of the platform. He heard a cheer go up from the passengers who were looking out from carriage windows; they were celebrating their expectation that they would soon be well on their way to their destination. Bert was increasingly concerned about the speed of their train; he put his engine steam brake into its first notch and heard the brake blocks drag on the engine wheels.

The foremost engine could be seen exerting itself strongly; its exhaust blast at the chimney emerging powerfully giving an indication of the work being undertaken by it. Clearly the Middlesbrough engine crew were showing no indication that they were preparing to coast to a gentle halt at the end of the platform as Bert had instructed.

Bert applied his engine steam brake more powerfully, he could feel it exerting a braking effect on the engine and slowing the passage of the train. The end of the platform came into sight. Bert waved Carol across the cab and put his engine steam brake on fully, but quite clearly they were going too fast for Carol to safely leave while the train was in motion.

"Why isn't he stopping Joe? Yuh told him didn't yuh?

"Yes." Joe gave a definite, clear response.

Bert's hand reached for the train vacuum brake lever. Joe knew that if Bert applied the vacuum brake the whole train would grind to a startling and definite halt despite the motive effort being exerted by their partnering locomotive at the front. Bert knew that such a dramatic halt would draw the attention of every onlooker to his engine; he wouldn't be able to just ease the vacuum brakes off and proceed within seconds. An emergency application of the vacuum powered brakes on every coach and both engines would mean stopping the train for a minute or two at the least.

Bert paused; hand on the wooden brake handle, precious split seconds ticked away and the platform continued to drift past tantalisingly. His hand started to apply the brake, air began to rush in through the air inlets; Joe watched unhappily, Carol prepared for the inevitable; but suddenly Bert stopped depressing the brake lever and the engine steam brake. He put everything into 'go' position and opened up his steam regulator.

"What the hell went wrong? He was bloody well supposed to stop!" Bert looked and sounded angry. Joe and Carol felt like shrinking while at the same time experiencing feelings of relief. "Looks like we stuck wi' yuh young lady. Only hope I don't live to regret this day. For Christ's sake let's hope we get through the tunnels wi' out anything going wrong." Joe nearly cheered. Carol Blanchard was going to stay on board and take her luck with them as they climbed the steep gradients and pounded through the two tunnels.

Joe stooped to the task of serving his engine firebox; to him the action offered an escape from any awkward questions raised by Bert. The engine was roaring at the chimney head with the torrent of heavy exhaust shooting into the sky. The blast on the fire raised the firebox temperature to a white hot heat that lit the gloomy cab with dancing shafts of incandescent firelight.

Although Joe had never before fired through a long tunnel he had received plenty of verbal advice from shed enginemen about how to perform when Sandsend-KettlenessTunnels confronted him. "Build your fire up well before you get into the tunnel. Have a good back-end on, no camel's humps in the middle. Burn the smoke off at the chimney head if you can before you hit the hole and don't fire while you're inside if you can possibly avoid it."

Bert vented his spleen on the long steel handle of the horn shaped steam regulator; he grasped it with both hands and forced it to full open position; he applied the steam blown sands to the shuddering great driving wheels and the slippery rails on which they struggled to urge the the train forwards, up the incline, towards the distant tunnel. The racket of thumping steel, the pounding exhaust blast and the roar of the white hot furnace electrified Joe's stooped and poised body as it fed coal from bunker to firebox. He was almost too excited to feed his hungry fire.

"Don't overdo it son. Don't get too much on or get a camel's hump in the middle." Joe nodded his response to Bert and left his fire and looked out through the cab window at the torrent of black smoke and exhausting steam at the chimney top. Its dense blackness told him that the fire was adequately fired. The five coaches comprised a relatively light load for the two engines; the train gathered speed even though the driving wheels on the Castlebrough engine spun repeatedly on the damp slippery rails.

"There's no wonder he stuck three times in that tunnel wi' rails like these. It's better for climbing and pullin' when rain's pouring down than when rail 's just damp and sticky like now." Bert shouted across the cab to both Joe and the young lady; she was now seated comfortably and confidently on the fireman's seat peeking out past the tarpaulin sheet to view the countryside; Joe had turned back part of the sheet and was looking out and occasionally conversing with Carol. Bert's mood seemed to have changed to a more carefree mood of apparent indifference to Carol's presence. Joe did not now feel that he was in immediate danger of receiving a 'rollicking' from Bert.

There was not much time for conversation, the noise of the pounding loco' drowned out all but shouted remarks or forced words to be spoken directly into an attentive ear. Bert had constantly to attend his controls and balance the steam fed into the engine cylinders with the needs of the driving wheels that shuddered for a precarious hold on the greasy rails. The appetite for steam expressed by the loco. kept Joe busy carefully feeding the white hot mouth of the firebox.

"Who do yer think's goner get blamed for all that muck the lassie's picked up on her face and clothes?" Bert leaned over and shouted the question in the direction of both Joe and Carol. Joe laughed and shouted back an appropriate response. Carol appreciated Bert's newly expressed relaxed mood; she muttered something with a grin in Bert's direction but it went unheard amongst the discordant noises of the struggling locomotive. She relaxed even more and removed more of the tarpaulin sheet and gazed seawards from the side of the locomotive.

The clouds had refused to lift and let the sun through to play on the rocky slopes of Kettleness headland. Grey clouds blanketed the sky from sea horizon to hilltop and from North to South. A small ship, hugging the coast for protection against marauding German ships and aircraft, made its way slowly southwards. The haze had become a patchy drizzle as the train climbed higher. Little jewels of mist, that had condensed on the cold sides of the water tanks, gave way to an anarchy of twisting rivulets pouring down to teem from the tank edge below and be abandoned to the passing ballast.

Where a root hold was possible grass and trees clothed the rocks and the soils on the way down hill from the high ridge on the left. Rocks and fissures and abandoned jet workings broke up the landscape along which the climbing single rail track wound. Telegraph poles stood at suitable spaces in the grassed border of the track. The train, spouting two columns of smoke and steam which fell back and trailed down the bank, snaked slowly up to its rendezvous with Sandsend Tunnel - the first of the two tunnels.

"When we hit the tunnel lassie, I want you all tucked up there on that seat." Carol had moved from her sheltered position on the fireman's main seat to the small fireman's ledge seat on the coal bunker. Bert had approached her and shouted his instructions.

He pointed to the corner of the seat she had occupied for most of the journey from Whitby Town. "I don't want you to to get a hot cinder in your eye by stickin' your head out in the tunnel." He crossed back to his side of the cab to attend his controls; he kept an eye out on the track but there was little which he needed to observe because the engine crew up front had the main responsibility for the safe passage of the train. Bert leaned over to Joe and spoke into his ear; "Better put that tarpaulin sheet back in place. It'll keep some muck off her, an' it'll stop her lookin' out when we're in the tunnel. You keep yer eye on 'er won't yuh? She's your responsibility."

Joe had been keeping his eye on Carol while he swung his firing shovel through its trajectory from the coal bunker to the fire-hole door. She was seated sideways on his seat with head leaning out to give her a vision of the track; she had her left foot on the floor boards and her right, with knee crooked on the edge of the seat, was resting on the raised handle of the front ashpan damper. More of her silk covered leg was visible than if she had been seated more squarely. Joe had to avoid his gaze appearing to alight obviously on her leg so it shifted about, he was uncomfortably conscious that she might think he was looking at her legs.

'Why does she come out in those awful silk stockings? Bare legs would be far more attractive - especially with her ankle socks.' The words were not spoken by Joe, they merely formed as un-expressed words in his thoughts; thoughts which he had to interrupt and apply to the task of fitting the tarpaulin sheet on the hooks around the opening on his side of the enclosed engine cab.

"Are you putting me back in prison?" She mouthed the question almost inaudibly above the engine's din, and she grinned charmingly at Joe as she moved into a more upright position so that Joe could re-attach the sheet. Her little tartan tam sat undisturbed on, held in place by a small hat pin. Her nose had collected a substantial smudge of engine dirt.

"You might end up in prison if anyone gets to know that you've been on here with us," he teased. He pulled his cap firmly onto his head and peered past the sheet out of the cab forwards up the line towards the spot where he could see the track enter the tunnel in the grey rock headland many feet above the sea.

He opened the wooden locker on the coal-bunker end and from within took a clean white sponge cloth. "This will do to clean some of the dirt off your nose end and your right cheek." He demonstrated on his cheek and nose where the smudges were located on her face. "Sorry that we don't have scented soap and towels for you. We'll try better next time you take a trip with us."

She laughed, took the proffered cloth and withdrew a small mirror from within a little purse taken from her pocket and proceeded to clean her face. Joe moved across the rocking footplate towards the beckoning figure of Bert Woodley.

"Tell her to use that cloth as a pad to breath through if the smoke gets thick in the tunnel." Bert was speaking closely into Joe's ear. "Tell her to wet it and it'll be even better for breathing through. Put some warm watter in the buckct, it'll be ready for dipping our cloths into." He paused and Joe turned away to do as he had been bid but Bert pulled him back for a final consultation. "If it gets very hot and smoky in there, tell her, and you take note as well, get down onto the floor where the air 'll be clearer. No need to panic tell her. It's alus like this."

Joe nodded urgently and responded,"Yes. Yes", then he conveyed the information to Carol; she was quite excited about the imminent trip through the tunnel. The thought occurred to Joe that she was a bit of a 'tom boy,' she didn't appear to be exhibiting the usual feminine concerns that men expected of women in situations of risk and daring.

He put the final touches to his fire preparations, he had a good thick, bright fire-bed with a good backend; no 'camel's hump,' no holes, just a good well prepared white hot fire. He felt pleased and for a moment the thought passed through his mind of the first hard journey he had done on the York passenger train with Bob Laker when he had nearly run out of steam pressure. He was more experienced now he conceded to himself.

To his mate Bert he assured, "She's ready now Bert. I'm not doin' anymore. She's got a full head an' a full glass. What do yer think? Will she tek us through wi' out any more firing?"

Bert took his cold pipe out of his mouth and inserted a piece of black plug. "We're about two train lengths away from the 'ole. Just round this here bend on the left. She should go through now", he replied in Joe's reaching ear.

The train, with its two straining engines, was hugging the side of the steep bank along which the line had been cut. Smoke and steam shot upwards from the two chimneys and came falling back down the bankside onto the train and the track left behind. Down to the right through the sheeted side of the loco' Joe could see the grassy bank of the cliff side slope away down to the seashore a long way below where the low tide had uncovered a beach strewn with boulders and pebbles. To the front he could see the distant stone portal entrance of Sandsend Tunnel; soon the foremost engine would be swallowed by it. Joe thrilled at the prospect as they stormed up the last few yards of open track.

"We're nearly there", Bert shouted to Joe. "Just goner give her a bit more." He switched the steam sands to stop the urging loco' from slipping her wheels; he opened his steam regulator to its fullest extent. The roar at the chimney top increased in volume as the whole of Joe's one hundred and eighty pounds steam pressure exerted its energy on the engine's three pistons. Joe felt the train surge forward more powerfully.

"Look out here lad," Bert Woodley beckoned Joe to join him and look out of his side of the cab; Carol took the invitation to include her.

"There's the 'ole, mile long she is." A yawning black hole was devouring the coaches of the train up in front. The work of long dead stone masons had produced a fine stone portal at the southern entrance to the famed uphill tunnel.

The moment the three heads saw it, was almost the moment of their absorption in the suffocating blackness of the bowels of the earth. Bert propelled Carol smartly back to her seat as the daylight, the falling thin drizzle and the drifting smoke and steam of their engine disappeared in the 'woof' of air rushing past them out of the tunnel. In the sudden darkness the dancing firelight fell upon the swirls of steam and smoke that shot in from the torrent tumbling past the open side of the cab. Like lost spirits of styx the illuminated wisps danced and darted magically in the hot square confines of the rocking and straining locomotive.

Unconcerned, Carol sat obediently on the fireman's seat with her feet resting on the wide pipe that ran along the front edge not far above the floor height. In her hand she held the white sponge cloth given to her by Joe. She was a dim figure in the firelit gloom and curling smoke but a thrilling companion to Joe who dutifully kept a watchful eye on his boiler controls.

Her gaze roamed interestedly across the range of white faced, circular gauges that stood at random across the boiler front. She knew which was the steam pressure guage; she had seen Joe's interest focus on it too many times for her not to note its significance in the life of the loco.'

The dancing white-hot coals which the loco's firm exhaust blast was rooting from the firebed and ejecting out through the chimney held Carol's fascinated attention. She viewed them falling through the blackness past Bert's open cab side and bouncing in the darkness along the boiler top which could be glimpsed through the foremost windows.

"Firework night," Joe spoke loudly into her ear."Great show we're putting on, an' no admission charge." Carol nodded agreement; she had her own thoughts but the noise of the loco' made expression of them a laborious affair. She, Joe and Bert seemed content to gaze, or move about the cab without speaking.

Bert stood adjacent to his engine's vacuum brake handle, reversing screw and steam regulator handle; all of which were in close proximity to each other. Smoke encircled him, the fire glow illuminated him oddly, his pipe hung lifelessly from his jaw. his right hand grasped the handle of the regulator; his cap was firmly pulled forwards on his head.

He wasn't looking at anything in particular or creating any impression that he was alert. Carol would have been forgiven if she had thought that the engine was driving itself, and that a driver was unnecessary; but Bert was in complete command, his eyes and ears were on the sounds of his engine and on the various gauge readings which the firelight illuminated. Joe likewise seemingly had little to do except carry on a difficult conversation with Carol and attend to his boiler water level and damper controls.

The Castlebrough locomotive performed excellently, Bert and Joe were very satisfied; she rolled in a pleasing manner on her six driving wheels as she raced through the velvet blackness of the tunnel. The rocking, smoke filled, firelit cab was an enclosed and complete world, the only hint of an external world being the black gleaming, wet drenched tunnel wall that raced past the open cab side.

"We're havin' to work hard with this train," Bert shouted across to Joe. "That feller up front's not pulling his whack."

"Mebbe he's short of steam again," volunteered Joe stretching across to be as close to Bert's ear as was possible. He paid attention to the sounds and efforts of the engine. He sensed that she was labouring hard but only Bert could compare the task imposed on his engine with similar tasks he had experienced in this same tunnel with other trains. Bert could not ask more of his engine; her steam regulator was wide open and Joe had the maximum steam pressure in the boiler.

Unexpectantly their engine wheels give a momentary shudder as she started to slip on the wet rails; Bert responded quickly, shut his steam valve and re-opened it at a lower level; he turned his steam sanding equipment into operation to spray sand beneath the flashing wheels to help them grip the rail.

"Mebbe she's slippin' up front too," Bert shouted into Joe's nearby ear. His engine slipped again despite the sand and reduced steam flow to the cylinders. Bert wrestled with the long, horn shaped regulator handle; he closed it down when the engine slipped and opened it up again when she found her wheels. The racing pistons, big ends and slipping wheels all sent their shudder of motion reverberating through the whole frame of the loco. The slippery rails now forced a slower rate on the train's progress.

Smoke and heat collected more easily in and around the more slowly moving loco. The three riders in the cab could see each other only faintly through the black sulphurous smoke that entered the cab only to be sucked into the eternal draught torrenting into the gaping firebox doorway. Carol held her clean sponge cloth close over her mouth and nose, her eyes appeared bleary and sore but friendly between the cloth and the curled fringes of her auburn hair.

Joe wondered if she regretted her situation, he hoped fervently that nothing would go wrong and result in her presence becoming known to the railway authorities. He soaked another clean white cloth by dipping it into the bucket of warm water, he squeezed it almost dry and gave it to her with a suggestion that she used it rather than the dry one she pressed to her face.

"Get lower down,"Joe leaned across and spoke loudly into her ear. "The air will be a little fresher down on the floor." She shook her head and articulated that she was still alright. Bert held a cloth to his mouth and wrestled with his slipping engine as it thundered on through the darkness and the smoke, its exhaust smashing up onto the roof of the tunnel.

Although only three or four minutes had passed, the journey through the tunnel seemed to take an age. Joe enjoyed every uncertain moment of the stinking, hot, shuddering experience; he wouldn't have missed it for anything, especially now that Carol was with them, and not even though it meant that he might miss his grandfather's funeral.

The thump of the exhaust on the tunnel roof altered suddenly; daylight and fresh air flooded in to the cab with an unexpected brilliance and grey clouds filled the small square opening in the roof through which heavy drops of rain fell.

To Bert's side a square, high stone wall replaced the wet black wall of the tunnel; in front of their locomotive and train which they were pushing, could be seen the shelf of land on which they ran, and which joined the exit of the Sandsend tunnel to the entrance of the shorter Kettleness Tunnel. Joe loosed the tarpaulin sheet from his side of the loco' so that he and Carol could look out to the mist laden sea and down the cliff to the boulder strewn beach below.

The healthy blast of the exhausting steam at the chimney reaching up into the sky was like music after the muffled roar in the tunnel. A feeling of elation and pride swept through Joe and clearly Carol's face exhibited similar enthusiasm. Both had acquired considerable dirt on their faces which were now more black than white.

"I wouldn't have missed that for all the tea in China," Carol mouthed as quietly as she could into Joe's ear.

"Me neither. Was great wasn't it?," he grinned and replied and then heard Bert addressing him.

"This next hole 'l not be much bother," he shouted across as he prepared his pipe for a smoke. "She's only a few hundred yards long, and then we've got a climb up a short hill to Kettleness." The tunnel enveloped them almost as soon as his words were spoken.

Smoke and steam again swirled in through the cab side opening; the firelight in the darkened cab probed outwards and swept the black shining walls of the tunnel that flashed past. Bert had to grapple with his slipping engine wheels again as the wet tunnel rails offered insufficient friction. He applied his steam blown sands and without too much difficulty kept her going.

With unexpected suddenness beams of daylight replaced the dancing firelight and grassy banks surrounded them as they exited from the tunnel.

"We're nearly there." Bert paused to light his pipe with the long paper taper." You'll see Kettleness's outer home signal soon from this side."

Joe stepped across the cab to Bert's side and Carol took the invitation to include her so she followed Joe and peered out across the grassy bank as they climbed ever upwards. The signal post with its drooping board told Bert and the driver of the leading locomotive that the road into Kettleness Station was clear.

Not much time elapsed before the regulators were closed and the train with its two locomotives rattled into the down line platform to the accompaniment of the muffled cheers of the passengers who had waited long and patiently.

Carol was confined to the cab and hidden totally from inquisitive eyes by a second tarpaulin sheet which was hooked and drawn across the other side of the engine cab.

Joe detached his engine from the rear of the Middlesbrough train and returned to his footplate to await instructions. Once again, he expected, to return to Whitby with Carol as their unauthorised passenger. Bert, however, had other ideas. There was another passenger train adjacent to his engine on the 'up line' in the next platform. Bert had ascertained that it was an ordinary service passenger train from Middlesbrough to Whitby Town.

"There's your ride back to Whitby, Miss," Bert said with an expression of relief. I'll get you on board in a minute after I've had a word with the guard."

After the Middlesbrough train, which they had assisted, departed and vacated the platform, Bert moved his engine along the platform track until it could be stopped alongside the guard's van of the adjacent waiting Whitby train. He passed through the cab doorway on Joe's side of the loco' and stepped across the gap between the waiting trains into the guard's van.

There was no one in the van, the guard was out on the platform. Bert said, "Come on. Quick, no one's looking," to Carol and Joe who looked at him across the gap between the engine and van. She obeyed without any show of enthusiasm and stepped confidently across the space and the ground below which was about six feet beneath her.

She was in the dark interior of the guard's van; Bert unlocked the communicating door to the train's corridor and guided Carol into a vacant seat in one of the compartments; her grubby looking condition had to be ignored. Before the train departed Joe was able to stand on the platform and converse with her through the open carriage window.

"I'm glad you've missed your eleven-ten train from Whitby. Now you'll have to travel To Castlebrough with us on the one o' clock train." He chuckled, "I don't think Bert's going to let you travel on the footplate with us though." She returned the humour and added thanks for her exciting journey through the tunnels.

"I wish I could be a fireman, It's not fair that only lads can work on the footplate." Joe agreed following that line of conversation until the train departed and Carol was soon only a distant colourful head and arm waving from the disappearing train.

* * * * * *

5
CONGRATULATIONS DRIVER.

Joe walked slowly back to his locomotive; he felt tired and hungry but he knew that he would not arrive home; (he corrected his thoughts,) arrive at the church he meant, for about another three hours. The forthcoming funeral blanketed his thoughts and dismal feelings crept over him.

'What a poor life Grandad had lived,' he thought, 'In the pits for nearly all his working life, little money or possessions; only his ten bob weekly pension, his clothes and the few things in his bedroom, The bedroom and the furniture weren't even his.' Joe found himself recalling how Dick Peace had described his twenty-four hour entombment in the pit after a fall of rock which killed many of his mates. Joe wondered how close his own experience in the Kettleness Tunnel came to being like the blackness of the pit in which his Grandad had been entombed.

He closed his mind to his memories and the coming funeral and looked around the landscape and the extending sea. The slight drizzle had abated; the horizon on the North Sea was clearly visible, a convoy of ships could be seen steaming southwards on journeys to southern ports or through the English Channel. Joe and Bert moved their engine and waited until the 'Director's Train' from Whitby West Cliff arrived alongside them leaving the road to Whitby clear for their engine.

They free-wheeled their engine at speed down the gradients through the two tunnels, the fast swaying locomotive with its banging steel parts, spinning wheels and grinding brake blocks thrilled Joe as he sat and stared into the rushing darkness and firelight. He knew now that he wanted to have a life on steam loco's, it far exceeded the rewards of working in the wood factory or as a railway porter; even, and he was now sure, better than being in the army helping to defeat the Nazi hordes that were being soundly beaten on the war fronts in Europe. He wondered how Bert judged the speed of the locomotive as it careered through the inky blackness; how he kept his rocking and rolling charge from leaving the rails and crashing into the tunnel sides.

After a while the end of the tunnel could be seen in the far distance, "Just like a tanner a long way off," Joe shouted to his mate who drew his attention to the small growing circle of light. He watched it until it grew larger and rushed upon them suddenly to leave them bathed in the daylight that poured down onto the sea and landscape. They ran down hill to Sandsend Station.

The journey to Whitby passed speedily and uneventfully; they were soon collecting the hooped tablet from the signalman in the Prospect Hill wooden signal cabin that straddled the line on the approach down to the Esk Valley. Their engine flashed beneath the twelve-arched brick rail viaduct that spanned the Esk; the widening river estuary spread out before them, its level increasing as the tide moved in.

The river surface shimmered and caught an unclear reflected image of the viaduct and the north bank of the river. The railway lines into Whitby lay out before them; their passage into Whitby Station clear and unchallenged, the only signs of railway activity came from the locomotives steaming and moving about in the small locomotive shed yard alongside of the main lines.

Soon their Castlebrough engine was standing at the head of five coaches in number two platform. Bert was chewing a piece of black twist and again irritating the uncomplaining Joe by regularly ejecting a stream of black spittle in the direction of the open firehole door. Joe sat reading a copy of 'The Locomotive Enginemen's Examination Guide.' He was trying to answer some of the examination questions he would be faced with if he were ever examined to be a driver.

In spite of his apparent interest in the book he was somewhat bored and inattentive; in the back of his mind he had carried with him all the way from Kettleness the hope that he would see auburn haired Carol when his engine arrived in Whitby. His hopes had been dashed. Nowhere on the train or in the station had he been able to find the girl who had intended to journey to Castlebrough and then on to York and her family.

One o'clock approached. The guard's whistle sounded and the engine and five coaches puffed noisily out of Platform Two; soon to be crossing the viaduct that spanned the Esk taking the rail track to the southern bank and six-hundred foot high peak at Ravenscar. From the track that took them over the viaduct that towered one hundred and twenty-five feet above the river the view was exceptional.

Joe felt no anxiety about his task of making the engine steam sufficiently well to enable them conquer the steep gradients up to Ravenscar and through the short but difficult tunnel. His first concern was the forthcoming funeral which he knew he must attend; he had never been to a funeral before, or seen a dead person in a coffin prior to yesterday; he was not enthusiastic about the event.

His second concern was for Carol, whom he now thought of as a close friend. Where was she? Would she get into trouble for being so dirty? Would she tell anyone that she had ridden on the footplate of a Castlebrough locomotive through Sandsend and Kettleness tunnels? Joe wished he could see her again if only to stress to her once more the importance of her silence.

When the train stopped at Hawsker he looked back along the train hoping that he might see Carol's head emerge from a carriage window. At Robin Hoods Bay Station where they had to stand and wait for a north bound train to come down the single track from Ravenscar, he walked back down the platform; at best he could he examined the passengers who were crowded into the five coaches. She could not be seen. 'Maybe' he mused 'she has travelled by road to Castlebrough to catch her York connection.' He climbed back on board of his locomotive.

"Why isn't anything being put into this front luggage van Bert? This morning when we travelled up to Whitby I helped load the front van."

"Don't know. Can't even guess," came Bert's disinterested response. He paused to light his pipe from the flame at the end of his long newspaper taper, then he continued, "The guard's comin' up. Has he got something to tell us?"

The guard supplied the answer. "We'll be here for another ten minutes at least. That chap at Ravenscar has just left. We could have been part way up there if they'd let us go."

Joe was disappointed, they were being delayed further; he would have great difficulty in arriving at Grandad's funeral in time for the service and to join the cortege to the cemetery.

"I'll go down to the signal cabin Bert and bring the tablet back as soon as I can. That might get us away a few seconds earlier," said Joe. He thought that the walk down the platform to the cabin would give him another chance to search for Carol. He dropped from his engine footplate onto the platform alongside the guard who was talking to Bert. He lit a cigarette and then as he turned to commence his journey the guard walked off in the same direction.

"Is there owt in this front van?" Joe asked the guard. "I've not seen any porters going in or out an' the door's is locked."

"Yes. There's summat in it. Got to keep it locked up. It's for Burton Agnes, t'other side of Bridlington. Have yer been that way," the guard replied to Joe and questioned him in turn.

"Yes, we work passenger trains and workmen's trains to Hull and Carnaby. I've been that way twice. Don't see much of a place when your on the footplate. I've been to Hull twice an' I hoped to go an' see the bomb damage but never had time to leave the engine, we was in such a rush to make it back."

"I'll show you the van. It's locked cos nowt else can travel in here."

Joe's curiosity was alerted but at the same time he was

disappointed. He had tried to open the van door in the first instance during his brief search for Carol; he had thought rather improbably that Carol might be riding in the van. She had ridden on their footplate, maybe she was riding in the van this time he had reasoned. The guard's remarks seemed to make it clear that she could not be in the van.

The guard inserted his tee shaped carriage door key, taken from his waistcoat pocket, into the van door's keyhole. With an air of mystery and no further explanation he opened the door and climbed inside the dark interior. Joe followed him, his cigarette glowed in the darkness. His eyes slowly accustomed to the gloom. The shaft of light thrown by the open door helped outline the interior of the van.

The guard walked across to the switchboard near the guard's seat and turned on the van interior electric lights just as Joe was beginning to discern the shape of the interior and the nature of the load within the dark locked van.

"He's going home poor lad." The guard was cleaning his spectacles as he nodded his head in the direction of a oak coffin that was placed length ways on the van floor; it was the van's sole occupant. Brass handles and a brass nameplate twinkled in the poor electric light.

"Aircraftman James Lupin. Age 19 years," Joe read aloud from the nameplate. "Only nineteen. Crumbs, he were young. I wonder if he were killed in the war."

"Don't know son. But there's plenty younger than him bein' killed in the war and not getting brung home fer burial."

"What's this note then?," Joe asked as he stooped to examine the label tied to one of the brass handles. "I see, yes it's an address in Burton Agnes."

"Mi own lad's been out in the Far East since forty-two. Missus gets rare up tight if she sees the telegram lad in the street. She don't sleep for days afterwards. Alus scared that the telegram might be for us." The guard and Joe paused in a respectful silence; Joe removed his cap and the guard followed suit. After a few seconds the guard added. "Bloomin' war. It's a curse on many homes. Glad when it's o'er."

Joe wasn't thinking of the war at that moment; the coffin's presence and its indicated occupant brought home the memory of his Grandfather's open coffin standing in the front parlour at his home. He remembered the sad thoughts and remorse that flooded through him when Jean Walton had accompanied him to his last viewing of his Grandad in the coffin.

He was thinking now that James Lupin's relatives would soon be surrounding the coffin as they wept and mourned the youth, rudely parted from life in the fulness of early manhood. How many of the mourners would cry and fret as he had done and register that it was now too late to make amends for hurts, intended or unintended? 'Death is a time for taking stock and adopting new resolutions' Joe thought as he stared down at the young stranger's coffin.

A distant engine whistle alerted them to their duties. "That'll be the chap comin' down from Ravenscar peak," said the train guard. "We'd better be ready for off." He locked the van door and Joe raced off down the platform to the signal cabin ready to collect the tablet when it was handed in by the fireman of the train approaching down hill from Ravenscar.

Before long he and Bert were driving hard up the steep inclines to Ravenscar and the short treacherous tunnel just before the summit. In the excitement of the demanding task Joe forgot about his failure to find Carol Blanchard, he forgot about the coffin and the corpse in the van; he forgot about his urgent desire to arrive home in time to attend the funeral at St James's Church.

While his engine footplate rocked and the chimney exhausted noisily, they journeyed through the dips and up the hills as he laboured away, on the moving footplate, building his fire carefully in preparation for a harder climb ahead. He intended to be well prepared for the short but steep climb through the beautiful rocky landscape; with the sea filling out the eastern aspect and the western reaching up to a high rocky ridge. A patchwork of green and brown fields, woodland copses and quarried areas, gorse and trees draped the whole of the bank which faced them for the two mile climb.

As they approached the steeper parts of the climb Bert Woodley opened the regulator wide to get the maximum tractive effort that his driving wheels would allow. The engine barked louder at the chimney top, Joe responded enthusiastically.

"Give her some stick Bert," he shouted in his mate's ear. "I want to be home before Sunday morning." Joe's dirty face grinned roundly into Bert's as he shouted his remark above the slow heavy pounding of the locomotive.

"We're goner be home by Friday, yesterday's Friday not next week's an' never mind Sunday," Bert yelled back as he prepared his pipe, he intended to have a smoke before he reached Ravenscar Tunnel. "You get yer back into it an' keep that needle standing up there where she is now," he said, tapping the pressure guage glass with the mouthpiece of his pipe.

The long steady climb and the sight of the beautiful bay and its beaches brought the heads of many passengers out through the windows. Joe gazed backwards at them whenever he could gain a few moments respite from the greedy demands of the furnace; he searched for the head of Carol although he was almost convinced that she must have stayed in Whitby. Overhead a number of heavy low flying aeroplanes heading towards the North Sea whisked Joe and Bert's attention skywards.

"Wellingtons," shouted Bert to his fireman, "With Beaufighters as escorts. On their way to Germany I'd guess. Seems a bit early in the day for a night time raid though. Mebbe they goner catch the Jerries just at twilight." Bert grabbed hold of the engine whistle cord. "We'll give 'em a blast on the whistle to send them on their way."

While Joe listened and watched Bert blasted a 'toot a root toot' twice on the engine whistle. The passengers leaning from the windows of the Castlebrough bound train understood Bert's whistled 'well wishes' to the low flying aircraft, they waved and shouted similar farewells to the plane crews. The whole train saluted the formation as it flew by.

Rain seemed imminent and the heavy sky promised a dense black-out that would not be relieved by moonlight. Bert sounded his engine whistle regularly during their slow uphill journey as a warning to traffic and pedestrians who might choose to use the unmanned accommodation crossings in front of their train.

Joe toiled on but with less urgency; his fire-bed glowed a healthy white heat. He knew that his uphill task was almost over; they were well past the brickyard which Bert had said would be their stopping point if they had to stop for a 'blow up'. Soon he would rest his shovel and talk into Bert's ear until they entered the hundred yard long tunnel with its treacherous 'S' bend track.

The tunnel lay only yards ahead; the engine was barking hard and gripping the rails with determination. Joe and Bert were both looking out as they entered the tunnel and the noisy exhaust blast became a muffled roar as the chimney head passed within the low confines of the tunnel. They were enveloped in the blackness of the tunnel, broken only by the brilliance of their engine fire which threw its beams out into the shapes and shadows of the black enclosed cab.

The steam sands blew vigorously at the wheels and rails; the engine held her feet and blasted her way with ease through the short twisting tunnel. The only thing which Joe missed was the presence of Carol as the journey evoked the memories of his earlier struggle through Sandsend and Kettleness tunnels. With the same suddenness with which they entered, they left the tunnel to meet the dazzling flood of daylight and chug the last few hundred yards to the top of the climb and pull into Ravenscar Station.

The downhill trip of eleven miles to Castlebrough went with surprising ease and speed; soon they were passing through the short

Gallows CloseTunnel in Castlebrough town preparing to run around their train and pull it into Castlebrough railway station.

The signal to advance into Platform Five fell into its clear position and Bert wrenched his train into urgent action. Now that his journey was almost finished he could hardly wait to arrive at the shed and make his way up Sander Road to the RailwayTavern where he might just obtain a pint of 'Moors and Robsons' before closing time.

Joe was in likewise haste; he was preparing to wash his face in water contained in the engine water bucket; he wanted to be as clean as possible for the dash to St James's Church. However, he was also planning to view the passengers leaving his train in the hope that Carol might be one of them. The train ground to a halt at the buffers of Number Five.

John Blanchard one of the regular station shunters stepped from the platform on to the step of Bert's A8 locomotive almost as soon as it had come to a halt. He opened the door and climbed into the cab.

"Will you push the train into Gas Up sidings for us Bert?" he said. Then as he saw anger flare on Bert's face he continued, "I'm sorry Bert but we haven't got a station pilot engine to shunt you. He's had to go to the shed and won't be back for half an hour."

"Nothing's ever bloody straight forward on this railway," Bert came back promptly and angrily. "We've been on for ten hours and you know we're booked to be shunted by the station pilot."

"Yes. You're right, but he's been called to the shed. There's a derailment on the points into the shed at the top end and the only engine outside of the shed to help pull him back on is the pilot. If you want to wait for him to come and shunt you, you'll be waiting a good hour." Bert grumbled and Joe expressed concern about arriving at his Grandad's funeral on time.

Bert spat some black twist juice into Joe's firebox. "Okay, the quicker the better, but I aint pleased. We've had extra work to do pushing a Middlesbrough man through Kettleness tunnel and then bringing back this later train."

The firmly built, pot bellied station shunter changed the subject. "You're looking grubby son, like you've been sleeping in the coal bunker." Joe was standing near to the cab side peering out onto the platform; he was watching the passengers as they left the coaches. His hands and face were blackened with oil and coal dust.

Briefly he told John Blanchard about the extra work through Kettleness Tunnels, he didn't mention the unauthorised ride that they had given to Carol Blanchard. He wondered about the surname Blanchard and wondered whether there could be any connection between Carol and the station shunter John Blanchard. He hoped not because he didn't like the blustering, teasing Blanchard.

"You've done a good job today then son. I heard that you'd got the District Locomotive Superintendent on the train. So Gaffard the Station Inspector says. Travelled down with you from Whitby."

Joe felt a little bit alarmed at the thought of the District Locomotive Superintendent being on board of his train, especially in view of some of the unauthorised things he had been doing.

The shunter continued, "He'll have been watching his time piece and checking you all of the way, an' counting the times you let her 'blow off' and waste coal."

"He'll give us a medal then won't he Bert?" Joe answered in the spirit of the shunter's conversation; he knew John Blanchard to be a persistent 'leg puller.' Joe would never forget the time when Blanchard had sent him down to the Station Inspector's Office, during Joe's portering days, for 'a long stand.'

Joe was convinced that he was seeking permission for one of John Blanchard's shunting loco's to be allowed a 'long stand.' Joe had stood in the inspector's office for thirty minutes and then been told "That's long enough, son." Go back to Mr Blanchard and tell him you've had the long stand." Joe was furious, he had vowed to get his revenge one day, but today the vow was forgotten. "What are you goin' to do about the coffin John" Joe asked the waiting shunter.

"Bury it I suppose," retorted the well built shunter, for ever for the joker.

"The coffin in yon end van. The coffin for Burton Agnes."

"Joe lad, if there'd been a coffin on board I'd known about it. I'd have had a wire about it." Blanchard shrugged off the remark about the coffin as if Joe was setting him up for a practical joke.

Joe saw some passengers drifting past his engine cab so he stepped from the cab to the platform with his last remark to John Blanchard, "Somebody will have to put that coffin on the train to Burton Agnes."

The train guard and Mr Gaffard the Station Inspector were about to approach the engine; they were asking Joe if the station shunter was on the footplate, when John Blanchard emerged from the cab. Joe had other purposes to which he desired to turn his attention. The train was beginning to disgorge its passengers onto the platform, passengers that included the usual smattering of servicemen and servicewomen.

Joe watched the emerging throng rather than paying attention to the remarks of the station inspector. He heard the shunter saying to Bert that he would have to keep him back a little while longer because there was a coffin in the front van which had to be transferred to the

Hull train which would leave soon.

"That means Bert that we want you to run round the train in Gas Up Sidings and bring the van containing the corpse back into number three platform and hang it onto the three o' clock Hull train."

Joe heard Bert complaining again about the station pilot being brought up from the shed to do the job, only to be assured that the pilot wouldn't get back to the station until after three o' clock. Joe's real attentions were elsewhere; his eyes were combing the bobbing heads and the trundling figures.

Suddenly he was rewarded; his eyes settled on an auburn head bobbing amongst the flowing crowd of passengers and porter's barrows. 'Yes, it is,' the thoughts almost formed into words; he felt a certain sureness about his conclusion that the head belonged to Carol even though the familiar tam was missing.

John, having moved away from Bert, broke into Joe's thoughts, "There's the Loco' Super I was telling you about. The feller in the black trilby hat, he's the one I said was comin' in from Whitby with yuh."

Joe's thoughts were on Carol and he felt irritated by John's intrusion into his thoughts but the shunter's insistence about the importance of the 'Loco' Super' left him feeling uneasy. "How do you know him?" ask Joe still only partly believing John's story.

"He's mi namesake. That's how I know him. Same name as mi self."

The auburn haired figure was almost clear of the crowd; it was Carol. She wore different clothes now; her face was neat and clean, her ankle socks had been removed and she now wore brown flat heeled shoes.

Joe had recorded John's remark about the black trilbied figure whom he could see being likely to come and show interest their locomotive.

Carol was also walking in Joe's direction with a smile of recognition on her face. Joe's subconscious was struggling with the anxiety that somehow the secret he shared with Carol might become the knowledge of the very important District Locomotive Superintendent; a man who would not, could not, ignore the fact that a young girl had ridden on Bert Woodley's footplate through Kettleness Tunnel. There was no concern on Bert Woodley's face as he leaned out of his cab with a lighted tabacco pipe drooping from his clenched jaw. He had not been listening to John's conversation with Joe.

The Yorkshire District Locomotive Superintendent for the London and North Eastern Railway Company was a tall impressive man dressed in a long black expensive looking overcoat. He carried a rolled umbrella and wore a blue tie in a hard collar. He looked towards Joe and Bert and their engine with a show of familiarity; almost as if he knew them well.

Joe Wade was beginning to feel decidedly uneasy; he hoped that his nervousness would not be visible. His anxiety grew more definite when he noticed that the auburn haired bright young Carol was walking with the Locomotive Superintendent and a lady who must have been of some relation to Carol or the Superintendent. Joe's heart nearly missed a beat when the three figures were seen to be quite obviously walking towards him and his A8 side-tank locomotive.

"Good afternoon." The superintendent nodded his head in the direction of the engine crew. Joe could now see that this tall impressive looking man had a small waxed black moustache. "You are the crew that brought this train from Whitby, aren't you?"

Joe and Jim articulated the word, "Yes" at the same time.

"You did well up the bank towards Ravenscar Tunnel, and very well through the tunnel. I don't ever remember coming through that tunnel quite so quickly and efficiently." He looked straight into Joe's face. " I always make a point of thanking the engine crew for a good journey. I'll get your names from your shed master on Monday and send you my personal thanks in writing from my York Office. Castlebrough men aren't you?"

"Yes, we are Castlebrough Men," Joe stuttered.

He felt nervously ill. He shook his head in agitated agreement. Carol exchanged a meaning glance with Joe as her father, the District Locomotive Superintendent commented about the technical superiority of the A8 locomotive on the gruelling gradients up the coast road to Whitby.

* * * * * *

6
A WATCH TO TIME TRAINS

Funeral music drifted out from the arched, brick portal of St James's Church on Sander Road. A thirsty and hopeful Bert Woodley was trudging towards the Railway tavern. A still black faced uniformed Joe Wade was placing a heavy Raliegh bicycle behind a bush by side of the church door. He was showing signs of the exertions he had made to arrive at the church.

At the curb on the road outside of the church two black funeral cars, with their sombrely dressed drivers, awaited the end of the service. Joe knew that he was late; he fretted over the fact but at the same time he felt relieved that he had not missed the funeral completely. The thought passed through his head that his Grandad would not mind his late arrival providing he were there for the mainpart of the service. He wiped his heavy greasy boots on the thick coco-fibre porch doormat and entered the church as quietly as was possible.

Four coffin bearers were just sliding the coffin containing the body of Joe's Grandad Dick Peace onto the plinth in front of the altar. The vicar was poised to begin his duties; the mourners were leaving the cortege and choosing their places on the pews. Joe joined his weeping mother, his silent serious faced father and his two brothers in a front pew.

They all exchanged sad looks as Joe managed to position himself alongside his darkly dressed, trembling mother; they seemed to express to Joe a gladness that he had managed to be present, but none spoke, almost as though the occasion forbade speech.

Joe became so buried in dreamy thoughts, brought on by fatigue, that the rituals of the ceremony went almost un-noticed. The solemn words of the service and the Vicar's expressed sympathy for the family drifted into Joe's hearing almost unrecorded. His eyes and thoughts were on the coffin and on the passing of his Grandfather Peace.

Joe was trying to evaluate the meaning of the life that had passed; trying to understand that Dick Peace had been sixty-nine years on earth, but was now gone, and yet left so little to show for those long slow years.

Grandad had lost his wife many years ago, tragically in her early womanhood. His one offspring, Emily had grown to be the mother of Joe and his two brothers; no unique earth shattering experience Joe considered but if she hadn't, he went on to concede in the lonely catacombs of his mind, 'I would not exist, neither would our kid Luke , or Tim.'

What a chance life is,' he proceeded to think while the words of the vicar drawled on in the distance. Joe was just trying to give some weight to the guilt feelings that he bore and which grew out of his conviction that he was blameworthy of having ignored the old miner who stayed his last few final years in the Wade household.

Joe was trying to recall whether he had himself meaningfully said 'thank you' for the regular 'spice money' Grandad had given him; whether he had really shown appreciation when Grandad had cleaned his shoes each week. All of a sudden he became conscious that the church part of the service was over and that the coffin and the re-formed cortege were moving off to the cars and then to Woodland's Cemetery.

"Why I ever got a job on the railways I'll never know" Joe whispered to Tim as he squeezed his smoke blackened, greasy figure into the undertaker's black Ford funeral car that stood behind the hearse.

All five members of his family and Mrs Walton were seated behind the glass partitioned rear half of the cab; all of them except Joe were tidily and appropriately dressed. Tim, the eldest son, was in the neat blue uniform of the Royal Air Force; the rest were in black or dark clothing. Joe felt ill at ease in his dirt and his locomotivemen's uniform, this made him mutter his momentary condemnation of his job on the railways.

It seemed however that the state of his dress did not matter; no one remarked on it. Indeed while he stood at the side of the open grave in the drizzling rain, with his boots turning up the mud around the grave edge, he felt appropriately dressed. 'How better' he thought, 'to pay respects to an old miner than be present at his funeral in coal soiled overalls and heavy boots.' Shortly afterwards in the living-room of his council house home when his family and the few mourners were eating sandwiches and drinking tea he offered the same thoughts to his Mother.

"I'm just glad you managed to get to the church on time." The harassed face of his mother articulated. "I was worried stiff, couldn't think where you were. Wished you'd never got that job on the engines. I never know when you're coming home." Emily Wade was on her favourite gripe to Joe and he bore it stoically while she returned to the topic of concern which he had raised with her.

"Grandad wouldn't mind how you were dressed." After a pause she continued, "He thought a lot about you. He told me in the hospital just before he died that you three boys made his life a lot brighter. Left you his watch, said he hoped you'd become an engine driver one day and use it and think about him everytime you timed trains with his watch." She rose and collected a heavy shiny pocket watch and chain from the dresser drawer and placed it in Joe's lap.

"Gee, thanks Mam. I'll keep it all my life." He paused, looked at the heavy steel watch which had ceased working at three o'clock on a previous day, thought deeply for an instant and then he started. "Crike Mam, I forgot to collect mi bike at St. James's Church I'd better go for it now. I borrowed it from Spinky so that I could get to the Church in time for the three o' clock service. I left it in the bushes, Spinky'll want it when he leaves the shed at four-thirty."

The blacked out streets of Castlebrough were quiet except for the noise of the occasional, dimly lighted car or double-decked bus that rattled along from stop to stop on the main roads. Very little moonlight found its way through the drifting clouds. Unlit gas lamp standards stood in silent acknowledgement of the four years of blackout and war.

Buildings presented themselves as faint silhouettes against the barely visible night sky; windows, where they could be discerned, displayed little shape and no light as the owners and the occupiers adhered rigidly to the black-out regulations. Air raids were not so likely now that the defeat of Nazi Germany seemed assured but the memories of early destructive raids on Castlebrough were sufficient to encourage an efficient blacking out of all properties.

Joe Wade, neatly attired in his grey utility suit and displaying parted, brylcreemed hair, sat on the well worn leatherette seat of a Sander Road number 'one hundred' United Bus. He was on his way into the town centre and to 'Hell's Kitchen,' a billiard hall down Huntriss Row. He showed little interest in the shadowy nondescript silent passengers who travelled with him. The conductress who collected fares in the dim blue electric light took his fare with barely an exchange of words.

Joe's mind was on the day's happenings; mostly on Carol and the District Locomotive Superintendent, on the coffins in the van and in the open grave at Woodlands, but also, quite happily, on the watch that his Grandfather had left to him and which had alerted him to the need to return Big Jack Spink's bicycle to the shed by four-thirty.

Joe removed the watch from his top jacket pocket where the chain secured it to his lapel; he raised it towards the little blue shaded electric light on the bus ceiling and looked at it for the hundredth time. It had already been lucky for him because Big Jack Spink the shed labourer, a belligerent and bellicose man would certainly have boxed his ears for not returning the bike on time.

The day had been a trying one but certainly a full one: now, although he was very tired he was going to end the day with a night at the town's leading ballroom on the seafront; he couldn't dance but that didn't matter; his mates would be there, so would the girls, and the 'booze.'

Tomorrow, Sunday, was to be an unusual day, he hadn't been rostered for work; he had the day off, and that meant to him that he would stay in 'kip' until dinnertime and pick up some energy. At the moment, as the double-decker bus trundled noisily through the blacked-out streets on its journey into town he let his mind fill with pleasant fantasies about a developing relationship with the pretty Carol.

'Hell's Kitchen' was a poorly kept billiards hall below the street level close by the Salisbury Hotel on Huntriss Row; it was a grim, sparsely furnished, somewhat grubby cellar rather than a 'hall' but it was a popular meeting place for men and lads in Castlebrough. Joe ran down the stone steps with the careless abandon that only a youth would adopt on steps in the black-out.

He entered through the single open doorway and around the partition shield that kept the inside light from escaping up the steps and into the darkness of the street. Nine billiards tables filled almost the whole of the rectangular flagged cellar floor. Cigarette and pipe smoke clouded the atmosphere and drifted through the light beams that fell upon the tables from the hooded electric lights above.

All of the tables were occupied and the seats around the room were filled by waiting men. Most of them were in their 'best clothes' but some still wore clothes that were designed for workplaces. Joe was a very different spectacle from the figure who had toiled so rewardingly through the tunnels on the way to and from Kettleness. He looked confident and vital; his blue eyes sparkled in his clean face. He expected his grey suit, brown shoes; and paisley patterned light blue tie in its hard collar, to make him an attractive proposition for the girls at the Olympia Ballroom later in the evening.

"Hello Joe; over here." Joe saw the figure of Frank Sutton coming towards him from the direction of the voice. Frank was a fellow engine cleaner at the shed; he was taller than Joe, black haired, with thin boney features and a capacity to indulge in eternal chatter. He shared many of Joe's interests; reading, snooker, dancing and politics but he drew the line at boxing and cross country running which were becoming activities of interest to Joe. They often exchanged papers, leaflets and ideas on religion and politics; they attended 'Worker's Educational Association Classes' on 'Current Affairs' in Roscoe Rooms - known significantly to some as 'Moscow Rooms' because of local communist activity and meetings in the rooms.

"Hi Frank, you got a table yet?"

"Yes - got a game fixed up with Johnny and Pusher. We've got number 'Six.' It's a lousy table; got more bumps than the Pennines but we didn't want to wait," Frank replied keeping up an unbroken conversation as they both walked towards number six table.

Johnny Marsay was dressed in his locomotivemen's uniform and only partly washed because he had only recently finished his shift at the shed and had dropped into Hell's Kitchen before making his way home. Johnny's broad cheerful face had no doubt been washed in the water of a greasy engine fire bucket.

Pusher was much older than the three youths with whom he was about to play snooker; he was about thirty-five years of age and was poorly and untidily dressed, he wore a grimy flat cap even though he was indoors and about to start playing snooker. Pusher was not his real name, no one knew his first name, he was Pusher Jackson to everybody. Pusher was the nickname he had acquired because of his habit of always having something to 'sell for a song on the Q T.'

The war had opened up many new possibilities for 'pushing' shadily obtained goods and Jackson did his best to exploit the opportunity. The Government had directed Pusher to work at the shed and earn a living instead of 'living off the parish relief' or the 'dole.' He was now an unwilling shed labourer who avoided doing as many of his allotted tasks as was possible.

Pusher's current strategy in Hell's Kitchen was "t earn a few baubles off the kids at snooker and then go off an' get a skinful." His short dumpy figure had a greasy look about it; his face was rubbery, squat and unshaven. His Park Drive cigarette burned away in his mouth until the billiard hall attendant stopped him smoking while he was 'on a table.'

Their conversation, quite naturally, centred on the shed. They exchanged tales about the Shedmaster Jack Franker; and about 'Mousey' a new cleaner who was locked in a cold firebox by the late turn cleaners last Wednesday evening. He hadn't been let out until well after ten o'clock when Jack Mild had gone with a blazing shovelful of fire to put in the box and 'put the engine in steam.' "Poor ole Mousey, nearly got his arse burnt raw, he did" said Johnny.

The drift into frivolity as the game of snooker progressed emboldened Joe to boastfully follow with his contribution.

"I took a bird through Sandsend and Kettleness Tunnels on 9881 today. Crackin' piece, had me on heat just looking at her. Bert Woodley were stark starin' mad but he couldn't do nowt cos I kept fixin' it so's she couldn't get off. He nearly had a fit when he saw her getting off the train at Castlebrough wi' her dad, only the District Loco' Super' of all people. God how ah laughed. Bert was messin' hisself."

Joe filled out the details for his unbelieving but attentive audience as the game progressed but he either forgot to say "Don't tell anyone else" or he believed that to do so would weaken the daring carefree image of himself which he was cultivating.

"The Second Front's coming soon," Johnny informed, changing the subject. He paid more attention to the politics and the course of the war than Pusher and Frank, possibly because many of his family were abroad in the forces.

"I wish I was going," was Joe's laboured response as he painstakingly endeavoured to sink the blue ball into the middle pocket. "Better than bein' at home shovelling coal."

"You'll be going to France alright - when the Second Front opens. So Browny were telling me today," returned Johnny. "In the First World War lots o' railwaymen; especially loco'men, single fellers, were taken over to France to run trains up to the front line. Lots of our drivers down at the shed went over; Blunkett, and Ward, and Jokes, they're alus on about France." He paused and returned his remarks to the game. "There, that's left you snookered Pusher an' the game hangs on it."

The conversation was suspended for a few moments while Pusher attempted to overcome the snooker only to fail. "Ye, they says the Second Front's coming anytime now," said Joe with more than the usual interest. "Can we do something to see that I get on it. I'd like to work on the French Railways. French birds is hot stuff they say, leastways they are on them French postcards." He paused to weigh up a careful shot.

Pusher was swearing and blasting because he and Frank were very close to having lost the game and they would have to pay up their 'tanner' bets. "I'll ask Nuttlefold on Monday. He'll know if anybody does. Mebbe he'll write to A.S.L.E.F. head office for me. Unions sometimes helps their members to go abroad to work."

"Ye, you can but I'm not a candidate," Johnny answered, "not now that I'm wed. Besides, I've got a few soldier's wives to look after until the war ends."

Johnny was well placed on the table to pot the black and win the game for him and Joe. The conversation paused and silence reigned while Johnny lined up on the black ball and then placed it neatly in the top pocket. "Howzat! Fork out Pusher, and you Frank." They cleared the balls from the table and made way for the next waiting pair of players. "The Second Front's coming soon there's no doubt, an' then the war 'll be finished. Rusky's knockin' 'ell out o' Jerries. Yeh, you try for Railway Transport Corp. Smithy's in it. I'm sure you'll get in."

Joe was interested in the new possibility; he had twice tried to join the armed forces to get in on the fight against the Nazis without success. He recalled his unsuccessful efforts to Johnny and remarked that this time he might be successful.

The three friends deposited their cues and snooker balls in the hall attendant's cubicle, and prepared to leave the hall. Pusher was urging for another game with the intention of recouping his losses but Johnny indicated his intention to make his way home after a call at the Railway Tavern.

As they left the hall Joe said, "I've got the day off tomorrow. First Sunday off duty for seven weeks."

"You're not Joe. Thought you knew or else I'd er told yuh earlier." Johnny expressed some surprise. A duty ticket went to your house from Bill Clark just as I was leaving work. Mason was taking it, told me you were being called out for six o'clock tomorrow morning

"Johnny, don't kid me on. I'm proper knackered workin' early all week," Joe pleaded.

"You know me. I don't kid on things as serious as that," Johnny returned with conviction. "You and Woodley's been called out 'cos there's no one else spare that can get nine hours rest in from today, You've to tek three dead engines through to Leeman Road Shed at York. District Loco' Super's got summat big on he's got to provide engines for. Clarkey reckons he knows that it's for the Second Front." Johnny could still detect a measure of disbelieve on Joe's face. "It's true Joe," he continued on a more serious note, "Honest, - bet you next week's wages on it."

However, Johnny could not resist adding a jest after he had quite surely convinced Joe about the truth of his message. "Mebbe the Loco' Super' just wants to see you and Bert Woodley now he's learnt from his daughter that she's had a ride through Sandsend tunnels wi' the two of yuh." The fact that Johnny was being mischievous showed in his eyes; Joe recognised it as such but he was by now convinced that a ticket had gone to his house calling him on duty at six o 'clock in the morning.

"Well, we're going to the dance aren't we Frank? I'll just have to miss a bit o' sleep tonight that's all. He plucked his inherited watch from his pocket, allowed a brief thought for his Grandad, and remarked on the lateness of the hour as the three friends climbed the stairway to the street. He finished his conversation with a confident "Tarah John, see you at the shed tomorrow when I get back from York," and turned on his heel to set off down Huntriss Row towards the seafront dance hall.

THE END